Wild Bill glanced [up at the ropes that]
bound him and th[...] her—
only to find that eve[n ...] the fugitive's
awed expression both[...] He stared deeply
into her eyes as he contin[ued] jimmying the wire
in the lock. Was she the type who fell for felons?
And had she lied about her identity?

"Shouldn't you watch what you're doing?" she
asked.

"Picking locks is like making love," he returned
softly. "It's better to do it by feel."

Spots of color warmed her cheeks. "So, why isn't
it working?"

He grinned. "It just did, sweetheart."

She stepped back gingerly and began rubbing
her wrist. "I'm free," she murmured.

But was she? Watching her, Wild Bill was sorely
tempted to never let her go....

ABOUT THE AUTHOR

When asked about *Bride of the Badlands*, Jule McBride had this to say: "My childhood road trips were full of wonder. White guardrails flattening to the asphalt reminded me of dominoes falling down...and lullabies were a magical mix of parental whisperings and softly playing radio music. I still love how bright the stars can look on a dark country road, the promise of sunrises through windshields and drinking good coffee from foam cups. The unique intimacy forged between fellow travelers compelled me to write *Bride of the Badlands*, where a couple discovers that the only true map is the human heart—and that sometimes, when paths cross, it really is forever."

Books by Jule McBride

HARLEQUIN AMERICAN ROMANCE
500—WILD CARD WEDDING
519—BABY TRAP
546—THE WRONG WIFE?
562—THE BABY AND THE BODYGUARD

JULE McBRIDE

BRIDE OF THE BADLANDS

Harlequin Books

TORONTO • NEW YORK • LONDON
AMSTERDAM • PARIS • SYDNEY • HAMBURG
STOCKHOLM • ATHENS • TOKYO • MILAN
MADRID • WARSAW • BUDAPEST • AUCKLAND

For John Walker Moore—

For each time I think the world's coming to its end, and I hear you say—in that West Virginia drawl tinged with the Carolinas—"No problem" and "I love ya, sis."

—Love you, too. I got a real hero for a baby brother.

ISBN 0-373-16577-3

BRIDE OF THE BADLANDS

Prologue

"Five foot nine, a hundred and thirty pounds, blue-eyed and with light blond hair nearly down to her butt." Mickey grinned, feeling more excited than he had the previous day—his sixteenth birthday—when he'd found the Blazer he was driving in the family carport with a bow on the hood. "And she's thirty, which means she's in the sexual prime for women."

"What is it for guys?" Darrell asked, sounding concerned.

Mickey's dog, Wolf, barked as if he wanted to know, too.

"Two more years, dude," Mickey said. "When we're eighteen."

"I sure hope I'm married by then," Darrell said glumly.

"I just hope we get the chick before the cops do." Mickey patted Wolf, then glanced at Darrell who was riding shotgun. "And that she doesn't look like Jill Jennings." A vision of the most sought-after blond-haired, blue-eyed dish at their high school popped into his head.

"*Every* girl should look like Jill," Darrell said evenly. "Much as I'm loving spring break, only she could lure me back inside Mrs. Paine's English class."

Yeah, Mickey thought, the woman they were chasing was way more interesting than her boyfriend, who sounded like an ex-hippie. He had sandy brown hair, a mustache and a tattoo. "But if the woman looks like Jill," he said, "I couldn't turn her in."

"Not even for five hundred bucks?"

"If we get her boyfriend, too, the reward'll be a thousand each."

"And I can get a car." Darrell nervously opened his orange hunting vest, exposing the pistol he was packing in the shoulder holster beneath. "I'm ready."

Feigning confidence, Mickey adjusted the shotgun in his lap, so that the long barrel pointed through the open window. "Isn't there something on that radio besides static?"

Darrell leaned forward and started wheeling the knob. "More weather," he apologized, settling on a station.

"Spooky as it is, I'm sick of hearing about it."

Darrell leaned back and ran his hands through his close-cropped brown hair. "Why don't they say something else about Bonnie and Clyde?"

Mickey smirked. "Think those are their real names?"

Darrell snorted. "Bet they're aliases."

"How are we supposed to conduct a manhunt with no information?" Mickey asked.

"Or a woman hunt?"

Mickey crouched closer over the wheel and followed the curve in the winding West Virginia road, half listening while the newsman talked about the weather. It *was* unusual for April. Temperatures had shot to record highs, hovering in the nineties, a good twenty degrees above average. The late morning sky was such a muggy gray that it looked like an August evening.

Mickey peered through the windshield. "Pretty whacko."

Darrell nodded. "Makes you feel like something weird is going to happen. Like maybe we'll catch Bonnie and Clyde."

Mickey grinned even though the weather was making him feel edgy. Overhead, the endless gray cloud ceiling was getting darker. Every once in a while the sky peeled open like the lid of a tin can. Heat lightning shot between the mountains surrounding the New River Gorge, then the sky snapped shut again.

"There it is!" Mickey exclaimed. "Turn it up!"

Darrell's hand whirled the volume knob.

"Criminals or victims?" the newscaster began.

"Can you believe the news guys are siding with *them?*" Darrell asked in disgust.

"No." Mickey wondered if they'd hear some new information.

They didn't. It was the same old story. Two native Texans, Bonnie Smith and Clyde Calvert, had inherited a large piece of property outside of Charleston. When they'd arrived in town, the land had been harvested of all its veneer-quality hardwood. Each tree had been worth at least six hundred dollars, and the earnings had totalled five hundred thousand dollars.

According to Langston Larson of Larson's Logging International, Bonnie, Clyde and their neighbor, Jason Morehead, had stormed into his Charleston office early that morning and held him and his partner, Clarence Smithers, at gunpoint. Then the trio had taken five hundred thousand dollars and fled in Jason Morehead's white 1950 Cadillac.

"The money's in a yellow duffel," Mickey said.

"Yeah" Darrell leaned closer to the radio. "They didn't mention that before."

Mickey wished the story wasn't so hard to follow in places. The main points were that there had been witnesses to the holdup, and the local police had offered a reward. They hoped to catch the criminals before they crossed state lines, to avoid FBI involvement.

Mickey didn't understand the part about the contracts at all. Larson's Logging International had produced legal contracts proving that the couple had agreed to let him harvest their land. According to Larson, the logs had been sold and he was just about to give the couple their rightful portion of the money when he'd been robbed.

But during the harvest, earth silt and oil had poured into a creek. Because the creek led to a fishing stream, the state now intended to collect a ten-thousand-dollar fine. According to Larson's contract, the couple who owned the property were liable to pay it. Bonnie and Clyde had refused.

"Did you get all that, dude?" Darrell asked.

Mickey shook his head as the newscaster announced that Larson's Logging International had been accused of shady dealings in the past. When the story broke, other people stepped forward, claiming that Larson and Clarence Smithers had illegally harvested their land of timber and had taken their money.

Mickey scratched his head. "Is he saying Bonnie and Clyde might have been robbed, instead of the other way around?"

"All I know is that if I catch them, I get a car," Darrell said.

"But why's there no reward money for Jason?"

Darrell shrugged. "They said he's eighty and uses a cane to get around. Maybe they don't think he'll get very far."

Mickey lifted a hand from the wheel and rubbed his temple, feeling confused. "But wasn't he the one with the gun?"

The announcer wrapped up, saying, "We're sending this one out to Bonnie and Clyde."

A newer cover of an old song began playing and, at the chorus, Roy Orbison crooned, "I fought the law and the law won."

Mickey sighed. "Tall and blond. That's the main point."

"Yeah, but one of these days—" Darrell's adolescent voice broke in midsentence "—I've got to find a girl like that who isn't on her way to the slammer."

"Don't worry, dude." A flash of inspiration hit Mickey. "In two years, she might be out on parole."

"And I'll be in my sexual prime for men!" Darrell snapped his fingers, sent Mickey a thumbs-up and said, "Cool."

Chapter One

"I'm thirty and on my first manhunt in over ten years...but where do I wind up?" Frannie Anderson muttered. "Lost."

It figures. She whipped her long blond hair over her aching shoulders with two practiced jerks of the head, almost wishing she was headed toward Helga, her mother's Swiss masseuse. Squinting her blue eyes, she leaned over the wheel of her father's white 1950 Cadillac carefully, so as not to upset her book-on-the-head posture.

She was trying not to panic, but everything in the West Virginia mountains looked the same. Curves, wooded hills on either side, stands of pines and stormy weather. She hadn't talked to a soul since early morning, when she'd stopped at a gas station outside of Charleston to ask for directions.

An elderly man had accidentally bumped Frannie with his cane, and the woman who'd apologized for him had looked so much like Frannie that they could have been sisters. She'd seemed very much in love with the young man at her side. The three were on vacation, just as Frannie was. But while she was heading for a week of white-water rafting, they were driving to Texas and then to a sanctuary in Mexico.

"If I could just find a rest area," Frannie murmured. She turned up her radio for company and tugged down the hem of her white silk skirt, hoping to keep it wrinkle free.

Not that anyone would see her suit. She'd already missed the Friday morning welcome breakfast at the New River Raft Inn and she'd brought a sportier outfit for the lobster lunch. With her luck, she wouldn't arrive until the cocktail social, and she still hadn't decided which dress to wear. The inn was one of many resorts that supposedly dotted the scenic New River Gorge, but Frannie didn't see so much as a power line.

Maybe she'd been a fool to come, but when she'd seen the pamphlet lying around her father's law office, she'd impulsively made a reservation for the week of her spring break. The male model on the back had convinced her it was time to get on with her life. Somewhere in her Chanel bag, pressed flat against the map she couldn't read, Mr. Suave was smiling. The tall, dark, handsome man sat on a rail above the white water with a champagne flute cradled against his suit jacket, looking as sinfully cool as James Bond.

And as rich. Frannie had bypassed the first marriage, which was supposed to be for love, because the man she'd hoped to marry had left her when she was seventeen and pregnant. Now she was thirty and headed straight for marriage number two—which was for money. Love didn't last. And only fools believed in men who didn't leave. She nodded absently and decided that she'd worry about the marriage for companionship when she hit sixty.

When the radio deejay segued from "Jailhouse Rock" into the Bonnie and Clyde story again, a chill went right down her spine. She could only hope she wouldn't run into the criminals. Or that the storm didn't break, leaving her stranded.

"Please," she said. "Just give me one sign of civilization."

She swerved toward the road's shoulder, threw the car into park and got out, slamming the door. As she beelined toward the seclusion of a bush, she glanced around anxiously and dug in her shoulder bag for a tissue. Not that there were any cars on the road. If there were, she'd have asked for directions.

Minutes later, she tossed her tissue to the wind and marched back toward the car, her three-inch heels stirring up the dust. The Caddy was now filthy, which meant her father would kill her, and the filmy white shell beneath her jacket was soaked with perspiration. If she wound up wearing her suit to the lobster lunch, Mr. Suave wouldn't so much as look at her.

She had half a mind to let out one of those primal screams, the kind people said were therapeutic, but she hadn't felt good enough to yell like that since her cheerleading days. She suddenly imagined her pamphlet fantasy man appearing from behind a tree with a bottle of bubbly.

And then she saw the Blazer.

A teenager in an orange vest was leaning against the passenger side door. Unfortunately, the kid looked like such a bonehead that Frannie had to wonder if he was lost, too.

"My savior!" She waved her arms as she approached. "Do you know where we are?"

"Yeah," the kid said. "And I know where you're going, too—jail." He flung open his vest, exposed a shoulder holster, and then drew out a pistol and pointed it at her.

"Don't shoot me," Frannie said flatly, stopping in her tracks. Scenes from the movie *Deliverance* played in her mind and her eyes cut toward the bushes. There was no way she could run for it, not when she had on heels and he had a gun.

"Put your hands in the air," another voice said. A new kid wiggled out of the Blazer, swinging a shotgun in her direction.

Stay cool. "Please point that weapon away from my face," she managed to choke out, illogically thinking that

Mr. Suave might not be as apt to notice a bullet wound in her extremities. ''I'm not going anywhere.''

The teenagers didn't move.

''Darrell,'' said the one with the shotgun, ''it's Bonnie Smith. Five-nine, blond, blue-eyed.''

Bonnie Smith! They think I'm Bonnie Smith! ''Five-nine?'' she called in shock. ''It—it's just my heels. They add a good three inches.'' She wasn't sure but thought she saw the shotgun waver uncertainly in the air. ''I'm not Bonnie Smith!'' How could these boys mistake her for a woman wanted for armed robbery?

''Mickey,'' Darrell said, ''could there be two white 1950 Cadillacs on the road?''

Mickey snorted. ''No way.''

''This car's my father's prized possession,'' Frannie said in a rush. ''And—when my lemon—'' She paused, briefly wondering if a usually trustworthy sports car could be considered a lemon. ''When it broke down again last night, just before I was leaving for my vaca—'' Her voice faltered. Guns and Mr. Suave seemed to waver like a mirage before her very eyes. ''For my *vacation*...well, Daddy said I could drive it. You see, he and Mother were going to North Carolina this morning and they were using the station wagon and—''

''Did Clyde and Jason just leave you?'' Mickey asked, cutting her off. He glanced around fearfully, but kept the shotgun trained on Frannie.

''No one left me!'' *Except Joey Florence.*

''Get those hands up,'' Darrell repeated.

When Frannie's hands shot in the air, her purse hit the dust and the contents tumbled out. Just as she realized that the pamphlet from the New River Raft Inn had fallen out and that her fantasy man was smiling up at her, a dog that looked more like a wolf shot from the Blazer cab. She heard a yelp, thought it was the dog, then realized it had come from between her own lips. *The next time I see Mr. Suave, I'll be at my own funeral!*

Her knees nearly buckled when the dog reached her. But instead of lunging for her throat, he started sniffing at her makeup bag.

The kids looked too darn dumb to kill her. Even if they pulled their triggers, they'd probably miss.

"Check my pocketbook." She tried to hide her fury, in deference to the guns. "My IDs will tell you I'm Frances Anderson."

Darrell looked at Mickey, then said, "Fake IDs! Cool!"

"Keep the pistol on her and I'll tie her up," Mickey said.

Tie her up? "Didn't you hear me?" she shrieked. She stomped her foot and the dog backed up a pace.

Mickey was rummaging in the glove box. After a moment he walked toward her with a fair-size piece of rope. She glanced downward and gasped. "He's taking my purse!" she burst out, watching the dog trot toward the trees. "He's stealing my wallet!" With a sinking heart, she watched the dog drop her bag to the ground. Just thinking about him salivating on the leather made her shiver. He hunkered down on his haunches and started digging with his front paws. "He's burying it!"

"Bring your hands down and put them out straight," Mickey said.

She'd been so intent on the dog that she hadn't seen Mickey.

"Hands out, Bonnie," Darrell called. "Slow and easy."

Frannie sighed shakily as Mickey leaned the rifle against his thigh. "My father's a lawyer," she muttered as she stuck out her hands. "Rest assured, he'll sue you for everything you're worth. Everything your parents are worth," she amended wryly.

"I am not Bonnie Smith!" she suddenly yelled, right in Mickey's ear. "If I were Bonnie smith, I would have an exciting life. I don't. My life is boring. Deathly boring. If I was Bonnie Smith I'd have a boyfriend. Remember? Bonnie robbed Larson's Logging International with her boyfriend, Clyde!''

When Mickey shoved her bracelets and watch upward and started binding her wrists, she sank into sullen silence. The rope was chafing. She could just see herself at the lobster lunch, constantly shifting the bracelets, to hide the red marks.

"Now," Mickey said, "Get in the back seat of the Blazer."

"Lovely," she muttered.

"Wolf," Darrell yelled. "C'mon, boy."

Somewhere behind her, Wolf barked.

And then she saw *him*.

The rough, unwashed wild man who was crouched down next to one of her father's whitewall tires. He looked so much like pure danger that she almost called a warning to the two teenagers. The kids had guns but the man looked positively lethal. She glanced over the space where his leather vest fell open and exposed his bare chest. How long had he been there?

Whoever he was, he had to be over six feet tall. Every inch was solid muscle. He tossed his longish, sun-streaked brown hair out of his face and met her gaze. Frannie couldn't see the color of his eyes, but could feel their intensity. She sure hoped they weren't brown. With his full beard, mustache, and dusty motorcycle boots, he matched Clyde Calvert's description.

"Please move," Mickey said.

Darrell raised his pistol, pointed it at the sky and pulled the trigger.

Frannie's shoulders jerked. Wings flapped in the silence. Birds took flight, arrowing into formation. And Frannie decided not to alert the boys to the fact that they had company.

"I—I'm going." Frannie took a quick step toward the Blazer. She tried to tear her gaze from the man's, but couldn't. He was good-looking, in an incredibly rough kind of way. Not that she cared. She just wished he'd rescue her.

Instead, he winked.

She gawked back. She was now close enough that she could see his eyes. They were brown, all right, the kind of chameleon brown that shifted according to circumstance.

He's Clyde Calvert! What am I going to do?

The man was creeping toward Darrell, moving with a predatory silence a tracker would envy, his thigh muscles flexing beneath his threadbare jeans. Watching him, Frannie felt a little faint.

Was her heart beating out of control because of the danger...or because of the raw, lithe power with which the man moved? Her stomach curled into a tight knot. She found herself wishing Clyde Calvert didn't have a girlfriend. *If he is Clyde Calvert.*

Frannie fought back a sudden whimper as she neared him. She was more convinced by the second that she was about to be shot. Or kidnapped. Or worse, she thought in terror as she looked at the man. How could she have felt an ounce of attraction for him? *I'm going crazy. I'm so scared that I'm going crazy.*

He looked as if he hadn't bathed in a few days and he had a bird tattooed on his shoulder. It was dropping an olive branch onto his very well-delineated bicep. She drew in a sharp breath. *Clyde Calvert has a tattoo!* What was it...Love-Hate written across his knuckles...Mother etched on his arm...a mermaid swimming on his chest? The newscaster hadn't said.

Leaves and twigs didn't make a sound when the man stood to his full height. He struck with the speed of light.

Darrell's rifle clattered against a rock. By the time Mickey turned around he, too, was falling—wordlessly and without preliminaries—to the ground.

"Dear heavens," Frannie whispered. "Did you just kill them?"

The man chuckled. "No."

What was that? Frannie wondered as she stared at the...bodies. A karate move? *Oh please. He's a karate teacher. Let him be a karate teacher.*

She'd hoped to meet her dream man this week. Her rescuer hardly qualified, but if there was one thing he didn't seem, it was real. When she stared at him, her knees quivered.

Wolf bounded past her and lunged for the man. *Maybe he'll go for the throat this time,* she thought feeling almost relieved.

But Wolf's large paws landed squarely on the man's chest. The canine nuzzled his nose against his new master and wagged his tail.

Frannie watched in astonishment as the man patted the dog once, perfunctorily on the head. Then he turned on his heel and strode toward her father's Cadillac. He bent without slowing his gait, picked up the pistol and shotgun, then tossed them into her back seat.

"Oh no," she croaked.

The man was sliding behind the wheel of her father's car, just as casually as you please.

"Stop right there!" she screamed, bolting after him. There was no way she was going to let this stranger simply drive off in her father's classic Caddy. If he did so, she'd surely be dead. Her own father would kill her.

The passenger door swung open as she approached.

In a slow, lazy drawl that might well have been Texan, the man said, "You comin' or not, sweetheart?"

HE WATCHED HER sling her silky-looking blond mane over her shoulders and coolly scoot in the passenger's side. When she tugged down her short skirt with her tied-up hands, he caught a flash of a white lace garter. She slammed her door hard and he suppressed a smile. Fortunately, he'd experienced plenty of danger in his lifetime. Which meant gunfire didn't get in the way of his checking out a sexy woman.

Whoever she was, she had legs to die for. Great breasts. Great everything he amended, his mouth quirking. He threw the gear into drive, did an illegal U-turn, then headed north. The lace of her bra was visible through her silk top, he noted when he glanced across the seat.

He figured he might as well feast his eyes since there was a small two-cell lockup not ten minutes away. He'd drop her off somewhere in the vicinity. By the time the kids regained consciousness, she and the sheriff would have them in cuffs.

He readjusted the seat and leaned back, meaning to enjoy the ride. The last vintage Caddy he'd driven had been hotter than tamales—and both he and it had been impounded. Fortunately, he hadn't had to hot-wire the vehicle this time around. He'd taken the keys so that the woman next to him could process her ordeal. He imagined that's what she was doing, since she was staring wide-eyed through the windshield.

"You all right, sweetheart?" he finally asked.

"Who *are* you?"

She sounded furious. He slowly turned his head and looked at her again. Her skin was as clear and soft-looking as a baby's behind. Her flashing eyes were deep blue, but he got the sense there might be a soul beneath them, the way there were fish beneath the calm surface of a lake's waters. He shrugged. "Some thanks I get."

She wrenched around in the seat. "Thanks? You're driving my car! Are you stealing it? Just tell me—are you Clyde Calvert? Are you going to kill me? Are you—"

"Going to—" *Kill her?* She looked like she wanted to kill *him.* Not that she could do him any real damage. Was she angry or in shock or just crazy? He was so taken aback that he couldn't help but say, "Maybe."

"You're car-jacking me," she said evenly, as if trying to convince herself of it.

Those guys must have shaken her up pretty bad, he decided. He lifted a hand from the wheel. "Whoa there—" The back of his throat went dry. Had rescuing her been a mistake? Maybe the kids had held her at gunpoint for good cause. Either way, looking through her creamy silk stockings at her legs was making his jeans start to pull across his hips. The traitorous response made him wish he'd been blessed with less testosterone. But he was the kind of guy who could go from "pleased to meet you" to "I'll die without you" in a second flat. Not that the feelings lasted.

"Look—" He shifted his weight on the leather of the seat, telling himself he was just getting comfortable. "First, I don't think car-jack should be a verb," he said. "After all, that's the tool one uses to *support* the car when the tires are being changed. Second, I'm not saying I've never stolen a car, but this would sure be the first time I took one with a woman in it."

He checked the rearview mirror, then stared into her eyes. The least she could do was thank him. He squinted. Who did she remind him of? The memory was slippery, intangible.

"Keep your eyes on the road," she commanded haughtily. "You're going to wreck my father's car!"

It *would* be Daddy's car. He averted his gaze and glared through the windshield. Everything about the woman spelled out Daddy's Money in neon. Including her high-handed righteous indignation. "Calm down, would you?" He was starting to feel genuinely sorry he'd saved her. "Who's Clyde Calvert?"

"Pull over and untie me."

Her voice had become as flat and dry as an overcooked pancake, a thought that made his stomach rumble. If it weren't for her, he'd still have his backpack—and his bologna sandwiches.

He sighed. "Those boys are gonna come to shortly, so I figure we best get to the cops as fast as we can. That way, they won't have as much time to get away."

"As if you are really taking me to the police," she snapped.

He'd known her less than five minutes and he'd already had it with her attitude. Where in the world did she think he was taking her? He screeched to a halt, right in the middle of the road, and on a curve no less. He threw the gear into park. Then he reached across the seat and grabbed her wrists. Feeling the wildly beating pulse points, his fingertips tingled where skin touched skin.

When he'd first seen her, from an elevated ridge on the mountain, he'd felt time compress. She was a class act. Cool and blond and dressed to kill. He'd felt as if a word he wanted was on the tip of his tongue. Only now did he realize that he'd never actually met her before. He'd merely seen her in his dreams.

She had a look that said everything in the world had gone her way. And dreaming of a woman like her had gotten him through some rough nights in prison. She was the kind of woman he always yearned for... but sometimes hated.

"Are you just going to stare at me all day?" she asked weakly. "Or are you going to untie me?"

He shot her a cynical smile. "What the lady wants, she gets," he said, not bothering to make it sound complimentary. He flipped open the snap of the leather sheath on his belt and drew out his hunting knife. It was his favorite, with a six-inch blade he kept sharp and polished.

"You sure are cagey," he commented gruffly, reaching for her hands again. When she tried to jerk away her wrists, he tightened his grasp in a natural reflex. He hooked a finger under the rope and tugged her forward. "Hold still or you'll get cut."

When he glanced at her face, he realized she was terrified. "Sorry I'm testy," he said, as gently as he could. "It looked like you were in a real mess back there. I know you're scared."

He ran the blade between her wrists and snapped the knot. The kid had wound the rope around her wrists a number of times, but touching her was making his skin sizzle, so he decided to let her finish unknotting herself.

As her fine-looking hands with their long, beringed fingers suddenly dropped limply to her lap, he noticed that she wasn't married. Not that it mattered. Women like her only went out with men like him temporarily—for a quick fling with danger. Then they went back to the kind of men they married. He slid his knife into its sheath again, scooted back behind the wheel and shoved the gear into drive. He punched the gas.

After a long moment she said, "Are you really taking me to a police station?"

He nodded.

"Thanks."

He could hear her voice wavering. "Those fellows sure shook you up."

"Not as much as you are."

His eyes shot to hers. "Me?"

She cleared her throat. "Just for a moment, of course."

What in the world could be scary about him? "Sweetheart," he said, "it looked like those two kids were about to blow your pretty behind off the face of the map."

"My—my..."

She looked appalled. *Pretty behind.* He'd been thinking it and the phrase had just popped out. He tried to concentrate on the road and decided she was one of those women who repressed her darker desires. "Who's Clyde Calvert?"

"Where have you *been?*"

He shrugged. "In the woods."

She started unwinding the rope from her left wrist. "Don't tell me," she said, "you're Grizzly Adams."

"So, where were *you* headed?" he couldn't help but ask. "To a bridge game?"

She tossed a length of rope between them on the seat, then began unwrapping the rope from her other wrist. "Clyde Calvert—who...er...by the way looks like you—and his girlfriend, Bonnie Smith, committed an armed robbery of a logging company this morning with an elderly neighbor named Jason Morehead."

Great. His heart nearly stopped beating as she filled him in on the story.

"And they took a half-million dollars," she finally finished.

He slammed on the brake and brought his face so close to hers that he could feel her breath. "I take it you happen to look like Smith."

"Unfortunately, yes," she said, leaning away from him. "I do. Those kids were trying to arrest me, probably hoping to get the thousand-dollar reward."

When he grabbed her hand, the warmth of her skin reminded him that he hadn't had a woman he'd really wanted for a while. Not that he hadn't had women toward whom he simply felt friendly. "So are you?"

She wrenched away, but he held her fast. "No!"

"I knew I should have kept you tied up," he muttered. He'd given up stealing cars years ago, but the idea of driving off with her and keeping her helpless was downright tempting. If she was really on the lam, he was in a heap of trouble.

"You might be Clyde Calvert," she said flatly.

He gazed down the length of her voluptuous body, wishing she wasn't making him entertain criminal notions. "I might at that."

Her eyes widened.

"But I'm not." He released her hand, not exactly wanting to. He put the car into drive again and speeded toward the police station. If she was Bonnie Smith, he was aiding a woman who'd committed armed robbery. He'd been around long enough to know that expensive jewelry, snazzy suits and fancy cars didn't make a woman honest. Out of habit, he couldn't help but wonder what had happened to the five-hundred grand, either, and suddenly he felt furious. He wasn't about to get roped into harboring a thief. "If you're not Bonnie Smith, what's your name?"

"Leslie Lewis."

He looked at her just long enough to see that she was lying. Had she done so because she was Smith or because she still thought he might be Clyde Calvert? He nodded. "Pleased to make your acquaintance."

It was an understatement. She had Wanted written all over her, he decided. Trouble was, he didn't know who wanted her most—him or the cops. And with his luck, the attraction he was feeling was of the fatal variety.

She sniffed self-righteously. "And who are you?"

"Bill," he said. "Wild Bill."

SHERIFF JOHN JACKSON'S lips were so close to the radio that he was tasting the metal of the grid. He glanced quickly at Kent and Tyler, his two good-for-nothing deputies. Kent was lounging lazily against the bars of one of the two cells. Tyler was staring in a mirror and combing his red hair as if he were sprucing up for a date, instead of preparing for a manhunt.

"Come again, boys?" the sheriff said. "Calm down and come again."

"We nearly got Bonnie and Clyde," a boy who identified himself as Darrell said. "I swear, we nearly got 'em!"

The two kids were talking in such an excited rush and over so much static that Jackson could hardly make them out.

"Bonnie and Clyde! We had our guns trained right on them! We had her tied up. But when Clyde came, they ganged up on us and knocked us out!"

The second boy's voice broke in. "The tire tracks go north! They took our guns with them in their Cadillac!"

"You boys all right?"

"Oh, yeah!"

The kids sounded ecstatic. The sheriff wished his own deputies were half as riled up about the case. But they weren't. Deputy Tyler had even defended the couple, saying he didn't think they were guilty.

"They got away!" one of the boys suddenly exclaimed. "So we don't get our reward, do we?"

Sheriff Jackson chuckled. "The reward's for any information leading to the arrest," he said. "So, you boys just start thinking about how you're going to spend all that money, and I'll intercept them here."

"I'M SHERIFF John Jackson," a man shouted. "Come out with your hands up."

Out? Frannie already *was* out. She had fled from her father's Cadillac and from the most intense hazel-eyed gaze she'd ever encountered. She hadn't even taken the time to get her umbrella from under the seat. Now she was running toward a small, brick, jail building. She just hoped her rescuer, who was every bit as grungy as he was gorgeous, would follow her inside and agree to be a witness to what had happened to her.

Not that she'd have to contend with him after she forced him to give a sworn statement. She'd made it safely to the police! Her heart swelled with relief. The police were going to help her! Wild Bill couldn't be Clyde Calvert, otherwise, he wouldn't have pulled into the precinct lot. She waved her arms wildly at the uniformed man with the megaphone.

"Two teenagers held me at gunpoint," she screamed, gesturing behind herself at the ever darkening sky. "They're just down the road. They had guns and—"

"Stop or we'll shoot," Sheriff Jackson barked through the megaphone. "Get those hands above your head."

Frannie slowed her steps, nearly stumbling over her own two feet. If she stopped, Wild Bill was going to wind up right beside her! She'd been anxious to talk to the police, but the primary reason she'd bolted from the car was to escape him. The idea that she could be attracted to a grubby man with a tattoo had terrified her more than teenagers with guns ever could.

But what was wrong with this picture? She stopped uncertainly and glanced around. Who were the officers yelling at? She gestured over her shoulder. "And a man," she called out. "That man in the car, Wild Bill, he stopped and—"

"If I were you, I'd put my hands behind my neck, right under all that pretty blond hair."

Wild Bill's gruff drawl had sounded right behind her. Just hearing it, she actually shivered. The voice had a rough, raw edge to it and every time he spoke, she started imagining him saying something sexy. She tried to tell herself that he sounded as if he'd had too much to drink the previous night, then attempted to cure himself by eating gravel for breakfast.

She glanced over her shoulder. The man's hands were clasped behind his neck and his eyes had gone flat and watchful. He looked serious. Dead serious. He stepped forward cautiously, so that he was right next to her.

"What—" Her mouth fell open.

"This is no joke, sweetheart. Just do it."

The man was probably honest, she decided. She'd never seen a look so earnest in her life. Still staring at him, she slowly raised her hands. "This is absolutely unconscionable," she managed to say.

"Well, it sure looks like they're arresting us," he drawled.

"For what?" she asked in shock.

"Armed robbery would be my guess."

"Oh no!" Frannie's hand shot toward her mouth, then changed directions and shot in the air again. "Not only do I look like Bonnie Smith, but you look like Clyde Calvert. There are just too many coincidences here to be believed. We have to explain...."

She felt his gaze drift over her, making her skin feel scorched beneath the cool silk of her white suit. His eyes lingered on her breasts and when she caught him looking, there wasn't so much as a hint of apology in his expression. She wished with all her heart that she could lower her arms. Or that the police would hurry up and come for her.

"Don't argue or they'll think you're resisting."

"Just too many coincidences to be believed," she repeated.

"Hardly coincidence."

She gasped. "What do you mean?" Had the man been tracking her or something? She watched the sheriff motion to a red-haired officer, indicating that he should move in and make the arrest. The guy crept forward carefully.

"You look like Bonnie," Wild Bill said, "I look like Clyde. You happen to be driving a 1950 white Cadillac—

which is a fairly unusual car around these parts—and then you just so happen to get lost."

"I always get lost," she said in protest.

He nodded as if it didn't surprise him in the least. "Then, right at that moment two teenagers are out looking for you, because they think you're Bonnie, and at the same time, I spot you from a mountain and—"

"And what?" Frannie suddenly snapped. It was the longest speech the man had made, his voice was so sexy it was driving her out of her mind and she couldn't believe any of this.

"That ain't coincidence. That's fate."

"What were you doing in the woods, anyway?" she asked coolly, watching the red-haired officer approach. "Meditating on the mysterious inner workings of the universe?"

"Leslie," he said gruffly. "Or whatever the hell your name is—don't get short with me. Your only other option was to save your own hide. And somehow I doubt you could have shot it out with those kids. P.S., I was hiking."

She sent him a steely stare, feeling furious. How had he guessed that she'd lied about her name? He was right about the fact that she couldn't have rescued herself from the teenagers, too. And the idea that fate had brought them together was one she definitely did not want to contemplate. "A shoot-out would have been preferable to this." What she'd meant was preferable to his company.

The red-haired officer was now standing ten paces away.

"Lie down on the pavement," the sheriff said through the megaphone.

Behind the red-haired officer, another policeman drew out his gun.

"Wild horses couldn't drag me down on that pavement," she said in disgust. "I simply refuse to lie down and ruin this outfit."

"I'm not getting killed over a Chanel suit," Wild Bill said flatly.

She realized that most of her anger was coming from the fact that the man seemed to have summed her up with a glance. "How do you know it's a Chanel suit? Do you secretly pore over *Vogue* in your spare time?" She smiled at him sweetly. "You know, when you're not communing with nature."

"Inner pocket, sweetheart," he shot back. "I read the label."

"On the ground!" the sheriff yelled. "Or we will shoot you."

"Know something else?"

She was pretty sure the man was intentionally trying to annoy her. "What?" She glanced at the officer with the gun.

"The way it hugs your curves makes me feel like I already died and went to heaven."

She was so surprised that she almost smiled, but she caught herself. Why couldn't she find a man who both bathed *and* said sweet things like that? She thought of the picture of Mr. Suave, which was buried in the hole that Wolf had dug, and blew out a sigh. Next to her, Wild Bill kneeled, then settled his flat belly on the pavement.

"You too, lady," the red-haired officer said.

She realized that two sets of handcuffs were dangling from his finger. He was so close that she could now read his name badge. "May I please use my hands, Tyler?" There was no way she could go from standing to lying down without them. She wondered why in the world she had to lie down in order to be handcuffed.

After a moment, he nodded. "Sure."

"I'm really not Bonnie Smith," she said, wincing when the white silk of her blouse touched the dirty concrete. She lay on her stomach, reminding herself that it would all be over very soon. They'd discover their error and apologize profusely. Then she'd demand to use their bathroom so that she could change. After all, she wasn't going anywhere near the lobster lunch in a filthy suit.

She lifted her nose from the pavement and glanced at Wild Bill, wishing she didn't keep feeling so compelled to stare at him. "Do you have a last name?" she found herself asking. "Or is Wild your first name and Bill your last?"

His mouth quirked. "It's Berdovitch."

"Wild Bill Berdovitch," she repeated, thinking that one look at the man would tell any woman how he'd gotten his nickname.

"We know he's Clyde Calvert," the red-haired officer said, sounding as if he thought they were trying to pull a fast one. "Two kids up the road already ID'd you both."

"Yeah," Frannie said dryly. "You're right on top of things, Tyler."

"Now spread 'em!" The sheriff yelled through the megaphone.

Frannie gasped. "Spread 'em?"

"Your legs." Wild Bill cleared his throat. "Spread your legs."

"I know the part of my anatomy to which he's referring!" she exclaimed, raising on an elbow and gaping at him. She slightly parted her legs at the ankles. With only that much movement, she could feel her hemline rise. When she glanced down she could see one of her garters. "Why is it taking them hours to arrest us?" she muttered.

"Because we're so armed and dangerous."

She glanced up and realized that Wild Bill's eyes were shining with pure devilment.

"What is so funny?"

"Sorry," he drawled, glancing toward her spread legs. "But you've got to admit that the police have all the luck."

She felt her cheeks getting hot. "Tyler," she said, staring at Bill pointedly. "Would you please hurry up and handcuff him?"

Chapter Two

"You don't understand!" Frannie kept her voice as low as it was urgent and glanced through the large glass window between the interrogation rooms. Next door, Wild Bill was being duly processed by the deputy named Kent. Why hadn't Tyler shut the darn door? If Wild Bill heard her, heaven only knew how he'd take his revenge. "I've never seen that man before in my life!"

"Doesn't sound as if you're above maligning him in the hopes of getting yourself out of a jam, either," Tyler said with humor.

"Listen to his drawl. Maybe he *is* Clyde Calvert!" Her eyes latched onto Wild Bill's chest. His vest was open and he was holding a numbered placard against his mat of golden chest hairs. He looked none too happy about posing for a mug shot.

Frannie blinked against the camera's flash. "I swear, I've known him less than a half hour!"

She heard Kent say, "Gee, Clyde. You could have smiled."

"Anything else you'd like me to do?" Wild Bill shot back. "Like flex my muscles?"

Tyler said, "Now, quit jerking around and give me your thumbs."

When she didn't, Tyler grabbed one and tugged it toward an ink pad.

She moaned, imagining her fingers—blackened, clutching a cocktail fork and digging into a lobster tail. She could just see Mr. Suave wincing at her manicure. *The Lobster Lunch!* She glanced at her wrist, then remembered the police had stolen her watch. "This is a French manicure!" she burst out. *And my jewelry's gone.* Her bracelets, watch, rings and diamond stud earrings had vanished inside a small manila envelope.

She watched in horror as Tyler rolled her second thumb over the ink, then pressed it on a sheet of paper. After that, he started fighting her for her fingers.

Next door, Kent said, "Turn left, please."

At least her partner in crime had an interesting profile, she thought dryly. High cheekbones. A nose that was straight enough to make him look a bit arrogant, but crooked enough that he didn't look pretty. It was hard to tell, but his jaw seemed strong and she found herself wondering why he'd grown that thick beard to hide it. *A disguise?* She gulped.

All the indignities they'd suffered—from arrest to fingerprint to photo—had left her with the distinct impression that he'd had precinct practice. In the car he'd made it sound as if he were a car thief. Surely he'd been joking.

How could she set the record straight? she wondered, staring at Tyler again. *Record!* She was going to have a record now. "Before today," she said calmly, "the only records I've had have been of the musical kind."

"Just a couple more fingers and I'm done. They'll be a little sticky." Tyler suddenly chortled. "But then they already were."

"Ha, ha," she said.

"Thing would move more quickly if you lovebirds would tell us where you hid the money. Where's Jason Morehead, anyway?"

"Please—" She leaned down so that she was eye level with the deputy. "Remember that dog named Wolf that I keep telling you about?" When the deputy nodded, she continued. "Well, that horrible dog buried my pocketbook. If you dig it up, you can see my IDs."

Tyler smiled up at her indulgently.

Her heart started racing. He was going to help her. "I'm a nice person!" she exclaimed. "I was voted most likely to succeed in high school. I was the captain of our cheerleading squad. My father's an attorney. So can't you see why it would be a little strange if I was to be arrested?"

"You've already *been* arrested," Tyler pointed out.

"Things like this just don't happen to people like me," she said, her voice rising. *But they do. They have.* An overwhelming sadness coiled around her heart.

"Well, I guess a nice girl like you shouldn't have hooked herself up with Clyde Calvert." Tyler sighed and leaned forward. "I'm fairly sure you two are innocent. I've got a great-aunt over in Boone County who claims *her* land was illegally harvested by Langston Larson and his partner, but she couldn't prove it. The truth will win out, but in the meantime, you'll just have to let me do my job."

"Do we even look like a couple?" she snapped. "Could you imagine us at the symphony together? A cocktail party? I have never even talked to a man with a tattoo, much less gone out with one!"

Her hands flew to her chest and she pressed her fingers against her blouse. "Look at me! I'm wearing a Chanel suit and I have a French manicure, which is now ruined because of your lousy ink pad." She pointed toward the window. "Now look at him. If anyone's the criminal here, who do you think is the better bet?"

She pounded her fist on the fingerprinting table for emphasis. When she glanced downward, she realized she'd left five perfect black fingerprints on her white silk shell. "My blouse," she muttered. "My brand-new silk blouse!"

Tyler held up his paper and grinned. "The ones on your blouse came out a sight better than mine did."

"Well, believe me," she shrieked, "I'm not trading." She was still glaring at him when he cuffed her wrists.

"I'm really sorry," Tyler said. "But we have to go next door for the mug shots." He smiled. "For you, we'll call it a photo session."

"You're a real doll," she said acidly.

While the deputy marshaled her toward the camera, she caught a glimpse of Wild Bill. Even though he was being shoved into a cell, she couldn't help but notice how broad his back was or how his snug jeans hung on his hips, showing off every blessed contour of his backside.

In a matter of minutes, she'd be alone with him, too. And steel bars would hardly protect her.

"It's MISERABLY HOT in here and this wretched cot is absolutely unhygienic!" Frannie had given up on yelling at the policemen through the bars because her throat had begun to ache. As much as she hated to let her jacket touch anything in the cell, she removed it and laid it across the uncovered mattress. Then she perched on the cot—so close to the edge that her behind threatened to plop off—and clasped her stained fingers together in her lap.

"Where do you think you are, sweetheart?" Wild Bill muttered. "A spa?"

"Furthermore, these policemen are positively inept," she continued, ignoring his sarcasm. "If they misfiled that envelope with my jewelry, I—I'll—" She sniffed. Fortunately, they had let her go to the bathroom alone and they hadn't discovered her secret skirt pocket, so she still had a hundred and forty dollars. Not that the money would do her any good. "Well," she snapped. "What are we going to do?"

"We?"

She watched Wild Bill recline on his cot and shove a grungy pillow behind his head. The heel of one of his motorcycle boots rested on the toe of the other. How could the man simply lie there? He looked so peaceful that he might well have been meditating.

Just because I've been treated like a common criminal does not mean I have to act like one. I will not give in to my temper! She rose from her cot, squared her shoulders, crossed her arms, and started pacing between her cot and the bars that separated her from Wild Bill. "Well, it *does* look as if we're in this together." She tossed her head regally. "For better or worse."

"Or for richer, for poorer," he said drolly. He sent her a long, level stare through the bars.

She realized his expression wasn't really serene. His glance traveled slowly down the length of her body and back up again, as if he were undressing an adversary with his eyes.

"Don't look at *me*," he said after a long moment. "After all, *you've* got that fancy French manicure to bargain with."

He heard every word I said. She strode as close to him as she could get before the bars stopped her. "What does my manicure have to do with anything?"

"It equals good morals, doesn't it?" He left his cot and was nearly nose to nose with her before she could move. For a minute, she thought he was going to reach through the bars and grab her. It wasn't exactly as if she could call the police. They'd probably think the man was merely claiming his conjugal rights.

She stared into his hazel eyes, meeting their challenge. The scent of his skin wafted toward her. He didn't smell of soap or shampoo or after-shave. Instead, he smelled of the woods—of new leaves and fresh pine, mixed with a little manly sweat. She became suddenly conscious of her breasts. Perspiration was making her shell cling to her skin.

"Pardon me for doing my level best to get myself out of here," she managed to say.

He merely glared at her. The intensity of his gaze was enough to make her flinch. Not that she did. But she realized that she was definitely attracted to him. How was it possible? Her heart started hammering as she thought of Mr. Suave. He was her type! She needed someone well employed. Someone who owned a suit to wear to her mother's cocktail parties. *Someone who can take care of me,* she thought in panic.

"From listening to you talk to that deputy, I'd say women with decently manicured hands might be as apt to lie as..." His eyes narrowed until they looked like almonds—a hard, shiny light brown, not quite ovals. "Criminals like me."

"I never said you *were* a criminal." She retained her surface cool, but her voice was starting to waver. When he shrugged out of his vest and casually tossed it behind him, to his cot, her eyes drifted over his chest. When his eyes fixed on hers again, she breathed in sharply.

"Well, you do have a tattoo," she ventured. She tried to keep her eyes on his but they flitted over his biceps. "And that leather vest...."

"Now, that should be enough to convict a man," he drawled.

He lifted his arms and his fingers curled around the bars on either side of his face. It was hardly the time to notice that his golden eyes were flecked with darker brown and rimmed by thick, sandy lashes. "Of course it's not," she said weakly.

"How come people like you are so damn prone to make snap judgments?"

"People like me?" She knew exactly what he meant, but her eyebrows shot up in protest.

He rolled his eyes.

Just looking at him, she suddenly wanted to defend herself. All he'd seen was the surface. The exterior of a now half-ruined outfit that her mother had bought. A car that didn't belong to her. A manicure her mother had insisted she have. "No girl can go on a husband hunt without a fresh French manicure," she'd said.

The man saw the image and nothing more. If he wasn't so judgmental himself, she decided, she might actually clarify things for him. But given his expression, she wasn't about to go into the saga of her many comedowns in the world. Or tell him about how much she'd suffered.

Her eyes fell as she thought about her son. She'd fought to have him—argued with her friends, with Joey Florence's parents, and with her own...and then Raymond had died.

She found herself glaring at Wild Bill Berdovitch. "Never trust a first impression."

He arched a brow lazily in her direction. "What? Are you a white-collar thief?"

She'd never stolen anything in her life. And the only thing she'd ever had stolen was her own heart.

"You know," he drawled softly. "I do believe you *are* hiding something."

"Nothing," she said quickly. She could be incarcerated with him for an eternity, and he'd never know that she felt as trapped in her own life as she did in the cell.

"Sorry I said all that to the deputy," she said, changing the subject. "But if you hadn't come along, maybe I could have talked those kids into letting me go."

He dropped his hands, rested his shoulder against the bars and leaned casually. Somehow, every time he moved, she felt her world go just a little more off kilter. She found herself anxiously wondering what he did for a living, even though she was sure that frank sensuality was his only stock in trade.

After a moment, he chuckled softly. "Sweetheart, it didn't look to me as if all that smooth talk was doing you much good with the deputy." His smile made his mustache wiggle. "Not that your wily ways are always so ineffectual, I'm sure."

She squinted at him. His voice had suddenly sounded almost cultured. In her father's car, he'd told her that car-jack shouldn't be turned into a verb with the surety of a grammarian. And yet, he'd made it sound as if he'd stolen cars. *Who are you?* Maybe he was really wealthy... He was obviously somewhat attracted to her. Yes, maybe he was hiding out, to write a novel or something and— She should have her head examined!

"I—I was simply trying to talk some common sense into him," she stammered. "I truly did not intend to use wiles."

His lips twisted into another quickly wrought, wry smile. "Now that's a real shame."

"Look, I simply came over here to talk to you because it's essential that we—" She ran her tongue quickly over her lips, wishing he didn't smell so dangerously enticing and that his eyes weren't such a rich, changeable brown. "That we get along."

His shoulders shook with unsuppressed laughter. "Just how well do you want to get to know me?"

"That's not what I meant," she said shakily.

"You're just lucky those kids didn't accidentally shoot you."

She shrugged. "My father's going to kill me."

"Aren't you a little old to be worrying about what your daddy thinks?"

Her temper flared, but she kept a lid on it. Undoubtedly, he thought she was spoiled. "Probably."

He scrutinized her face, then nodded as if he'd won a formal debate. He turned on his heel and strode back to his cot. He lay down again, making a show of stretching out his legs. They were long, but couldn't exactly be called lean. He was a little bowlegged and his thighs were well muscled, like the rest of him.

Talk about wiles. She straightened her posture, turned gracefully and strode back to her own cot in what she hoped was an equally self-possessed manner. She made sure her heels clicked rhythmically on the tile floor and swung her hips just enough that he'd notice. She'd spent enough time staring in various mirrors to know darn well what she looked like—and right now, she hoped he was getting an eyeful of what he'd never have.

When she reached her cot, she spun around daintily. Then she perched on the edge of the mattress and folded her hands again. She glanced at him with faint disdain. She'd rather walk across hot coals than have the man guess she was attracted to him.

She shut her eyes and tried to conjure the long lost image of Mr. Suave. He swam hazily around in her mind. Had he been as tall as Wild Bill? Just how dark had his hair been?

When she blinked, her eyes opened on the vision of Bill lying calmly on his cot with his tanned hands clasped over his chest. Unwashed, unshaven, and tattooed was one way of putting it. Criminal was another. But the longer she looked at him, the more he seemed as wild as a wooded mountain, as primitive as a rushing river and as untamed as the coming spring storm.

When he looked at her, his eyes seemed to say that he could take a woman places she didn't even know existed. Even scarier was the fact that Frannie found herself wanting to go. And wherever that place was, it definitely wasn't civilized.

She ran her hand from her chin, down her neck, nearly between her breasts and back up again, swiping away the droplets of perspiration. Heat pooled in her belly.

If she didn't get sprung soon, trouble wasn't even the word for where she was going to find herself.

HE JUST WISHED she'd quit dreamily running her fool hand beneath her collar and down between her breasts. At least an hour had passed. The only excitement had been the visit from the two boys who had attempted to arrest his cell mate. While they'd made arrangements to collect their reward, the woman had screamed at them. Through the barred-in window above his iron headboard, he could see that the storm still hadn't broken.

He watched her pat herself with a tissue the red-haired deputy had brought for her. What he wouldn't give to touch the rounded, slender column of her throat with that kind of familiarity.... Of course, he'd probably wind up strangling her. He'd never met anyone so condescending in his life. If she knew the thoughts he'd been entertaining about her— ladylike as she was—she'd let herself sweat like a pig, he decided.

In his latest fantasy, he'd walked across his cell, clutched two of the bars that separated them, then stretched them apart, the way men did in cartoons.

He stared at the ceiling now, which was was wide and flat and blankly white. But the whiteness of it reminded him of her cool white suit. She didn't exactly look virginal in it, but she sure looked soft.

And older than he'd thought. There were tiny lines at the corners of her eyes. A sadness touched her blue irises at times, making him think she didn't quite add up. He doubted she was Bonnie Smith, though it was possible. Either way, under all her grooming—the suit, the manicure, the jewelry—trouble was brewing.

He'd dated numerous women like her. And they were all the same. They wanted a quick motorcycle ride and an introduction to the wilder side of passion. Years ago—when he'd had little going for him except good looks, a bad attitude, and a worse reputation—he hadn't minded. He hadn't missed those lovely ladies when they'd run back to the buttoned-down types they always wound up marrying, either.

Now he minded. Still, they were fun while they lasted, he thought, glancing back at the woman in the opposite cell. Was her name really Frannie Anderson? It was what she'd said when they'd booked her. It was how he'd think of her, he decided, even if he called her Leslie Lewis.

As Frannie patted her throat, she made a show of staring at the front desk. Actually, she wasn't staring at anything—just away from him. It was a simple matter of chemistry. Some well-kept women just couldn't resist grungy men in leather. And when it came to cool blondes who smelled of hundred-dollar-an-ounce perfume, he was as helpless as a newborn.

Each time he looked at her, he felt the age-old tightening of his belly, a warm tug of arousal and a dryness that hit the back of his throat. He forced himself to focus on the fact that she'd gotten him into trouble—at a time when trouble was the last thing he could afford.

If they were running the prints, they'd figure out he wasn't Clyde Calvert, at least. Maybe they were already digging out a fat, dusty file on William H. Berdovitch. Given the fact that his hunting knife was longer than was legal, he didn't know if that was good or bad. Either way, he and Frannie would walk. A list of technicalities a mile long would trail behind them. He decided he might also sue.

"What's he saying?"

Frannie's husky voice floated between the bars, sounding raw from all the yelling she'd done. She sounded as if she'd just gotten out of bed or had just decided to get into one.

Bill cocked his head and glanced at Sheriff Jackson who was on the phone.

"We've got to get him to Moundsville," the man was saying. "For her, we need a woman's lockup." There was a long pause, then the sheriff chuckled. "Yeah, makes you wish it was the electric chair, now doesn't it? Well, I figure they'll get five to ten, depending on whether or not they tell us Jason Morehead's whereabouts and where they put the money."

So much for the men in blue having identified him correctly.

Moundsville. He suppressed a shudder. That was one prison he didn't intend to see the insides of again.

"Have four cars waiting," Sheriff Jackson continued. "When my two deputies get there with the paddy wagon, you can provide escort on the drive upstate."

"Moundsville?" Frannie called out. "What's Moundsville, Wild Bill?"

Bill swung his legs over the side of his cot, then stretched them out, crossed his ankles and glanced at her. Her skirt still looked neatly clean and pressed, even if there were dark smudges on her blouse. He could see the lacy outlines of her bra, even at this distance.

The way she called him Wild Bill cracked him up. He smiled as reassuringly as he could. "Moundsville's a prison."

Her eyes looked so round and blue that he wished he could have said that Moundsville was a country club, a golf course or a hair salon...someplace where she might feel more comfortable.

Not that he'd exactly feel at home in Moundsville. In fact, there were probably still guys inside who wanted him dead. For the first time, he glanced toward the front desk and thought about escaping. There were only three of them—the sheriff and the two deputies. It would be foolish, but he could do it.

But his life, as he knew it, would be finished. He rubbed his jaw, his fingers riffling through his beard and massaging the scar beneath.

"Isn't this a prison?" she finally asked.

He shook his head. "Afraid not, sweetheart."

Her cool reserve had vanished and she looked downright frightened. He wondered why he wasn't more pleased. After all, he'd spent the past hour thinking about breaking down the wall of her haughty composure. Except, of course, they'd been in bed while he was doing it. Now, he wished he was as young and crazy and wild as he used to be. Then he would just break them out.

"What?" the sheriff yelled. "There's no license plate on the Cadillac? How can we ID the car as Jason Morehead's if there's no plate?"

"There's a plate!" Frannie yelled. "What happened to it? That plate would prove the car belongs to my father!"

Something as concrete as a license plate didn't just disappear. Had the woman been driving a stolen car? Once, in Las Vegas, he'd met a woman who was cheating the casinos. She'd been every bit as beautiful, well-groomed and cultured as the woman in the opposite cell. Was Frannie really Bonnie Smith?

"So, what's this about Moundsville?" she asked again. "What are they going to do to us?"

"Transport us, sweetheart."

TYLER HAD DECIDED against the leg irons. Instead of using them, he'd merely handcuffed her and Bill together. "Go ahead and get cozy," he'd said as he led them inside the paddy wagon. "After all, you two won't be seeing each other for a while."

Frannie tried to tell herself that the last thing she wanted to do was to cozy up to Wild Bill. Still, doing otherwise was impossible. His left hand was attached to her right. They were seated side by side on a metal bench. Through the wired-in side windows, she could see the mountains. Even though she kept imagining escaping into them, she remained right where she was—with Wild Bill's thigh pressed hard against hers.

"They didn't even try to call my father." Frannie watched the brick jailhouse recede in the distance as the paddy wagon pulled away. They rounded a curve and the building vanished from view. She thought of her jewelry, hidden away in the manila envelope, and wondered if she'd ever see it again.

"Not that he would have answered," she continued. When she glanced up, Wild Bill was scrutinizing her face. "He and my mother went to North Carolina. They borrowed somebody's cabin."

He looked at her as if he couldn't decide whether to believe her.

"It's true, Wild Bill!" she burst out.

He suddenly grinned. "Just Bill's okay."

The wagon hit a pothole. She bounced, then resettled uncomfortably on the hot, hard metal seat. Outside, the clouds had turned almost black. Up front, Kent and Tyler's heads bounced in response to the wagon's lousy shocks. The deputies seemed to be arguing.

Not that she cared. Wild Bill—just Bill, she mentally corrected—had looked truly disturbed at the mention of Moundsville. Somehow, she supposed she'd manage, but she was beginning to wish she could take Bill with her. He'd know what to do.

Her hand suddenly lurched onto his thigh. She glanced down at it and gasped.

"Sorry."

Apparently, he'd forgotten they were handcuffed together and changed the position of his hands. Not that he did anything now to correct his impropriety. Her right hand rested on the soft denim of his jeans. Beneath her fingers, she could feel his muscles quiver.

"Er... Leslie?"

It took her a full moment to remember that was the name she'd given him and another to wonder why she'd lied. Of course, she'd done so at first in case he was Clyde Calvert, but now she was sure he wasn't. "Hmm?"

"They'll straighten it out," he said softly. "Don't worry."

"I am not worried," she said levelly, even though she was. When they hit another pothole the cuffs jangled and his hand grazed hers. Her jacket was still at the station, and the blondish hairs on his arms whispered against the whole length of her side.

"Think positive," he said with irony. "If you're really Bonnie Smith, you'll get off on a technicality. I think they were just so glad to have some action around here that—"

"But I'm not Bonnie Smith!" The least he could do was believe her, since no one else did.

"In which case, you can sue as well."

The whole situation had become so absurd that she couldn't help but smile. "I can't believe you're considering the financial angles."

When he shrugged, he jostled her shoulder more than was necessary, gently bumping against her and forcing her to lean against him. She fit perfectly in the crook of his shoulder.

"Speaking for myself," he drawled, "I could use some cold hard cash." He sent her a lazy smile. "Of course, given the fact that you're decked out in the Chanel wear that nearly got me killed, I guess money's not one of your priorities."

"Why no," she said, mocking his drawl. "I concern my-self with French manicures, benefits for the arts and civic duties."

"You sure seem more civil than you did two hours ago."

It was true. The more this nightmare continued, the more she was starting to feel that Wild Bill was her only friend. "What kind of people are going to be in this place?"

He didn't say anything.

"Murderers?" she croaked.

After a long moment, he nodded.

"They would never—*could never*—do such a thing!" At the mere thought, she had to fight not to reach over the inch that separated their hands and grab his.

"I hope not," he said gently. His low, throaty chuckle filled the back of the paddy wagon again. "Even if they do, my money's on you. You'll chew them up and spit them out."

Forgetting how close he was, she turned abruptly. The man's looks were definitely star quality. All he needed was a bath. What had she been about to say? A second passed. Another second passed. Finally she said, "Do you think I'm a barracuda or something?"

"Absolutely cold-blooded."

Was he teasing or not? "I'm not a criminal!" she said defensively. "I'm warm-blooded!"

His face came toward hers by almost imperceptible de-grees. His lips had to have been a good six inches away. Then they were four... then three.

"You sure are," he said in a near whisper.

Frannie leaned back. "I think you're flirting with me," she blurted out. "And I think it's inappropriate. First, we're headed to a prison. And second, we're entirely ill suited."

"You are, anyway." He glanced at her, his gaze lingering on her breasts. Her cheeks warmed and she realized he was calling attention to the smudges on her blouse. What was left of her suit did look rather limp.

"Ill suited," he said. "Yes, it was a bad joke."

"At least I bathe." Even as she said it, she couldn't help but smile.

"So do I!" He threw back his head and laughed.

"Just not often?"

"So, you picked up on that fact of life, did you?"

"I'm not sure you and I should discuss the facts of life," she shot back dryly.

He shrugged. "Actions always do speak louder than words."

She laughed. When she did, she realized she didn't feel nearly as scared. "I can't believe you're trying to pick up a woman in a paddy wagon."

"There's not a whole lot else to do." He lifted their cuffed hands and shook them, so that the metal jangled. "Besides, I feel attached to you."

She glanced around. "If this is where you go on a first date," she said, "I'd sure hate to see where you go on a second."

He shot her a long sideways glance. There was concern in his face, but his eyes were twinkling. When his lips parted and their corners twitched into a smile, the tips of his mustache curled mischievously.

"No, you wouldn't," he drawled.

Her mouth went as dry as dust. "If you're so rough-and-ready, tough guy," she found herself saying, "then why don't you just break us out?"

"Don't think it hasn't crossed my mind."

He sounded serious and she wished with all her heart that he actually would. Before she thought it through, her palm flattened. It was as if feeling the rock hard solidness of his thigh could take her all the way back to 6:00 a.m. when her alarm had first sounded . . . and none of this had happened.

"If I break you out of here, what are you going to do for me?" he asked. "After all, you got me in this mess in the first place."

If he started blaming her, she'd kill him. "This is not my fault."

He shrugged.

"You mean you wouldn't mastermind my escape out of the goodness of your heart?"

He flashed her a quick grin. "You mean you thought a criminal like me *had* a heart?"

Another pothole sent them flying again. Somehow, as their hands jostled together, hers wound up in his. Her chest constricted and she felt breathless. *You might as well hold his hand. After all, you're never going to see him again.*

She gazed into his eyes. "Wild Bill, if you got me out of here, I'd marry you for life."

He blew out a playful sigh. "That's too bad."

His hazel eyes suddenly reminded her of old wood, the kind that had been polished for so many years that it gleamed in varying shades of brown. Almond browns. Golden cat-eye browns. Reddish clay browns. Deep chocolate browns.

Finally, he said, "I'm hardly the marrying type, but I'm reasonable and I *would* settle for less."

"I'm not about to ask for what," she said with mock gravity.

He gaped at her. "Maybe I was just thinking about a kiss, sweetheart."

When she giggled, her voice had a hysterical edge. "Well, that's too bad 'cause I'm not the kissing kind."

"Ah . . ." he drawled. "But I think you're lying."

And she was. She couldn't so much as look at his mouth without wondering how his lips would feel on hers. Past all his defenses—underneath the beard and mustache and beyond the granitelike clenched jaw with which he locked his features into place—she was beginning to think he might be a nice guy.

Not that she'd ever be serious about him. Mr. Suave was still out there somewhere—with a clean, nicely upholstered convertible and a band of gold. *Not that it matters, because I'm going to prison,* she thought in sudden terror.

"I've wanted to kiss you all day," Bill whispered.

He started leaning toward her and she decided she'd let him. It had been a stressful day and she was worried about where they were going and—

His lips lurched away.

The paddy wagon was swerving off the road. Had they wrecked? No, the deputies were stopping.

Bill's mouth, kissably pursed just a second before, was gaping open. He stared at the double back doors of the wagon, looking as if he'd forgotten her entirely.

And Frannie told herself that it was just as well.

BILL WATCHED in morbid fascination as the doors swung open.

"Run!" Kent yelled.

They were in the middle of nowhere, stopped near a high fence that stood against the mountains. Bill remained stock-still, with Frannie pressed against his side.

"C'mon!" Tyler appeared and started waving them out. Then both he and Kent ran back toward the cab.

She gasped. "They want us to escape?"

He nodded. They had rotten timing, too. Why couldn't they have waited until he'd kissed her? Frannie got up, pulling him with her. Her movements seemed to be motivated by confusion, rather than a desire to flee.

When he and Frannie reached the side of the paddy wagon, Bill stopped in his tracks. He felt Frannie bump into him, her breasts pressing against his side. "Sweet heaven," he muttered.

"Guess that's what they meant when they said Bonnie and Clyde have inspired hero worship," Frannie said.

Bill had been referring to how soft she felt against him, but he stared at her, anyway. "You didn't mention that."

"Excuse me," she said, suddenly sounding testy. "In all the excitement, I must have forgotten. A number of people stepped forward, claiming that they'd been robbed by Langston Larson, and so a lot of people think that Bonnie and Clyde are actually innocent. They—"

The ripping sound of duct tape stopped her cold. Bill glanced toward the mountains. Then he looked at her. Then he glanced down at the cuffs. It sure was tempting.

"I'll cover Kent's mouth with the tape," Tyler said. "You just sock me. We've got to make it look like there was a struggle, Clyde. I mean, don't hurt me...just—"

"We're not struggling!"

Frannie's shriek was so heartfelt that Bill gasped. When he put his hand on his hip, hers whipped upward, following suit. He felt her hook a finger through his belt loop.

"There goes my nail," she muttered.

"I'm not punching anybody," Bill said.

But he was itching to. He could see the bleak facade of Moundsville as surely as if he were standing in front of it. He thought about the lousy food and the lack of light. *No women.* He glanced at Frannie again.

"People will think we let you go," Tyler nearly wailed.

"You *are* letting us go," Bill corrected.

"We do not want to escape," Frannie said succinctly.

These days, Bill liked his women honest, but he still couldn't help but wish that she wanted to take off with him.

"Look," Tyler said, "there's not much time. Like I told Bonnie, my own aunt's been ripped off by Larson. So, the two of us—" he started taping Kent's mouth "—we decided to help you out. When I drove your car around back, I tossed the plate into a garbage truck that was on its way to the dump. Kent switched your prints with old ones from the drunk tank."

Bill's heart dropped to his feet. "You didn't."

"Oh, Bill!" Frannie clutched his waistband as if for support. "They'll never identify us."

"No, ma'am." Tyler reached inside the cab, grabbed his radio, and yelled, "They've escaped! We're only about a half mile away from picking up the escort."

Bill groaned. "I ought to kill you for this."

"Just clip me," Tyler said.

"With pleasure." Bill lifted his left fist, but realized Frannie was attached. He quickly shifted his weight and caught Tyler's jaw with a right hook. It wasn't exactly his best work, since he was left-handed.

"Assault and battery." Bill watched the deputy's head swing downward. "Great."

Frannie looked as if she were in shock. As she turned and tugged him toward the fence, Bill's whole life flashed before his eyes. He could go back to jail for what he'd just done. Of course, if they'd destroyed his prints, there was no real proof that he'd been inside that cell. He tried to remember what he'd touched. If he ran, the sexy lady next to him might well turn out to be deadweight.

A siren sounded in the distance.

And he realized that they might get shot if they stayed.

"Are we going?' she asked, sounding ready.

"Aw, hell," he muttered.

As they took off, he realized she was lightning fast. He shoved the rounded toe of his motorcycle boot into a diamond-shaped square at the exact second that she speared the fence with the pointy toe of a high heel. Their connected hands reached for purchase in a way so timed it could have been choreographed.

"Guess you owe me a kiss," he managed while they struggled toward the top.

"The kiss was only if you broke me out," she said without missing a beat. "They let us go."

"Indian giver," he muttered, watching her swing a shapely-looking leg dexterously over the top.

Chapter Three

Frannie fled like the wind, glancing over her shoulder toward the fence. As she'd swung her leg over it, she'd lost one of her shoes. It had clattered down the wrong side and now she was unbalanced. Even worse, her lungs were burning and her side was aching and— "My stocking just ran!"

"What do you want me to do?" Bill jerked his head in her direction, but kept moving at a dead run. "Carry you?"

"This isn't my fault! Don't you dare blame me for what's happening. Don't you—"

"I *will* carry you."

"Absolutely not."

She couldn't see the river, but heard the sound of rushing white water. Beyond the fence, the wooded terrain had become a dark jungle of brambles and low-lying tree limbs. She was so scared, she felt numb. Thorny switches waved toward her face like mammoth insect tentacles. Gnarled tree roots clawed at her ankles. Twigs snapped, crackled and popped beneath her feet like burning kindling.

But she wouldn't have let Wild Bill Berdovitch carry her if he was licensed by the airlines.

In midstride, she hopped, grabbed her remaining shoe by the heel and wrenched it off. Wielding it in her left hand, she swung it like a machete, swatting at branches and bugs. Her right hand swung far forward, making her lurch. "Quit jerking me around!"

"I mean to get us out of here before we get shot!" Bill exclaimed, without slowing his pace.

What had possessed her to run? And how was she going to get rid of the two hundred pounds of pure male to which she was handcuffed? With no shoes and the knuckles of his attached hand rapping hers, she could hardly hope to impress him with her physical prowess, either.

"You've got on boots!" she shrieked breathlessly.

"Keep your voice down," he threatened.

She kept running. But her heart was beating in wild panic. Wild Bill had turned mean. Maybe he really was Clyde Calvert. Maybe he was going to kill her....

He stopped dead in his tracks. She slammed right into the hard wall of his back. Where was the white water? She'd heard rushing, but the river—as swift as it was here—wasn't creating that sound. Her eyes darted down the river bank.

"Oh, no." She sucked in a breath, her pulse pounding. "The New River Raft Inn." How could she have missed it? There was a sign on the landscaped lawn. Brightly colored yellow rafts were already inflated and tied to the end of a dock.

Bill was panting, catching his breath. "Been here before? Know anybody here who could—"

Help us. She shook her head quickly. "No."

He nodded curtly. "Keep yourself down low." He crouched, pulling her down with him, then started creeping toward the dock. "I've got a cabin downriver. We'll steal a raft."

She squatted far down on her haunches, mindless of her exposed garters. Hunkered next to him, she started mirroring his catlike movements as they approached the dock. Her free hand clutched her shoe and her cuffed hand brushed back and forth against his thigh. He'd said steal. Were they really going to steal?

When they reached the river, he tried to walk right into the water. She hesitated but he tugged her arm so hard that her cuffed hand plunged beneath the surface.

"It's freezing!" She shoved her bug-swatting shoe into the waistband of her skirt and waded in, her heart sinking with each inch of skin that vanished below the surface. Icy water seeped through her stockings, hit her upper thighs, then soaked her panties, making her lower half tingle. Her breasts dipped down and came back up again. If she stood up straight, she could keep that part of her anatomy out of the water, but her nipples were pebbling against her scanty bra. And the lace was as transparent as her blouse.

Her breath caught in her throat. Below the surface, she felt the current move like the raw energy coursing between her and Bill. Swift and sure and too fast. She glanced uncertainly in the direction from which they'd come. The sirens had been wailing. The police would shoot them if they went back.

She glanced at her top again, blushed, then looked at Bill. His eyes merely said she was an albatross around his neck. She mustered her haughtiest tone and said, "I suppose the water temperature doesn't bother you."

"No—" he'd quit panting "—it doesn't."

"Perhaps this is where you bathe." Her glance was as icy as the water. "When you bathe."

He sighed and nodded at the complicated knot that fastened one of the rafts to the dock. "Just help me untie this."

"We can't steal a raft." She glanced nervously toward the New River Raft Inn. The cocktail social! People were congregating on the veranda.

"Like hell we can't."

Both Bill's hands shot to the knot and her cuffed right hand whipped right on top of a thick, coarse rope. The knots looked more complicated than the ones that plagued her when her jewelry got tangled.

"We've got to get out of here, sweetheart."

He was right. She started digging into one of the knots. "Nail number two," she muttered, watching its white tip peel off her finger like a sticker.

With the coming storm the air had turned as thick and dark as molasses. Gnats buzzed beside her ear. Her eyes darted toward the cozy, yellow-looking light inside the inn. People milled about, holding wineglasses. Not one of them had been arrested. Not one was running from the law.

Suddenly, she choked. There he was. In the flesh. Mr. Suave—or the spitting image of him. The man was tall, his tastefully short black hair neatly parted on the side. Even from where Frannie was, hunkered down in the water, she could tell that his cream suit had cost a fortune. He strode onto the veranda, carrying a highball glass. *The New River Raft Inn,* she thought, the promo copy sounding in her mind. *Where singles meet for the adventure of a lifetime.*

"Are you going to help or not, dammit?" Bill sounded furious.

"Please, just shut up," she said levelly. "And stop all that cursing. I'm sick of hearing it." Her hands had fallen still on the dock rope and she couldn't have cared less.

"Now don't you start getting testy on me, sweetheart."

Testy wasn't even the word for it. Not fifty yards away, her dream man was leaning on the veranda rail.

"Now I know this is probably the worst thing that's ever happened to you in your uneventful little life," Bill continued, his hands still flying over the rope. "But I am not going to put up with your attitude. Other people undoubtedly do, but—"

"My life is not uneventful," she snapped.

"Oh, no?" An end of the rope slapped the water as he pulled it from the coil. He grasped the next knot. "So, what's your idea of a good time? Lunching with the alumni association?''

''I put myself through college and don't go to alumni parties.'' Was Mr. Suave really looking at her? She glanced at Wild Bill. What she'd just said was a lie. Her parents were putting her through college and she hadn't graduated yet—much less considered being an alumni—but she was more than pleased to see the grudging respect in his eyes.

''I take it you like the pull-yourself-up-by-your-bootstraps type,'' she muttered. Which, she thought, with a faint twinge of disappointment, she was not. How could she even feel attraction for the man when Mr. Suave was within view? She sniffed and grudgingly started helping him work the knots again. ''I always had a lousy reputation, if you must know.''

Bill winced. ''I doubt it.''

''Wild and wanton,'' she shot back. ''Other kids weren't even allowed to play with me. Not since I was about age five. And now I run my own accounting firm in San Francisco. I'm quite a success.'' *Lies.* She glanced at Mr. Suave, who was looking over his shoulder, talking to someone. *It could have been me.*

She turned back to Bill and realized his gaze had landed on her breasts. She didn't have to look down to know that the darkened tips were visible. Pure lust was in his eyes. He'd clearly forgotten about the raft and their escape. ''I live in San Francisco,'' she managed. ''With my husband.'' She buckled her knees, so her breasts vanished beneath the water. ''We bungee jump for excitement.''

''Lots of bridges in San Francisco,'' he drawled. His gaze traveled to the rope and he started untying the knot with a vengeance.

''Hey there!'' a man yelled.

''Someone's spotted us,'' Bill muttered.

''Mr. Suave.''

Bill's gaze followed hers. "Who?"

She didn't respond. Instead, her hand slipped over Bill's. With a final tug, they jointly freed the rope from the dock. The end that remained attached to the raft trailed in the water.

And then Mr. Suave started pointing at them. Just as her eyes connected with her dream man's, she felt Wild Bill's free hand plunge beneath the river's surface. Water rippled against her thighs as his fingers passed. She squealed. Had the fool man actually grabbed a healthy handful of her rear end?

"What do you think you're doing!" she screeched.

"Just get your butt in the boat, lady."

His fingers squeezed her backside, then he hoisted her up with a loud splash and shoved. She shot out of the water like a leaping fish and belly flopped onto the inflated rubber. "Ouch!" she exclaimed as her cheek collided with an oar. Her right hand wrenched around unnaturally, the metal of the cuff grinding against her wrist bone. Then Bill rolled right on top of her. The heel of her bug-swatting shoe stabbed her in the stomach.

Bill righted himself, pointed toward an oarlock and said, "Paddle."

She could still feel his fingerprints on her icily numb backside. She glared at him. "We have to push off."

"Your friend Mr. Suave is on his way," Bill drawled, "so I suggest you hurry it up."

Mr. Suave was jogging toward them, his arms akimbo, but Frannie took the time to very daintily stick one of her slender feet outside the raft and give the dock a kick. The swift current gave them an extra shove. Bill was already paddling. She shot her dream man a parting glance, then whacked her oar against the water.

"They're taking a raft!" Mr. Suave yelled.

And somehow, he didn't seem so desirable, after all. In fact, as she felt the wind lift the damp ends of her hair, she decided he might have been a bore. But they were taking a raft—*stealing!* And the police were chasing them!

Big deal, she thought in panic.

If nothing else, the sheer physical exertion of paddling would help to get Wild Bill out of her system. And maybe all the lies she'd told him would keep him off her back. Literally. Her heart started beating double time. She told herself to concentrate on paddling and forget about what she was doing. And with whom.

Fortunately, the current was shooting them downriver at a brisk clip. Maybe Bill really thought she was a big success now. She was glad she'd informed him there was a man out there who loved her enough to marry her, too. Plus, San Francisco was on the opposite side of the country. Bill wouldn't look her up.

If she lived!

Her hair was blowing crazily behind her. Stray strands whipped against her face, stinging. Along the riverbank, resorts zipped past. The New River Raft Inn where she was supposed to be twirling under soft lights with Mr. Suave and a glass of bubbly had vanished.

Suddenly, Bill quit paddling and stared in front of them, looking worried. Her left hand stilled on her oar and she tugged her right, to get his attention. At the pull of the cuffs, he glanced her way.

"What's that sound?" she croaked.

"The rapids."

Terror seized her heart. "I thought these *were* the rapids!"

"No." He shook his head. "And it looks like we're about to go over Skeleton's Waterfall."

It hardly sounded promising.

"JUST LIE DOWN and hang on to me, sweetheart!" He hoped she'd heard him over the rising roar of the river. "I've got my hand wrapped around the rope. It's right over the side."

Bill shimmied his back against the wet bottom of the raft, lying flat with his head propped against the protective, bubbled side. He just hoped he wasn't taking his last breaths.

Unfortunately, his cofugitive wasn't letting go of her oar. She wasn't lying down, either. A wave hit the raft and washed over them, water soaking them both to the bone. Bill squeezed her fingers.

When she wrenched around to stare at him, her eyes were such a magnetic blue that he wondered if she was really married. Women who looked that good didn't usually make it far past legal age before someone claimed them. And yet she hadn't been wearing a wedding ring. He decided she'd been lying about both San Francisco and her husband.

"I'm a lousy swimmer," she wailed.

"Swimming in this wouldn't help. Lie down!"

Instead, she clutched her oar more tightly, as if she'd rather hang on to anything but him. A second later, the paddle snapped from her hand, thwacked a rock and splintered.

"I said, lie down!"

Bill raised his head and glanced over the side. Jagged rocks jutted above the river's surface. The water had turned so white and frothy that it looked as if it were boiling. The raft suddenly spun, sending them downriver headfirst.

Bill gave up, glanced at where her hand was cuffed to his, then jerked hard, pulling her right on top of him. Her lips landed a mere inch away from his own and he could feel her body press down the length of his. He looped his free wrist more tightly around the rope at the side of the raft.

"I know you'd rather die than put your arm around me," he shouted. "But since we're handcuffed together, I'm going to the bottom of the river with you if you go."

The speech hadn't been necessary. She curled her head against his neck, the scent of her sweet-smelling, wet hair flying at him on the wind.

Just then, the raft slid over a flat, mossy rock. Apparently, it served as a natural ski jump. Because as soon as the raft left the rock, it sailed through the air. They were on a magic carpet of inflated yellow rubber. Only the fact that they were cuffed together kept her from flying away like a scared bird.

The raft smacked the surface hard. As they pitched in a semicircle, she rolled off him. He watched her body unfold like a silk shirt. When their arms pulled taut, he tugged on the cuffs and she rolled right back into his arms.

This time she got the point. While he tightened his grip on the dock rope, her free hand wedged under his back. He gasped as her legs wrapped tightly around his hips. Now she wouldn't be going anywhere, not unless he lost his grip on the rope. *Good.*

Or was it? She was so wet and cold and shivery against his chest that he wanted to moan.

"Just hold on!" he yelled.

"I am!"

As good as it felt, he could still lose her. He was starting to get dizzy. Whether it was because the raft was now spinning in circles or because her long legs were squeezing him like a vise, he didn't know.

"There's more water in the raft!" White spray splashed her face and she sputtered. "We—we're going to drown!"

"There's not enough to sink us yet and we can use the weight."

"Swimming's just the one thing I always hated!"

Suddenly, they bounced. She flew upward. He had to fight not to drop the rope and grab her. But the cuffs brought her back. She settled on top of him again. Somehow, her legs got beneath him and her ankles locked together beneath his hips.

With more weight in the raft and life jackets and helmets, they'd be fine. He glanced around, but the current was so swift that he couldn't see much. And she was on top of him. The longer she lay there, the less he cared about where they were going.

At least his skin was getting a good washing. He'd felt self-conscious about his grunginess ever since he'd first laid eyes on her.

As if realizing he was thinking about her, she lifted her face from his chest. She looked terrified. He didn't know whether it was from the white water or because she had begun to feel what she was doing to choice parts of his anatomy. Not that he could help it. She was squeezing him tighter than any lover ever had.

"I'm losing my grip!" she shouted.

He couldn't help but smile. "On reality or me?"

She didn't bother to respond. But a brave smile settled on her lips. And somehow it made him feel good.

He just wished the water wasn't jostling and tossing her every which way but loose. Her breasts were crushed hard against his bare chest and her thighs against his felt like steel. His cuffed hand was now squeezed between them. There wasn't any available entertainment, other than staring into her eyes. "You okay?"

"No!"

Thunder clapped and lightning zigzagged through the sky. It looked as kinetic as his jangling nerves felt where she was touching him. White light was coursing through his veins, and in spite of the icy river, his skin was starting to burn. Unfortunately, water wasn't exactly the best place to be when lightning struck. Unless the electrical currents were merely of the sensual sort and the water was in a Jacuzzi.

He heard a great rushing sound and his chest constricted.

"We're coming up on the—" his voice broke as they whipped around "—waterfall."

"I've got you good," she yelled. The rest of what she said was lost to the wind.

Damn good. But the rope was cutting into his wrist. The only relief for the chafing was the cold water rushing through the bonds that held him. And desire. Her bunched skirt was chafing his zipper every bit as much as the rope was his wrist. Suddenly, he wanted to groan, knew he could, knew the sound would be lost in the wind.

Somehow, he restrained himself.

But where was that damn waterfall? If they didn't hit it soon, he decided he might give in to the urge to press himself hard against her.

To hell with living, he thought. If he was going to drown, he could think of no better way than with his mouth against hers.

The raft tipped.

Whoosh.

Ice water rushed between them. They were headed straight down, over the falls, completely immersed. The raft swept out from under them, though he still held the rope. She was clinging to him so tightly that he couldn't think straight. He opened his eyes, but only saw a wall of water. He snapped his stinging eyes shut again.

And then he lost the rope.

Somehow—never in his life would he know how—they wound up side by side. They shot out from under the fall as if pushed by a mighty hand and the raft slid beneath them with the ease of a dining room chair.

As soon as he could see, he gulped down a breath. He felt glad to be alive—until he remembered the police. Her wrist flopped against his hand, pulling on the cuffs. He hoped there'd be something along the bank he could use to pick the locks. "You okay?"

She swiped her face with the back of her free hand. After a long moment, she offered a waterlogged laugh. "Great."

"Better than a roller coaster," he commented.

She grinned back at him. And she looked beautiful. Her makeup, light as it had been, had washed off, leaving only the natural woman beneath. Her hair was drenched and fat droplets of water clung to her eyelashes. All her haughty composure had vanished. He watched her swing her hand from her jaw to her chest and rest her splayed fingers on her breast, right over her heart.

"It was actually kind of fun," she said breathlessly.

He squinted at her. "You can't mean that."

"But I do. I mean, it was—"

She paused and panted, trying to regain her breath. He couldn't help but think about making her breathless by some other means than a near-death experience.

"It was kind of—"

"Exciting?" The evidence that he'd found it exciting remained pretty plain if she bothered to look. He was still having fantasies about hauling her right to the riverbank and—

"Exciting's not even the word for it," she said.

At that moment, they stopped moving. The river around them fell still. Everything was quiet. Dead quiet. They bumped something solid. She sat up and then he sat up. The riverbank.

"After you," Bill said.

She stepped daintily from the raft even though her remaining shoe had disappeared. Her stockings were in shreds. And they looked fabulous, he thought, tearing his eyes away from how her pale legs gleamed through the glistening tatters. When she caught him looking, a red stain spread over her cheeks. He half suspected she'd been checking out choice parts of his anatomy, too.

"Turn around," she said levelly.

Whatever she intended to do, he wanted to watch.

She sighed. "I have to take off my stockings."

The last thing he wanted to do was turn away. But he did. He could feel her shimmy, her hip bumping his.

"I'm done," she finally said.

He glanced at the ground. The tattered silk, he could handle. But her wet, lacy garter belt was on top of the little pile. She intended to leave it behind and he had to fight not to pick it up.

Instead, he said, "Who's Mr. Suave?"

"The dream man I was supposed to meet on my vacation." She didn't exactly sound pleased.

"You mean I don't qualify?" he couldn't help but drawl. When she didn't respond, he tugged at her wrist. "Just c'mon," he muttered.

"Where are we going?"

How the mention of some fantasy man could turn a woman sulky was beyond him. He pointed. "There's another resort on the other side of that stand of trees."

"I suppose we're going to steal again?"

"That's right, sweetheart," he returned as he tugged her up the riverbank. "It's sheer luck that we wound up here."

As they walked, he found himself wondering what he was going to do with her. His eyes roved over the ground, scanning for stray pieces of wire. It had been ages since he'd picked cuff locks, but doing so was like making love—once you learned, you didn't forget.

Would he release her? He tried to tell himself that he was as anxious to be rid of her as she seemed to be rid of him.

And yet he wanted her. Having her might be easier if she didn't think she could escape.

"Why are we going to this place?" she suddenly asked.

"Stables."

"We're stealing a horse?"

Her voice had leapt with sudden excitement. He glanced at her and wondered if she wasn't taking to thievery a little too quickly.

He shook his head as if to clear it of confusion and decided he'd finish figuring her out once they reached his cabin. Not that it would be difficult. She was rich, spoiled and occasionally imperious.

No, he'd uncuff her as soon as possible, he decided. Then he'd start making the necessary calls and straighten out this mess. He could listen to the radio, too. He had yet to hear about Bonnie, Clyde and Jason Morehead from an objective source. He glanced from the ground and realized the stables weren't ten yards away. "Put your arm around me," he said.

Since they'd left the waterfall, her high-handedness had seemed to return by degrees. Her pale cheeks were still flushed, possibly with excitement. Still, with the dawning knowledge she was alive and intact, she was starting to view him warily again. He didn't blame her. Maybe she was smarter than she looked.

"We'll act like a couple," he explained. "Put your arm under my vest, and I'll keep mine behind me. At a distance, no one will realize we're wet. They won't see the cuffs and they'll think we're just looking at the horses." She did as he asked without argument and he sighed in relief.

"You really think someone would mistake us for a couple?" she muttered as they approached the barn.

"No," he couldn't help but drawl. "They'd think I'd have better taste."

She didn't bother to contradict him. Instead, she said, "I do look pretty pathetic."

He wanted to tell her that she looked pretty. Her legs were bare and he could see her slender feet and pink-painted toes. But he suspected the woman had an ego the size of King Kong, so he kept his wits about him—and his mouth shut.

Inside the barn, a man waved at the two of them. At a distance, he'd undoubtedly mistaken them for tourists. Bill stopped in front of the first stall. The horse was ancient. It looked like a real plodder who'd given one too many a skittish kid a trail ride.

They kept moving.

He was scanning the dirt floor for wire again, when she tugged his wrist. He glanced up and into her smile. It wasn't his imagination, he decided. Off and on, the woman was really starting to look as if she were having a good time. He followed her gaze.

The plaque above the door said Nightmare.

Bill grinned. The animal was dark and sleek, young and well muscled. Bill's kind of horse, even if he was a trail horse.

"But how are we going to ride with the handcuffs?" she whispered.

Good question. He silently lifted the latch of the stall and crept inside, with her close on his heels. He upturned a water bucket and placed it beneath the animal, for a footstep. "You're going to have to ride facing me."

"I'll take the reins." She glanced at Nightmare. "Or mane as it were."

"You ride?"

"All my life."

He hated the fact that his heart suddenly skipped a beat. Was it possible they both loved horses? Even if they did, he decided he was doing the driving. "Sorry, sweetheart," he said. "But I rode in my past life, too." He shot her a penetrating glance. "Unless you're really just afraid of horses and too terrified to get on."

She stepped onto the bucket faster than he could have said boo. And then his hand flew into the air. She flung a leg over the animal's back with such speed that he didn't catch so much as a flash of her underwear. He was still feeling vaguely disappointed when his gaze landed on a piece of wire. It was short and thin. Perfect. Should he uncuff her?

He would have, but she was already on the horse. And they were in a hurry, weren't they? He stepped onto the bucket and mounted so that he was facing her.

"Is someone in that stall?"

The voice sounded faraway. Bill glanced toward the stall door. He'd left it open, for a speedy escape.

"Throw your legs over my thighs," he whispered, suddenly wondering if he really could ride bareback, one-handed and with a woman handcuffed in front of him.

"Who's there?"

The voice came closer. Her legs settled over his and her skirt bunched toward the tops of her thighs. Bill glanced down and felt his mouth go dry. Hoping to get his mind off her, he gave the horse a solid kick in the hindquarters. As racy as the thoroughbred looked, he didn't budge.

"Have you ever even ridden a horse?" she snapped.

He'd had it with her. "Is there something else you'd rather see me ride?"

That shut her up. He kicked again. And Nightmare bolted. Bill grabbed the mane with his free hand and galloped past a concerned-looking groom.

"Yeah—" Frannie suddenly clamped her hand around his waist as if she weren't too happy about it "—I'd like to see you ride off into the sunset." She smiled at him and batted her lashes. "Alone."

"I said something, not somewhere."

"Then I'd like to see you ride a porcupine."

He couldn't help but chuckle. Their cuffed hands came to rest on her bare thigh, making him long to touch her intimately. "Ouch, sweetheart."

"Where are you going?" the groom screamed. "That horse is resort property!"

"He's running after us!" Frannie glanced over Bill's shoulder.

"Come back or I'll call the police!"

She suddenly burst out laughing and Bill found himself grinning.

"Don't bother," she shouted. "They're already after us."

Bill headed straight for the mountains, feeling the hot rush of breezy air ruffle his beard. The sky was nearly black, but the rains hadn't come. Frannie's breasts brushed against his chest and he realized that her clothes were nearly dry. His jeans, which were of heavier fabric, still clung to him like a second skin. His vest was ruined.

Even though they were headed uphill, they settled into an easy rhythm. As Nightmare strained, pulling Bill forward, Frannie leaned backward. They rocked in the cradle of the animal's back as gently as if they were in a hammock. Bill's winces must have convinced her that her loose legs were bouncing against the horse and sending mixed messages because after a while, she set her lips in a grim line and locked her legs around his back.

From there on out the ride was sheer heaven.

Or hell, depending on how he looked at it. Her hind end kept scooting forward until she came in contact with him. Then she flushed and squirmed back toward the horse's mane.

At one point, she said, "I guess this isn't all bad."

It wasn't, but he wasn't about to let her know how he felt. "We're in trouble."

"I haven't heard a siren or shotgun lately," she said sweetly.

"Now's when you're going to tell me you're Bonnie Smith, no doubt," he said with practiced grimness.

"Who knows," she shot back. "Maybe I am."

"RIDE'S OVER," Bill said.

If the man really had a cabin in the mountains, Frannie sure hoped she could walk the rest of the way. She refused to contemplate what riding facing him had done to her senses. Before she could compose herself, the fool man dismounted, pulled her down with him and hauled her into his arms. Then he gave the horse a sound smack. Nightmare bolted merrily in the direction of home, tossing his head and shaking his mane.

Frannie wiggled free and slid down the length of Bill's body. As soon as her feet hit solid ground, her hand shot to her hemline. She'd inadvertently used her cuffed hand, and Bill made an unnecessary show of helping her tug down her skirt. She sighed and glanced around. The woods were beautiful, even in the dark, dangerous weather.

"I thought you said you had a cabin just over the mountain," she finally said huffily, wishing that she couldn't still feel his fingertips whispering over her skin.

"That mountain." He raised their cuffed hands and pointed.

"Excuse me," she ventured. "But I'd like to point out that we're now stuck on the edge of a cliff."

The grin that lit up his features was particularly annoying. "That's what the basket's for."

She eyed it as they approached. The rickety planked wooden cage hung beside an old scenic lookout post. Its sides were partially meshed with chicken wire. A cable stretched across a drop that took her breath away. "I've been in airplanes that have flown lower," she muttered.

When they reached the basket, he said, "Ladies first."

"You're a real gentleman," she returned dryly.

"No, I'm not."

It was an understatement. He was a rake, through and through. She almost wished the darn horse would come back. "Are you out of your mind?"

He merely chuckled. "No don't be such a basket case."

To add insult to injury, the man's jokes were just terrible. "You really are crazy," she said with conviction.

He nodded as if insanity were an asset.

"This is a scenic overlook," she continued, stamping her foot. "A gorge. I'm not taking a basket over what must be a thousand-foot drop."

"Closer to two thousand. We're near Spruce Knob."

His lazy half smile curled his mustache in a way that made him look almost pleasant. Grit and grime had washed away in the rapids. Looking at him, she realized she'd never kissed a man with a beard or a mustache—and she suddenly wanted to.

Sheer panic got her moving again. She jumped into the basket as if she could escape him. Not that she could. For a second, their cuffed hands stretched over thousands of feet of thin air. She just hoped lightning didn't strike them. Could the basket withstand the rains if they came?

To avoid looking down, she riveted her gaze on Wild Bill's face. She didn't know which was worse, watching the teasing glint in his eyes or looking down at the drop.

She forced herself to look down as if it didn't bother her in the least. The river was a thin gray line. There were tiny dots that could have been people or rocks. Between the planks in the bottom of the basket there were spaces. *I'm going to throw up.*

"Ready?"

"Sure." She fixed her gaze on the bottom of the basket. The contraption looked about as safe as her running partner. She decided against checking out whatever mechanism he was operating to get them going.

When the thing moved, sliding along the cable above, the fingers of her free hand twined through the wire and clutched the metal. She'd hoped it would be a one, two, three, down-the-hatch kind of experience. But she wasn't that lucky.

"You're really scared."

In the cramped confines of the basket, his voice sounded closer than was comfortable. "No joke," she snapped murderously, not feeling the least bit guilty for taking her vertigo out on him.

They'd almost reached the other side when the basket hit a snag in the cable and jerked outward. It didn't go far, but enough that her heart dropped to her feet and came back up again. The contraption swung in ever smaller arcs, like a pendulum.

Then she realized *his* face had gone dead white.

Were they trapped now? *Maybe he's as terrified as I am,* she thought, feeling vaguely victorious.

"Get down!" he said gruffly, pulling her into the bottom of the basket.

She landed nearly in his lap, her eyes wide. "What?"

"Cops," he said. "On the top of the mountain."

Sure enough, through the cracks of wood, she could see men with rifles checking over the ground where they'd just walked. She stared at Bill's face. His eyes were alert, watchful.

"Should we give ourselves up?"

He shook his head. "They don't know we're here and I'm not going to risk getting shot."

Chills raced down her spine. Guns. Tattooed men. Baskets. Where was she? "I can't stand this."

He smiled at her. Against her will, she found that smile—so gentle and reassuring—start to melt her heart.

"Sweetheart," he whispered, "just look into my eyes."

It was definitely better than looking down, or looking through the cracks at the men fanning over the mountain.

"What's that supposed to do?" She stared into his hazel eyes. "Mesmerize me?"

"Just don't panic."

Cold hysteria gripped her throat. "There's nothing beneath us but thin air. If you stand up and get the basket moving, the police might shoot you." She suddenly envisioned herself handcuffed to a dead man.

His mouth set in a grim line. "I realize that." He moved their cuffed hands, so that his palm molded over her knee. He squeezed. "But I'm not gonna let you fall or get shot."

His husky voice was so calm that she almost believed him. She glanced toward the cliff side opposite. The police weren't pointing at the basket—not yet.

Bill shifted his shoulder, lifted his free hand and grazed her cheek. Even though his fingertips were rough with calluses, she was sure she'd never felt a touch so soft. His head angled downward, his lips just a breath away.

"Feeling better?" he whispered.

"A little." She glanced at the men on the cliff. Some were in uniform, some weren't, but they all had rifles. She wasn't sure, but it looked as if they were considering leaving.

She realized Bill had snuggled his shoulder closer, and she had the distinct impression that he was going to kiss her. "You can't do this."

"Kiss you?"

"Yes. If that's what you were going to—"

"Am going to do." He smiled. "Ever been kissed when you're hiding from the cops and stuck in midair at two thousand feet?"

How could the man contemplate such a thing under these circumstances? Her mouth went dry in a way that no amount of lip licking would correct. "Can't say as I have," she croaked.

His gaze traveled from her eyes, to her lips, and back again. "There's a first time for everything."

She glanced toward their pursuers. "And a last."

He chuckled softly. "But I've got you trapped."

"That's not fair." Her voice lacked conviction.

"All's fair in love and war." His voice was low and incredibly sexy.

Listening to it, she actually forgot that she was suspended precariously in space held by nothing more than a basket and the strong arms of a man named Wild Bill Berdovitch. "So, which is this?" she managed. "Love or war?"

He shrugged. "Beats me."

And then his lips claimed hers with a shocking familiarity. His tongue followed with a startling vengeance. It plunged between her lips, so hot, so savage that the sheer drop below and the police with their rifles and Mr. Suave and everything else she'd ever known, including the loss of her infant son, vanished.

And she thought, *I'm alive. Truly and completely alive.*

She didn't even understand what he said when he drew away and whispered against her lips.

She gasped. "What?"

His tongue slid between her lips again, before she'd realized he'd said, "We'll be fine. As long as they don't call in the FBI."

Chapter Four

"My name is Reed Galveston," the man boomed as he bent beside the fence and retrieved a high heel. "And I'm from the FBI."

The county cops who'd gathered near the fence stepped back and widened the circle they'd formed around Reed. Reed knew he sounded like he was shouting even when he talked, but his assistant, Carly Sharp, should have been used to it. Nevertheless, he noticed that she jumped, too.

Reed shoved the toe of the high heel in his back jeans pocket, then glared at the two deputies who'd been transporting the prisoners. "So, how'd you lose them?"

The deputies flushed, telling Reed everything he needed to know. He shook his head in disgust and turned to Carly. "They let them go. Can you believe that, Carly?"

"No I can't, boss," she said quickly.

"Well, they did," Reed said with finality.

"We don't know if the...er...escapees have crossed state lines," Sheriff Jackson said defensively. "Which means that—"

"I'm out of my jurisdiction," Reed finished. Media attention had already made the case larger than the local boys could handle. Reed put his hands on his hips and viewed the landscape. "Your boys let my prisoners go, so I'm taking over your investigation."

"I'll call in to headquarters." Carly skedaddled back to their car for her cellular phone.

Reed nodded, and glared at the deputies again. "So, why'd you let them go?"

The mean squint in his eyes got them talking. As the story tumbled out, Reed nodded, not feeling at all surprised. After all, Larson Logging International had a reputation for illegally harvesting veneer-quality wood. The townsfolk—including the deputies—were convinced that the money the suspects had taken from the logging office was rightfully theirs.

"And so you let them go?" Reed finally shouted.

The deputies nodded guiltily.

"Carly!" Reed yelled.

"Coming, boss!" She streaked toward him and stopped breathlessly at his side, flipping open a notebook.

"I want our people to cover the whole area. Check the resorts up and down the river. Interview the people who Bonnie Smith and Clyde—"

Carly was watching him expectantly, her pencil poised just above her paper.

He guffawed. "You swear their names are Bonnie and Clyde?"

Carly's lips twitched. "Can you believe it?"

"No, I can't." He shook his head and went right back into action. "I don't care if their names are Laurel and Hardy, I want interviews with everybody—their grade school teachers, friends, prom dates—right down to the doctors who delivered them."

Carly scribbled furiously.

"And get me Larson."

Carly blew her bangs out of her eyes. "Will do," she said, pulling a cellular phone from her back pocket.

"Well, I'll be," Reed suddenly muttered. He charged right next to the fence, with Carly on his heels like a bloodhound. He reached through a metal diamond and plucked out a wisp of stocking. He held it between his thumb and forefinger while Carly rustled up an evidence bag. Reed dropped in the scrap of fabric. "Pure silk," he commented. "She lost it going down."

"I'd agree, sir."

He rolled his eyes. "Are you saying you think Reed Galveston could have been wrong?" From his back pocket Reed whipped out the high heel he'd found earlier. He slapped it against his palm, turned it one way and another, then held it up for Carly to see.

She crinkled her nose and stared into the instep. Then she wolf whistled, muttered the designer's name, and said, "That'd be a year of my salary, boss."

Reed wanted to chuckle, but he didn't. "Is that a hint?"

Carly smirked. "It's hard enough to keep up with you when I'm wearing standard issue boots."

At that, he did chuckle. "So, Carly, mind telling me why a woman from a farm—and a fugitive, no less—would be wearing silk stockings and a shoe like this?"

She shrugged. "I just don't know, boss."

"Well, find out!" Reed boomed.

"THEY'RE GONE," Bill whispered against Frannie's lips.

Who? she wondered vaguely as he pulled her to her feet. He started jimmying the cable, but all she could focus on was her wet, swollen mouth. The friction of his beard was still warming her cheeks when they reached the other side of the gorge.

"C'mon." Bill lifted her from the basket, one-handed.

As her filthy feet connected with the earth, she felt as if she weren't stepping out of a basket at all—but into her future. Her tingling lips made her wonder if fate had decided to be kind. Had it handcuffed her to husband material?

The kiss had been of the sort that could change a woman's life. Had it transformed Wild Bill into a prince? No, the man was just as burly and hairy as he'd been before and no amount of white water could wash off that tattoo. He didn't look like the type to keep a well-appointed guest room in his cabin, either, she thought in sudden panic. The primitive passion of his lips had been a real learning experience, but she decided she'd better put a quick halt to the situation. "I...uh..."

"Go ahead and spit it out."

It sounded as if he knew what was coming. Just looking at his golden hazel eyes and feeling his dangling hand brush hers made her heart race. He'd led her to a cleared path and was taking it slowly, as if conscious of her bare feet. "If Bonnie and Clyde don't get caught soon..."

"Hmm?" He suddenly tugged at the cuffs and pointed. "Watch those brambles."

She stepped around them. Even though the air was unseasonably hot, the soil still smacked of recent winter and her feet felt cold. "Well, we might be stuck together for a while...."

"Oh, don't worry," he drawled. "I'll have these handcuffs off in a jiffy. And you can escape the big bad wolf."

Was he trying to make her feel guilty? "Well, I just don't think—I mean, I didn't mind you kissing me back there, but—"

He glanced over his shoulder, toward where their joined hands swung above the path. "It takes two to tango."

She stared at him, slack-jawed. "I didn't mean to imply otherwise. But since we don't know each other, I don't think we should..."

"Maybe not." He lifted a thorny switch, waited until she'd stepped beneath it, then let it drop.

She realized she'd wanted him to protest. "I must have lost my head," she explained, determined to appear as unaffected by what had happened as he did. She watched his mouth compress into a line. How could lips that kissed like that look so grim? "And I told you I was married."

Even in the growing darkness, his piercing glance shot to her soul. "Now, are you really?"

"No."

He nodded curtly. "I didn't think so."

She stared down contritely. Red scratches streaked down her bare legs and dirt was caked under her toenails. Little bugs were running around on the ground. She thought of Mr. Suave and suddenly felt a bit depressed. "Why?" she asked huffily. "Don't I look marriageable?"

Bill shrugged. "I kissed you, didn't I?"

"That's not exactly a marriage license," she shot back.

"Thank God." Then he sighed. "One kiss. And what does a woman want? A proposal."

She glanced at the trees and rolled her eyes. "Are you really getting testy just because I don't want a repeat of what happened back there?"

He chuckled softly. "Probably."

For long moments, she merely continued next to him, under the dark cover of the arching branches. His arms swung widely, so he kept jerking her forward.

"And quit pulling my wrist!" she finally exclaimed.

"It's not my fault we're cuffed together."

"It's mine?" When he didn't respond, she sniffed haughtily. Not that there was much air to be had. It was as thick as the foliage surrounding them. In fact, she was starting to feel breathless. She reminded herself that they'd hit another incline and that Wild Bill's proximity had zilch to do with her respiratory shutdown. But with every step, hundreds of his muscles moved. They rippled the way water did when hit by a stone.

"Where's this cabin of yours, anyway?" she snapped. "At the top of Mount Everest?"

"Changing the subject?"

"We weren't exactly conversing."

Before she knew what was happening, her wrist jerked, her body snapped around and the man had backed her up against a tree. When he raised his left hand, her joined right followed and wound up high above her head. Her knuckles scraped the bark as he pressed the length of his body against hers, and lightning struck as if to punctuate the danger.

"Want to know why you don't want me kissing you?" he asked in a husky whisper. "I mean, really?"

The way his eyes dipped over her made her suddenly conscious of her attire. But right now even her ink-smudged blouse couldn't detract her attention from the eyes that held hers.

"Do you?" he said, glaring at her with a gaze that said *I dare you.*

"I'm sure you're about to tell me." She tried to act as if the way he'd trapped her was the furthest thing from her mind. It wasn't. His vest was open and his bare chest was crushing her breasts. Against her thighs, his legs felt as hard as the tree behind her.

"Because you'd rather worry about your daddy's car, and the suit you ruined that Daddy bought."

She gasped. "I can't believe you said that!"

"It's true."

His lips were so close she thought he was about to kiss her again. "Think whatever you want," she said coolly.

"Tell me the truth."

His coarse voice now sounded silkily persuasive, and her pulse began beating against her throat with a dull, thudding ache. When she squirmed against the tree in an effort to elude him, the bark scratched her back, snagging her blouse. "Seeing as you've resorted to caveman tactics—" she squared her shoulders "—I assume I'll have to answer anything you ask."

"When we were kissing—" his gaze dipped to her mouth and his tongue darted out, touching his mustache "—didn't uncomfortable scenarios flash through your mind?"

Nothing like those in her mind now. "Scenarios?"

"We kiss . . . we make love . . . you take me home. . . ."

With every word, his mouth seemed closer. The phrase *make love* echoed in the still air. The wedding, she suddenly thought. That came next in his list. "And then?" she murmured.

"And then your daddy shoots me dead."

Of course she'd imagined how Wild Bill's tattoo would wiggle when he shook hands with her father. She turned away from his lips. "I'm thirty and don't live with my parents!" *More lies.*

He shot her such a long, level look that she turned scarlet.

"Okay." She glared at him, deciding it was going to take more than a man of his ilk to make her dishonest. "I do."

"Mind telling me your real name?"

She pursed her lips.

"Okay. Mind telling me why you lied about what it was?"

The man could obviously read her like a book. It was infuriating. "You could still be Clyde Calvert. Or. . . somebody else."

"Somebody else who's equally dangerous, you mean?"

Her mouth went dry. Unfortunately, it wasn't from danger, but desire. "Frannie Anderson," she nearly whispered. "And under the circumstances, I think a lot of women would have lied."

The corners of his mouth curled into what might have been a smile, but wasn't. "Maybe you should have continued to trust your instincts."

Just as lightning lit the sky again, the fingers of his cuffed hand twined through hers. Her instinct was to run, but wherever she went, the man was coming with her. "Why's that?"

"I spent time in Moundsville for grand theft auto."

Her heart started hammering and she tried not to gawk. He'd hinted as much, but she hadn't wanted to believe it. Only the way his eyes had her pinned kept her from turning tail—that and the fact that she was cuffed to him and squinched between his torso and a tree. She gulped. "Grand theft auto?"

He merely gazed at her through eyes that had turned deep amber in the dark. Steady eyes. Penetrating eyes. Expressive eyes that said he didn't know which to do first—kill her or kiss her. He finally blinked. Then he turned away—without any forewarning—and hauled her back onto the path.

"Don't worry." His gruff voice floated over his shoulder. "These days, I manage to hold down a regular job."

No matter how hard he squinted, there was no hiding the gentleness that occasionally touched those eyes. Perhaps he'd taken a wrong turn in life, but she had a gut feeling he wasn't dangerous. Yet her instincts were sometimes dead wrong....

She mustered her best conversational tone, as if to call a truce. She'd just pretend that ex-cons counted among her best friends. "So, what do you do for a living?" *Now I sound as if we're at one of Mother's cocktail parties!*

He shot her a long sideways glance, then smirked. "Used car salesman. I had a lot of contacts."

"Right. Someone from whom you stole cars offered you a job?" The man was clearly put off by the obvious class difference between them, but he was willing to overlook it. "You're jerking my chain."

"About being an ex-con?"

"No, about selling cars."

He ducked under a tree branch. "Real estate?"

His tone, so volatile moments before, now seemed to tease. Sometimes, he sounded lower-class. Sometimes, he sounded well educated and accomplished. He was a hard man to get a grip on. Even worse, he was piquing her curiosity about his job status. Mechanic? She slid on a mossy rock and righted herself. "Psychiatrist?"

He shot her a droll glance. "Maybe I just do a little brain surgery every now and again."

"Or stun juries with your mental acumen and closing arguments," she returned, thinking of her father.

He burst out laughing. "A lawyer?" His gleaming white teeth lit up the dismal evening.

She nodded with mock gravity. When he conversed like a normal human being, he could be fun. "While in prison, you went to college. You turned your life around—"

"A hundred and eighty degrees by the sound of it."

"And began to royally prosecute others," she continued, "who, like you, had broken the law."

"You sure I don't just fix broken shoes?"

"Seriously," she said, thinking that if he'd just tell her it would put her mind to rest. "What do you do?"

Instead of answering, he said, "Home sweet home."

Her gaze followed his—and landed on a tumbledown shack.

HIS ONE-ROOM CABIN wasn't much. And now that Frannie Anderson was inside it, Bill wished it was nicer. "If I'd known you were coming," he began as she preceded him through the door and he flicked on the lamp, "I would have..."

What? His gaze flitted around the empty interior. There were cracks between the unfinished floorboards and no curtain over the window next to the bed. Kindling was in a cardboard box near the fireplace. When his eyes landed on the only piece of furniture, his mouth went dry. The old iron-frame feather bed was so small he barely fit in it.

"Installed some French doors with those pretty billowing curtains?" she finally suggested.

He found himself smiling. She had a tart tongue and an imagination—two things he absolutely required in a woman. Still, hers was a brand of woman he was better off without. He could see the future in the crystal balls of her blue eyes. His resentments would kick in. He'd blame her for growing up with all the things he hadn't had. They'd fight. Tears, protests, end of story.

Or would it end that way? He'd kissed her senseless and all but accused her of being a pampered princess. If there was one thing he knew better than cars, it was women, and she should have been hysterical by now. Maybe she was in complete denial about what was happening. She was pretending they hadn't been arrested, that they weren't cuffed together, and that the law wasn't on their tails. Was she denying his lustful glances?

"Maybe you'd have bought a TV," she finally prompted. "Or had your cook truss up a duck."

"I'm afraid all you're gonna get—" he pointed toward his small refrigerator in the makeshift kitchen "—is bologna."

She winced.

"I like bologna."

"You would."

He felt a rush of temper—until he saw how her lush, pouty lips were quivering with a suppressed smile. She wasn't laughing at his poor man's victuals.

"Give me a minute and I'll fix you a bologna dinner you won't forget." He shot her a quick smile. "I'll do it up special."

She chuckled. "Bologna à la mode?"

"For you, sweetheart? Almondine." He started toward the bathroom, and made it two paces before she pulled him to a halt. He glanced at her. "What?"

"No way," she said flatly, eyeing the only interior door.

How could he have forgotten she was still attached? He decided he was getting used to it. He toyed with the idea of not setting her free. "Guess not." He glanced around. "C'mon." He led her toward a chopping block component which, in tandem with the refrigerator, served as his kitchen. He rested their cuffed hands on the block.

"Now you're going to behead me?" She sounded nervous.

"Be-hand," he assured as he opened a drawer and riffled through the contents. He pulled a thread of wire from a roll and held it out. Then, he nodded toward his wire cutters. "Could you cut that?" He watched her inexpertly pick up the tool.

"Drats," she said. "I just wish I wasn't right-handed."

He looked at her. "And I'm left-handed."

She shook her head. "We sure have all the luck."

"At least you didn't have to punch a deputy with your right hook."

"*My* right hook would have been fine." As she snipped the wire, a crack of thunder shook the cabin's foundations. She shot him a droll glance. "But don't tell me. If you'd used your good hand, the man wouldn't be alive to tell about it."

"That's right, sweetheart." His shoulders started to shake with laughter. "Now, hand over that wire." Three metal links separated the cuffs. There was enough space between them and the wire was long enough that he could use his left hand to release her.

"You can really pick a lock like this?"

He glanced up while he jimmied the wire. He wasn't sure why, but something about the awestruck look in her eyes kind of bothered him. He suddenly hoped she wasn't the kind of woman who fell for felons. Lord knew, he'd seen enough women like that when he was in the joint. There were convict groupies, just as surely as there were cop groupies.

"Don't you think you better watch what you're doing?"

He was staring into her eyes. "Picking locks is like making love," he said, not bothering to lower his gaze. "It's better to do it by feel."

A flush crept into her cheeks. "So, why isn't it working?"

He grinned. "It just did, sweetheart."

She glanced down. "I'm free," she said in a shocked voice, stepping back a pace and rubbing her wrist.

Just looking at her, he wished she wasn't. The cuff that was still attached to his wrist swung down and hit his thigh. He decided to fool with it later, since he'd have to use his right hand to pick it. "As soon as I'm out of the bathroom, you're welcome to take a shower. I'll turn on the radio, get on the phone and see if I can't explain what's happened to the cops."

Or maybe he wouldn't. Her long, thick hair was disheveled and strewn with leaves. Her pouty lips had been kissed berry red. And there was a tear in her blouse. She looked positively wild. He'd been a fool to take off the cuffs. "I'll find you some clothes, too." *Maybe.*

"NO ONE'S GOING TO ENVY me my tailor," Frannie said. She stared down and twisted, trying to get a look at her own behind.

His only lamp contained a low-wattage bulb and he found himself readjusting his weight on the bed and squinting. "Lady," he said flatly, "those are my best jeans."

"I'd sure hate to see the worst ones," she shot back.

He shrugged. The jeans he was wearing were in tatters, and he hadn't bothered with a shirt. But he thought she looked great. She was at least five-six and generously curved. Beneath the black T-shirt, he could see her ample breasts swinging free. He'd poked an extra hole in his belt so his pants would stay on her—even though he'd just as soon see them fall off.

As he leaned down to pick up the phone receiver, the cuffs clanked against the radio on the floor. After he ate, he was going to have try and free himself again. In order to do so he'd have to use his right hand, which was virtually worthless.

"Still dead?" she asked as he replaced the receiver.

He nodded. "The storm must have hit somewhere. Power lines are probably down." There was no phone and the radio was pure static. The light occasionally flickered. "Ready for that bologna?"

"If we must." She headed for the bed, then stopped in her tracks. She glanced around, as if searching for a chair. There weren't any.

As soon as he stood, she casually moseyed over and perched on the quilt. "Oh, my heavens," she murmured when she leaned back and sank into the mattress.

"Feathers," he called, heading for the refrigerator.

"It's so soft!"

So was she. And he should know. He'd rubbed wrists with her all day. He frowned at a bag of marshmallows in the fridge, and decided he'd die if he didn't kiss her again. "Mind white bread?"

"Yeah, but I'm so hungry I could eat a loaf."

As he pulled out his last soda, then slapped together four sandwiches, he wondered if anyone had discovered the truth yet. All it would take was a few leads—or spotting the real couple—and the cops would realize their error.

If it weren't for the circumstances, he might be enjoying himself. Frannie's damp, mud-caked clothes were still piled in a corner of his bathroom floor—except for her bra, which was rinsed and hanging over a towel rack. When he'd gone in to take his shower, he'd felt a little angry since she was obviously used to having people clean up after her.

Then he'd found his cabinet open and smiled. The fact that there was nothing but a toothbrush, toothpaste and a box of condoms inside hadn't seemed to bother her. Not that there was much action to be had way up here, he suddenly thought, but a man could hope.

Why didn't she seem more worried, though? He was terrified of running into a trigger-happy cop. If they hadn't yet figured out that he and Frannie were innocent and if they tracked them here . . .

He piled the sandwiches on a plastic plate, shoved the soda under his arm and headed for Frannie, saying, "Pretend it's fresh baked sole."

She scooted toward the foot of the bed. "You don't live here?" she asked, as if the thought had just occurred to her.

"No. I've got a place in Charleston."

"Where you work as a used car salesman?"

He nodded, seated himself and put the sandwich plate between them. "I'm just starting to fix this place up." When he cracked the soda tab, the fool cuffs clanked against the can. He offered her a drink while he bit into his first sandwich.

"Diet," she commented, taking a swig. "A man after my own heart." She lifted a slice a of bread and peeked. "No condiments?"

"Not unless you want marshmallows or herbal tea."

She giggled. "*You* drink herbal tea?"

"If I did, I wouldn't tell you about it." She fell silent and he watched her eat. "Aren't you scared?" he finally said.

She polished off her second sandwich and washed it down with the soda. Then she handed the can back to him. "Scared? When I have a tea-drinking lock-picker like you to protect me?"

He guessed she had a point. The fact that he was a tough guy was hard to miss. She fell silent again. He glanced at the soda can, feeling conscious of the fact that her lips had just touched it. He gulped down the remainder and then dug the wire from his pocket and set about picking the cuff lock. As long as the wire was, it was flimsy and the lock of the cuff was right against his left wrist. He jiggled the wire with his right hand until the lock finally gave. Then he tossed the cuffs to the mattress and put his and Frannie's dinner plate on the floor.

As it had several times before, the light flickered, but this time it went out, bathing the cabin in darkness.

"Great." He peered in her direction. "I don't have any candles."

"We could build a fire," she suggested.

"In this heat? Besides, I don't want smoke coming from the chimney, in case people are still looking for us." He felt her stretch out her legs on the bed. Her bare feet nearly touched him.

"This weather is really weird." Her voice had lowered, becoming husky, as if in deference to the darkness.

He nodded and stretched out, wishing their heads were at the same end of the bed. His hand rubbed over the quilt and hit the cuffs. He picked them up and toyed with them for something to do. "With weather like this, I should have known something bizarre was going to happen," he finally said.

He wasn't sure whether he was referring to their arrest or to the fact that they were now lying side by side. Outside, an electrical white flash zigzagged toward the ground. He heard a final crack of thunder. Then the skies opened and the rains came pouring down. The storm came with fury, as if—like his desire for her—it had been pent up too long. Water pounded on the tin roof and slashed against the window. When the lightning flashed, he realized Frannie was staring at him.

"Guess we're stuck, just listening to the storm," he said.

"Well, there's not much else to do...."

Sure there was. It was his life's ambition to be stuck in a cabin during a storm with nothing to do but be with a beautiful woman. "You wouldn't happen to be afraid of storms, would you?"

"Oh," she said. "A little, I guess."

He almost burst out laughing. He was sure storms didn't scare her in the least. His next line was "Maybe you'd feel safer snuggled next to me." But that was too corny. He might drink herbal tea, but he was still an ex-con. "Look," he finally drawled. "I've been cuffed to you all day. And ever since I kissed you, the taste of you has lingered in my mouth. So, why don't you just do me a favor, sweetheart, and kiss me again?"

The pause was so long that he had plenty of time to berate himself for not using the more standard come-on. Maybe it would have worked. He wished the lightning would give him a sliver of her expression.

It didn't. So he just lay there, listening to the hard rain pelt the roof. Now that he was in bed with her in the dark, he realized how badly he wanted her. Maybe it was wanting all she represented, too—a nice life, a family, a house somewhere that a man could call home.

Then he felt the spread pull as she crept toward him.

She leaned close, so close that her breath fluttered against his cheek. When she kissed him, she missed his mouth. He was so surprised at the touch of her lips on his mustache that he merely smiled. And then he turned his head, found her mouth and covered it with his own.

The way she responded was unbelievable—beyond his craziest fantasies. Her tongue was every bit as wet and wild as the rain and as uncontrolled and tempestuous as the storm that had raged inside him all day. Her arms clutched his shoulders and he pulled her flush against the length of his body, wanting her to feel how hard she was making him.

Her long, lithe limbs were strong and yet soft. Some women felt as if they might break. They were too small and weak and bent too pliably. He was afraid of hurting them.

Not her. Her strength didn't equal his, but as she arched against him, he knew she was a match. He pressed his full heavy belly against her. Then he plunged the spear of his tongue between her lips, catching her moan, the kiss striking with all the speed and intensity of the lightning. Molten heat sizzled from her lips to his groin. Like hot, liquid metal, it flowed through his veins, burning, then cooled into hard steel.

Where there's smoke, there's usually fire, Bill. And you better watch out, in case she's trouble.

When he drank in her flavor again—his tongue diving and surfacing—the warnings vanished. He was hard and hot and ready. When her hand slid down his side, he grasped it and guided it across his stomach, trailing fire, then pressed her palm hard against his zipper. Her warm fingers cradled around him and all his emptiness was replaced with a longing he could never deny.

"I want you," he whispered.

"I—I..." Her raspy voice caught and her palm glided toward his belly again. "I just don't know if..."

When the protest died on her lips, he swiftly raised on his elbows and stripped off her T-shirt. He unbuckled her belt, then peeled his jeans from her legs. In the darkness, his fingers traced the silky lace of her panties. He left them on, crouching over her and kissed her from her breasts to her panties. His beard tickled her belly until his wet tongue found the nub of her desire.

Her hips began to twist beneath him, and she moaned.

She wanted him. Her perspiring hands and whimpering lips and wrenching hips begged for him. He hoped she wouldn't deny it. He was no fool. And he knew she was used to wanting gentlemen.

But he wasn't one. He teased her through the elastic of her panties, then touched her long enough to be certain of her desire. He found her mouth again and while his lips savagely took hers, he rolled his callused thumbs over the peaking tips of her breasts, until she thrust herself against his hands.

"I'll be back," he whispered, no longer even attempting to hide the raggedness of his voice.

As he headed for the bathroom, he undid his belt. The most intimate part of him pressed against his jeans, chafing the fly, hard and insistent. He sighed, wishing he knew her better. Or at all, he thought, grabbing a handful of foil packets.

When he returned, he stood above the bed for a moment, staring down. Lightning flashed and in the sudden streak of illumination, he saw her naked, save for her panties. She was long-limbed, with the kind of backside he could grab on to and the kind of breasts between which he could lay his head. She had legs that belonged nowhere other than wrapped around his hips.

"I—I'm not sure how I feel about this," she whispered breathlessly from the darkness. "It just kind of got out of control."

It sure did. He rolled beside her. "You want me." His voice was so raspy it was almost a croak.

"I—I do."

No joke. Her heated skin scalded him everywhere they touched. His hand slid over her breasts and tummy, then dipped beneath her waistband. He touched her intimately as he leaned and kissed her, and assured himself that what he was feeling had nothing to do with love. It was pure lust. And he was a man who'd seen it all and generally took what he wanted. With his free hand, he unzipped himself, then kicked his jeans and briefs from his ankles. In a quick motion, he stripped off her panties, put on a condom, then settled between her legs.

She gasped. "Maybe we shouldn't—should just—" She was panting so hard that she could barely talk. "Just stop right here."

He'd never forced a woman in his life. Never would. Trouble was, this one wanted him and was denying it. "Want me to cuff you again?" he couldn't help but ask.

"I just don't know. I mean, I want you," she said, her voice suddenly urgent, "I really do."

A soft smile touching his lips, he leaned agilely, lifted the cuffs from the mattress and took a deep breath. He could barely believe it, but instead of protesting, her fingers twined in his hair. He slipped one of the openings around her wrist, then locked the other around one of the rails of the iron headboard.

Save for the rain, the room fell so still that she might have quit breathing.

His eyes had adjusted to the darkness and he leaned back, gazing down the length of her. Her cuffed arm was raised and a beautiful line stretched from her fingertip, all the way down her throat, to her breasts and beyond. He traced down the line with his tongue.

"Don't worry, sweetheart," he said throatily, feeling her thighs part as he poised himself above her again. "You're safe with me." And she really was, he thought as he drove inside her with one deep thrust.

Her free hand nestled in his hair, then flew toward the bed rails. She gripped them tight and her legs squeezed around him, pulling him deeper inside. He didn't even try to hang on to his control. The minute he'd entered her, it was lost.

Somewhere, far away, she was gasping. Her lips found his, slammed down on them hard, then she flung her head back and murmured ragged incantations against his shoulder. He reached above, his fingers closing over her cuffed hand. He could feel her starting to climax, and suddenly her hips moved uncontrollably and cooing whimpers rained down around his ears.

Hearing that, he took his pleasure. Over and over, he drove into her, riding her with the fury of the storm they'd been riding out together. The world was mercifully simplified.

No one was chasing them.

They weren't fugitives from the law.

Only raw elements mattered. Flesh and bone. Desire and relief. The storm and the calm that would come in its wake.

And a woman Bill suddenly wanted more than life.

Chapter Five

"Our suspects are in that cabin on that hill and we're stuck," Carly moaned.

"Yeah," Reed muttered. "Why'd I do the world the favor of getting out of bed this morning?" He stared at the deputies in disgust. Four of them knelt in the mud, pressed their shoulders against the back bumper of Reed's recently commissioned county Jeep and shoved. Two of the four were the very same men who'd let Reed's suspects go.

"Push," Sheriff Jackson yelled from the driver's seat.

Leaves and sludge sputtered from beneath the whirring tires, every bit as fast as the curses that spewed from between Reed's lips.

"Maybe if we put boards under the back tires to increase the traction..." the deputy named Tyler began.

"Do you see any boards on this hill?" Reed asked in a lethal tone.

"No." Tyler flushed. "Well, do you want to—"

"What I want is to get up this hill!" Reed shrugged out of his black rain slicker and slung it over his shoulder. His hands shot to his hips and he snorted in exasperation. "Our suspects are right up there!" He pointed. The escapees were farther away than his tone would have indicated, but up the hill, he could see the small, secluded cabin, half-hidden by trees.

"What good's a four-wheel drive in mud like this?" Carly asked rhetorically, shaking her head.

"None whatsoever!" Reed spat out. When he pulled his boots from it, they made slurping sounds. "We'll be up to our necks in this if we walk. And by the time we get there, they'll be in Timbuktu."

The Jeep chose that moment to up and die on them.

"They flooded it," Reed spat out. "C'mon, Carly." He whirled around and started stomping up the incline.

"Since we've only got leads on Bonnie and Clyde, where do you think Jason Morehead went?" Carly asked, scurrying after him.

That bothered Reed more than he wanted to admit. Where had Bonnie and Clyde managed to hide their eighty-year-old neighbor?

"And what did you think of Larson, boss?"

"Dirtier than last week's laundry." Reed's frown deepened as he mulled over the interview he'd had with Larson and his partner the previous evening. Larson was a big lumberjack of a man and his sidekick Clarence was short and slight. "So's his partner."

"Clarence?" Carly prompted.

"Yeah," Reed snarled. "That weasel in the business suit. Both of them are shadier than a willow tree in the Sahara."

"Willows don't grow in deserts, boss," Carly returned.

"Doesn't matter," Reed shot back. "'Cause I mean to put 'em both where the sun don't shine at all." He turned toward his assistant just as her boot slipped in the mud. When she pitched forward, Reed caught her hand—and wished he could ignore the silkiness of her skin. She smiled up at him sweetly.

"Thanks, Reed," she said in a breathy voice.

"Just watch where you're going," he said gruffly. He turned away and started taking the hill in longer, mud-splashing strides, wishing he wasn't too old and decrepit and mean for her. Besides which, with one failed marriage behind him, he knew that women and the FBI didn't mix.

"I want those contracts," he suddenly boomed.

"Contracts?"

"I want every contract Larson and Clarence have made that says they can harvest wood. Maybe the couple in that cabin got ripped off. Not that it makes any difference to me—"

"Of course it doesn't," Carly put in quickly.

"I want to interview the witnesses to the contracts, and to see Larson's books and receipts."

"Will do."

Reed decided he'd never met a woman who was so darn competent. The way she filled out a regulation rain slicker was equally impressive. "I want Larson to feel as if he's been audited by the IRS, not the FBI."

"Anything you want, boss."

"Don't I wish," Reed muttered, wondering if he'd been referring to his case—or to his assistant.

FRANNIE WIDENED THE SLITS of her sleep-swollen eyelids and stared past Wild Bill and through the open window. Sun filtered through the tree leaves and dappled the ground, burning off the magical morning haze. Her eyes drifted shut again.

Even though Bill was next to her, yesterday seemed like nothing more than a fantastical dream. Last night, just a clash of bright images and sensual sounds.... Could it really have happened?

She could still hear thunder rumbling in the mountains. And mighty cracks and booms, mixed with moans of pleasure. She could see white bolts of light sizzle in the air, illuminating slivers of glistening skin. Sometime in the night, Bill had released her and made love to her again in a tangle of arms and legs and lips, until his relentless passion turned gentle and his kisses had become as soft as the old feather bed.

No, it wasn't a dream.

And she didn't really know Wild Bill Berdovitch.

She clutched the quilt to her chest and groped beside the bed. As she reached for her panties and the jeans and shirt Bill had given her, the handcuffs fell to the floor with a loud clank. She tried to ignore the sound and squirmed into the clothes. Next to her, the man was as naked as the jaybirds outside.

And on top of the covers. He was on his side, leaning away from her and peering through the open window. Frannie's eyes flitted to his shoulders, then remained pinned there like showcase butterflies. If only their lovemaking hadn't been so fast and furious.... If they'd talked, the transition to morning might have been less awkward.

How was a decent woman supposed to face a virtual stranger after a night like that? And why was it always the woman who felt responsible for smoothing over life's embarrassing moments? Let him do the talking, she thought.

But he didn't say a word. In fact, he glanced over his shoulder and pressed a finger to his lips, indicating that she should remain silent.

It was difficult not to scrutinize every inch of him in the broad light of day, since he'd pleasured her body like a man possessed. But what if he was Clyde Calvert? No, the only thing criminal about him was the way he'd touched her. Her cheeks got hot. "Morning," she ventured, once her shirt was on.

He glanced over his shoulder and pressed his finger to his lips again.

Why was the man's first gesture to tell her to be quiet? *Not a good omen, Frannie.* She may not have been handcuffed to husband material, but last night had convinced her she wanted to find out everything she could about Bill.

"We're in the middle of nowhere," she forced herself to say brightly. "Afraid the birds will hear us?"

He didn't so much as look at her.

"What's your problem?" she muttered defensively. She realized the radio on the floor next to them was playing soft music. She filed that away, wondering if the man actually listened to the station. Somehow, the idea of the gruff, tempestuous ex-con drinking herbal tea and tapping his foot to orchestrated versions of rock and roll songs made her want to giggle. She didn't, but it took the edge off the fact that he was ignoring her.

"The radio's on," she murmured. "That means the phone might be working." *We can straighten out this mess. I'll be free of Mr. Terse and Unreadable within the hour.* She glanced at Bill again, not feeling at all sure she was ready for their adventure to end. She wanted those strong arms to hold her, just once more. Suddenly, he held out his hand. *Now, that's a sweet, romantic gesture.*

Maybe he was as embarrassed as she was. Her mouth went as dry as dust. Maybe he even wanted to make love again. She hoped so. But she couldn't—not yet. She'd never had a one-night stand before. Not that her longer term relationships had exactly panned out. She thought of Joey Florence, who had left her to raise her infant son alone, and knew she had to be cautious. If it hadn't been for Wild Bill's torturously sweet kisses, she'd never have let down her guard in the first place.

She reached out, rested her hand in his and squeezed. "I'm glad last night happened," she said softly. "So I want you to understand why I can't pursue a relationship under these peculiar circumstances...."

He slowly turned from the window. When his gaze landed on hers, his eyes narrowed. For a long moment, he looked as if he couldn't decide what to say. She wasn't sure what she saw in his expression. Anger? Surprise? Disappointment?

Please let it be disappointment. Make him want to get to know me, too.

"Sweetheart," he finally said gruffly. "I'd hardly call a roll in the hay a relationship." He glanced at their joined hands. "What I wanted was my pants."

She dropped his hand as if she'd been burned. "Well, let me get them for you," she snapped. She pulled his jeans onto the bed so fast that one of the pant legs slapped hard against his bare thigh.

He forwent underwear and kept staring through the fool window while he dressed. He was still refusing to look at her.

"Could you hand me my boots?"

Her eyes widened. "You look like a grown-up to me. Why don't you get them yourself?"

He shot her a piqued glance. "Please?"

She sniffed, reached down and tossed his heavy motor-cycle boots on the bed. "Anything else I can do?"

"Yeah," he said. "Be quiet."

"No wonder you seemed so nearly starved when we made love," she couldn't help but say, her heart sinking like an anchor. "Somehow, I doubt many women would put up with you."

He nodded. "That's about right."

She'd never had a man touch her the way he had. Apparently, for him, it hadn't meant a thing. She watched the muscles of his back ripple as he tugged on his boots and almost decided that with some men, a woman could overlook lousy manners. She squinted at his tattoo. A dove with an olive branch seemed an interesting choice. Why would a man as rough as he was go for something so symbolic?

And what was he looking at? Frannie stared past him, as if he weren't even there. Outside, the ground was muddy, but it was a sunny morning. The new green shoots on the trees shone with rain drops, and tiny yellow wildflowers dotted the hillside. It was spring in all its glory. And, in spite of Bill's coolness, her heart welled with the promise of new beginnings.

"Maybe you're inclined to commune with nature in the morning," she tried, feeling as if she were speaking to nothing but the thin air. "Next thing I know, you'll start humming and stand on your head in bed, in some yoga position or something."

"Right, sweetheart," he muttered softly.

She lifted the phone receiver from its cradle, listened to the dial tone, then replaced it, wondering if Bill had tried to call anyone yet. Not that she'd bother to ask. She cocked her head toward the voice on the radio reading the morning news. "I can't believe it," she murmured. "Oh, my..."

"Please," Bill said, sounding exasperated. "They're giving a report on Bonnie and Clyde."

"But he just said—" According to the D.J., the money that Bonnie Smith, Clyde Calvert and Jason Morehead had taken from Larson Logging International was in a bright yellow duffel bag. She hadn't heard that before!

"I saw them!" her voice rose excitedly. "They were at a gas station where I stopped for directions!" She grabbed Bill's arm to get his attention.

"You saw them?"

She nodded. "I stopped at a gas station not long after I crossed the state line from Pennsylvania." She sucked in a quick breath and let go of his arm. He looked impatient, so she rushed on. "There were three of them. I remember looking at the woman because even I could see that she looked a lot like me."

"Did they say anything?"

Her eyes shot to his. "They had the duffel."

"The duffel?"

"They just mentioned it on the radio," she said. "The money they took was in a bright yellow duffel." Her eyes narrowed as she searched her memory. "They'd bought some breakfast stuff from the vending machines...."

He sighed. "Breakfast?"

"Bonnie was having one of those awful apple tarts. You know, those ones that are usually stale and—"

"I don't care what they ate," Bill interjected huffily.

"Excuse me!" She glared at him. "But I'm trying to remember every detail. They said they were going to Texas."

"You were eavesdropping?"

Her lips parted in astonishment. "It's a good thing I was," she said defensively. "Besides which, they were right in front of me. And—" her voice suddenly rose to a feverish pitch "—I didn't think you cared about such superfluous details!"

He merely nodded. "I don't."

She pursed her lips and crossed her arms defensively over her chest. "Well, they were headed to Texas," she continued. "I remember feeling envious because I'd love to go to the Badlands. I've never seen the Badlands before. I mean, there just seems to be something so magical about—"

"The Badlands are in the Dakotas," he said, sounding testy. "What did they say?"

She ignored his question. All her life, she'd thought the Badlands sounded so interesting and different, and she'd long thought of going to Texas just to see them. "I thought they were in Texas."

He squinted. "You thought *what* was in Texas?"

"The Badlands," she burst out.

He stared at her with utter contempt, as if to intentionally remind her of how bad her sense of direction was. *So what if my life hasn't gone where I wanted it to, you oaf!* She suddenly decided she'd rather be on a bed of nails alone than on a feather bed with Wild Bill Berdovitch—even if he *was* dressed.

"Guess you didn't pay much attention in geography class," he finally commented.

Her mind had been full of prom nights, the car she'd gotten when she was sixteen, new cheers for the football team and Joey Florence. "Well, excuse me for being a cheerleader!"

"You were a cheerleader." He nodded, as if to say, it figures. "Some cheerleaders study, I'm sure," he added.

"Well, I didn't. Okay?"

He leaned an elbow in the windowsill, stared out, then fixed her with his gaze again. "Are you going to tell me what they said or not?"

She couldn't help but smirk. "Maybe—if you're nice."

He shot her a look that could kill.

She stared back, determined not to let his eyes intimidate or seduce. "They said they were going to the Badlands... er...I mean, Texas. And then they were—" She shut her eyes and concentrated. When they fluttered open again, she said, "They were going to Mexico. They were going to seek sanctuary in Mexico. Sanctuary. That's the exact word they used."

"All right," Bill said.

"All right, what?"

Instead of responding, he turned and literally rolled on top of her. Even though he kept rolling and then stood up, everything from her breasts to her toes kept tingling. Pinpricks of awareness teased her skin with all the maddening insistence of a first flirtation. It was as if the whole weight of him had been on top of her for hours. Her body had both fallen asleep and jolted wide-awake—all at the same time. "What?" she finally croaked.

"There're two people coming up that hill." He pointed through the window. "They'll be here in about twenty minutes."

That was why he'd been looking outside! She gasped and crawled toward the window. Ducking low, she peeked over the windowsill. She didn't see a darn thing. "There's nobody out there!"

"I figure they're cops."

She whirled around and stared at him, then suddenly wished he wasn't so undeniably good-looking. He'd become more appealing since last night, too. "I don't see a soul!" He was looking at her as if she had the mental acumen of a flea, so she stared through the window again. Then, she sucked in a sharp breath. In the distance, two tiny dots were moving beneath the cover of the trees. "Oh, I see them now," she said with worry. "You really think it's the police?"

"Who else could it be?"

"Neighbors borrowing a cup of sugar?" she ventured with a fleeting smile.

As bad as his jokes were, he could at least have chuckled. He didn't. Instead, he leaned over her in such a lithe, quick movement that she scooted reflexively toward the bed's edge. The thought flashed through her mind that he really was Clyde Calvert and that he was going to grab her and hold her hostage. Then she realized he'd grabbed the pillow. He was Clyde Calvert and he was going to smother the only witness to his escape! No. He'd had ample opportunity the previous night, she assured herself.

She watched him carefully as he unzipped the pillowcase and shook it above the mattress. She was less surprised about the cash and checkbook that tumbled out than she was about the credit cards. The man possessed a ream of them—including the much coveted Gold Card. She grabbed all of them the second they hit the quilt. Then she crossed her legs, Indian style, and scrutinized them.

Her eyes scanned the cards for a name. Sure enough they said William H. Berdovitch. *But that could be an alias.* She quickly reached for the checkbook. William H. Berdo-vitch—and it showed a Charleston address.

"The cops are on their way," he said grimly, "and you're fantasizing about shopping?"

She was tired of his barbs—cops or no cops. "What's the *H* for?" she said sarcastically. "Heironymous? Homer?"

He blew out a quick sigh, pulled on a T-shirt and tucked it in with two quick stabs of his hand. "If those are cops, they'll now be here in fifteen minutes."

"They'll be here in fifteen minutes, whether they're cops or not," she pointed out, deciding she liked trying his patience.

He tugged his charge cards from her hand and shoved them into his back pocket. Then, he reached under the mattress and came out with a set of keys. Next, he kicked the handcuffs so they slid beneath the bed. Finally, he grabbed a small army-issue backpack from under the bed, ran around the cabin stuffing items inside, then he returned.

"Going down to meet them and invite them in for tea?" she inquired drolly. He was getting ready to move, so she decided she'd better be ready. She hopped from the bed, retrieved her bra from his bathroom and stuffed it into her jeans pocket. "I know," she continued when she plopped on the bed again, "you're going to knock them out with Celestial Seasonings Sleepytime Tea and then make your escape."

"They were headed for Mexico?" he asked.

They? She was still thinking about the police, and then she realized he was talking about Bonnie, Clyde and Jason. She gasped. "You're going after them?"

He stomped to the cardboard box that contained his kindling, pulled out a stick the length of Frannie's arm, then came back to the bed and slapped it into her palm. Her fingers closed around it reflexively.

She waved it in the air as if it were a magic wand—one that would make him tell her his game plan. "You're walking to Texas?" she prodded.

"Riding."

Her eyes narrowed. He did have a set of keys. His jeans were tight enough that she could see them bulging in his pocket. Still, she hadn't seen a car. Not that one would be of help, given the mud outside.

"Well, I guess I'm ready," she said, standing up. She smiled in his direction and batted her lashes. "These days, I'm traveling light." Maybe he'd given her the stick to use in lieu of a machete, in order to help facilitate their escape through the woods. She glanced down, realized she lacked shoes and frowned.

She drew in a deep breath, decided filthy feet hadn't killed her the previous day, then glanced at the stick again. It wasn't a bad idea to use it to beat back the bushes that would undoubtedly lie in their path. She realized he was staring at her, looking horrified.

"You're not coming with me," he said flatly.

She stared at him wide-eyed. "You were going to leave me here?"

"I *am* going to leave you here."

"Over my dead body!"

"If that's the way you want it." He glanced toward the window. "Eight minutes," he said, in a tone that indicated she'd been seriously holding him up.

She was so shocked that she didn't know what to do. Hurt too, she realized. The man had blown hot and cold all the previous day, only to make love to her with more heat and raw energy than she'd ever experienced. It hadn't affected him at all and now he was ditching her. Even worse—he was tossing her to the cops like a bone!

She leapt from the bed and advanced on him, her bare feet slapping on the wooden floor. She waved the ridiculous stick. "I can't believe you!" she sputtered. "You're leaving me here to face the cops alone! Is that what this—this stick's for?" A sudden rush of temper made crazy energy sizzle along her nerves. "What am I supposed to do with this thing?" She ignored the fact that Bill ducked beneath the wildly swinging stick. "Fend off a bunch of policemen who have guns? Jab them with my big weapon? What kind of man would leave a woman in this situation?"

She stopped in her tracks and gaped at him. Then she watched in sheer amazement as Wild Bill headed for the bed again. He snatched up the empty pillowcase and returned.

Images of shoot-outs played through her mind. Of course, it wouldn't really be a shoot-out, since only *they* would have guns. She, of course, would have a stick. She would be a lone woman trapped in a cabin while men with guns and megaphones and handcuffs slipped into bullet-proof vests and readied themselves to charge inside and arrest her. Darn it, maybe they'd just start shooting. They'd take up positions behind the trees and— She could almost hear the shots ring out. "What do you expect me to do?" she wailed.

Holding the pillowcase between his thumb and forefinger, Bill lifted it into the air. Then he hung the white cloth on the end of the stick. "Surrender, sweetheart," he said softly.

"SURRENDER?" she burst out.

Bill wrestled his old prize Triumph from behind a bush, nudged up the kickstand, then edged it toward the creek bed. The creek, usually a meandering trickle, had swollen with the heavy rains. Fast-running water cut a wide path down the mountain—and away from the police. Gripping the handlebars, Bill pushed the motorcycle into the center of the creek, easing the tires over leaves and pebbles. He figured he could ride all the way down to the road. Meantime, the cops would be stuck in the mud. Riding through the creek meant he wouldn't leave footprints or scents that dogs could follow, too.

Things would be fine if he could force himself to ignore Frannie Anderson.

"You really think I'm going to surrender?" she wailed again.

He told himself not to turn around.

But he did. And felt like a cad. She was standing at the edge of the creek, looking as serious as she did forlorn. She'd rolled the cuffs of his oversize jeans above her perfectly rounded knees and her bare feet were submerged beneath mud. The line of filth stopped at her ankles. When she pulled up her feet, the wet earth slurped at her skin, making indelicate smacking noises. Black mud splashed onto her pale calves. It was a sight to behold.

So was the wild uncombed hair that blew around her. His clothes were baggy on her, but he knew darn well what all was beneath them after last night. If she hadn't started right in on him this morning about not pursuing what she'd falsely called their relationship, he might have been inclined to bring her along, he decided. Hell, he wanted to bring her along in spite of it.

But he'd couldn't abide being stuck with a woman whose sheer presence teased him—and whom he couldn't have. Nothing, he decided, would be more excruciating than having her ride tandem when he wasn't to so much as kiss her. The look in her eyes this morning had said she still wanted him. And that she was still going to deny it.

"Please," he finally said, "just go surrender."

Instead, she plastered a falsely bright expression on her face and slung the stick, complete with pillowcase, over her shoulder like a hobo's makeshift pack. She stared down at her feet pitifully, then squared her shoulders with resolve and marched right into the creek.

He turned around abruptly and started pushing his bike downhill, wondering why he'd let her hold him up for so long. Now he'd have to go some distance before he could start the engine.

He could hear her splashing behind him.

When she was next to him, she said, "You clearly didn't notice, but I believe I did surrender quite a lot!"

He arched a brow in her direction and realized with a sinking heart that getting rid of her wasn't going to be easy. Even worse, his old affliction was kicking in. He'd gone from "pleased to meet you" to "can't live without you" in twenty-four hours flat. Trouble was, every time he looked at her, he started to fear that the feelings might last. Surrender? What on earth was she talking about? He tightened his grip on the handlebars. "Excuse me?"

She sniffed haughtily. "I surrendered myself to you last night!"

You would have thought he'd taken the crown jewels. And maybe he had, he thought. It had been a night of lovemaking he'd never forget. But she didn't want him and he wasn't the type to beg. "I don't exactly remember you surrendering, sweetheart," he found himself saying gruffly. "I mean, you sure seemed like a willing participant."

He wasn't sure but thought tears might be starting to gather in her eyes. He hoped not. He just hated it when women cried. If she cried, he told himself, he really was going to leave her right there, in the middle of the creek. Was she upset because *he* was leaving her—or because he was leaving her for the cops?

"You're a very mean man," she nearly whispered.

"And you sure know how to lay on the guilt," he returned. He pushed the cycle around a pile of driftwood and wondered if he could get away with starting the engine yet.

"Well, you should feel guilty for leaving me here like this!"

If she'd just surrender, the way he'd asked her to, the worst thing that could happen would be that she'd find herself in a jail cell again. "If you were in jail, you might not get the cuisine you're used to, but it would lessen the risk of a trigger-happy cop taking a shot at you. I'm trying to protect you." He shot her a quick cynical grin. "Besides, I bet you could sweet-talk them into bringing you some nail polish."

Her gaze shot to her hands. He'd known it would. She looked so depressed when she looked at her fingertips that he almost felt inclined to offer to paint them for her.

"You just can't leave me here like this!"

"Because you've got a bad manicure?" he asked dryly.

"No," she said, her voice suddenly catching. "Because I can't go home."

He wanted to stop but kept moving. He'd run hot cars over countless borders, and even though he lived on the right side of the law these days, he could smell a cop from a mile away. They were close. "Why can't you go home?" he finally asked. Was she Bonnie Smith? *No, she's who she says she is.*

"I just can't," she said. "That's all."

He slowed his steps and squinted at her. She was on the run, all right. There was panic in her eyes. But from what? A job she hated? A bad marriage? An abusive boyfriend? He decided that she could go home, but that she didn't want to. Did he dare to hope that a woman like her could fall for an uncouth cuss like him?

For a moment, the only sounds were her splashes and the flowing water parting on either side of his round-toed boots. He sighed, thinking that her body fit his like a long lost puzzle piece. And that she didn't have shoes. He swung his leg over the seat, then glanced behind him. "Fine."

"Fine?"

"Just get on."

A second later, one of her long legs swung in behind his and she shimmied forward, wrapping an arm around his waist. She tossed the stick toward the bank, but missed. It caught the current and fishtailed in front of them.

He glanced over his shoulder again. "You on?"

She nodded.

Now both her arms were around him, clinging tight. He wanted nothing more than to turn around and make love to her—the cops be damned.

He glanced in his side-view mirror. Now that the woman had gotten her way, she was actually grinning. Her breasts pressed against his back and he could feel her breath flutter against his neck. Not five yards away his pillowcase snagged on a branch and waved in the breeze as if waving them goodbye.

As he turned the key, all he could think was that he was making a terrible mistake.

And that it felt good.

Chapter Six

"Can we make another pit stop?" Frannie screamed. When she bobbed her head, trying to get Bill's attention in his side-view mirror, her new helmet slid over her eyes and obscured her vision. The helmet was bright red, with the words *Speed Demon* sprayed in gold on both sides. They'd found it attached to a parked motorcycle outside a town called Boone and while Frannie adored it, Bill had looked none too happy about committing the theft.

She only wished he'd managed to steal her a pair of shoes. She tilted her head back so that she could see beneath the rim of her helmet. Locks of Wild Bill's hair flew from beneath his headgear, the stray strands tickling her nose. She squeezed his flat abdomen insistently with one hand, almost wishing he had love handles to hang on to. With her free hand, she touched his hair. The wind had combed it into fine silk. When she yanked it, he turned his head to the side.

"You have to stop *again*?" he yelled. The emphasis was on *again*.

"It'll just take a minute." How could Bill drive for so long without a ladies' room? Men's room, she corrected as her hand dropped from his hair and wrapped around his muscled stomach again.

Even though the engine was roaring and the wind was flapping by her ears, she could imagine Bill sighing. If anything had convinced her he didn't want her company, it was the last seven stops. Still, in spite of his professed pique, she kept catching him watching her in the mirror. Perhaps he was angry because she'd said she didn't want to sleep with him again. But didn't he understand that a woman had the right to get to know a guy first?

When he slowed, she glanced around anxiously. He wouldn't make her go outside—would he? They were taking back roads, but he'd found gas stations every other time. Her last trip to the wilderness had sworn her off bushes altogether. After all, she'd just come from behind one when Mickey and Darrell held her at gunpoint. Besides which, she felt grimy and needed to wash her face. If only she'd managed to keep her pocketbook, which had contained her brush and makeup....

Not that it mattered. All day, Bill had tried to establish a distance between them. Periodically, she started to wonder why she'd felt so attracted to him...and then she'd remember the feel of his arms wrapped around her hips while he showered kisses on her belly. If a man could make love the way he did, there had to be something more to him personality-wise. Didn't there?

''Well, go on,'' he said tersely.

She shook her head to get the helmet out of her eyes and felt a rush of relief. Somehow, Bill had turned off a pleasant country road to the main drag of some small town. ''But you're not even stopped yet,'' she protested.

''Well, get *ready* to go,'' he said over his shoulder.

Every single word out of the man's mouth seemed calculated to make her feel lousy. ''If I'd known you were going to be this way,'' she said as he parked, ''I wouldn't have come.'' She swung her leg over the seat, got off and glared at him.

He looked at her as if to say, *Why did you?*

She ignored him and fumbled with her helmet strap. After a long moment, his hand shot upward. In a split second, he'd released the strap from the myriad series of buckles. As soon as the helmet was off, she tossed her hair behind her with two quick snaps of her head. "Thanks," she muttered.

"No problem," he said gruffly. "But hurry it up."

I'll take my good old time. "Late for the ball, Cinderfella?" she tossed over her shoulder, as she headed inside the station.

Just as the attendant handed her the keys to the ladies' room, a midnight blue BMW convertible pulled to the curb. On her way out, Frannie nearly collided with one of the passengers. "Excuse me," she murmured apologetically.

The woman, a well-coiffed brunette in her twenties, stared right through her, then said, "I need the ladies' room key."

Frannie almost giggled. Miss Priss was wearing an exact replica of the white suit Frannie had worn the previous day. Glancing at the BMW, Frannie realized she was secretly glad hers was in the shop. If she hadn't been driving her father's Caddy, then Mickey and Darrell wouldn't have tried to arrest her and she wouldn't have made love to Wild Bill and—

"She's got it, ma'am," the attendant said.

The woman's smile wavered. Her eyes dropped over Frannie's black T-shirt, oversize jeans and filthy feet. She pointedly averted her gaze and stared through the station's plate glass window. Her eyes seemed to land on Bill.

He was leaning casually against his bike, looking dangerous. The sleeves of his tight, white T-shirt were rolled up so that his tattoo was as evident as the grim set of his mouth. He peeled off his leather riding gloves and slapped them against the thighs of his threadbare jeans.

"I'll wait," the woman said shakily.

In all her amusement over the woman's attention to her and Bill, Frannie had forgotten where she was headed. "I won't be long," she assured.

"As you can see, I'm hurrying!" she called to Bill as she passed him. She headed around the side of the station, chuckling. Whether it was because she was intentionally annoying Bill or because of the woman in the station, Frannie didn't know. Just how many layers of wax toilet coverlets would Miss Priss use, seeing as Frannie—biker chick extraordinaire—had just used the john?

"A lot," she whispered to herself, sluicing warm water over her cheeks. She patted her face dry, then squinted in the mirror. Her hair was wildly disheveled, but her eyes looked brighter than they had in years. She grinned. "You motorcycle mama!" she said to the mirror.

She shoved the key into her back pocket and headed outside again. It was amazing, but the woman's reaction to her hadn't been offensive. Instead, it had cracked her up.

As she slapped the key into the woman's hand, she almost laughed out loud. Why? *Because I've never dressed in clothes like these. And before today, I'd never been on a motorcycle or gone any farther west than Pittsburgh, Pennsylvania.*

She wasn't going to let Bill Berdovitch ruin her sense of newfound freedom, either, she thought, stepping onto the shady curb. The pavement felt cool beneath her bare feet and when she stretched and glanced at the sky, it seemed bluer than a royal blue crayon.

Bill was still leaning against his motorcycle, with his boots casually crossed at the ankles. One hand was now on his hip. The other hung idle in a long, unbroken line of well-delineated muscle and sinew. All the man needed was sunglasses. The riding goggles around his neck ruined the rebellious image.

Just looking at him, Frannie suddenly wanted to hoot and holler. Last night he'd loved her like he meant it. Had that changed her overnight? She hadn't felt so good since high school. *And why shouldn't I yell?* she thought with an impish smile. She didn't know these people—not the attendant, or the woman from the BMW, or the kids in the old, yellow VW bus that had just pulled in. But was her motive really to get Bill's attention?

She filled her lungs with air and then belted out the first thing that came to mind. "I feel fabulous!"

Heads turned and people stared. The BMW woman rounded the corner and Frannie waved jauntily in her direction. Then she laughed. She'd spent half her life learning to be heard in crowded football stadiums, so her yells were powerful. She grinned at Bill. Not that he smiled back.

And then she saw the boot shop. She gave her cantankerous driver a final wave and headed toward the store. The fact that Bill might leave her gave her pause, but then she did have a hundred and forty dollars hidden in her pocket. Her mother had always coached her to "Keep a dime for a phone call" when on a date....

Of course, she wasn't on a date, calls were a quarter nowadays and she meant to hang on to her money if she could. Last night—when Bill had made love to her as if he'd become accustomed to her body long ago—she might have shared.

But not today. Because maybe she didn't need him. Maybe she didn't need a man at all. Twenty-four hours ago, she'd intended to use her vacation to husband-hunt. But now? If Bill left her, he'd become just another Joey Florence and Frannie would buy a bus ticket. Maybe she'd go to the badlands, too, instead of back to Pennsylvania.

But Bill was following her! She stopped in front of the boot store, her eyes roving over the display. Not a moment later, she saw Bill's reflection in the window glass.

"I'm not buying you a pair of six-hundred-dollar boots," he said flatly.

A smile touched at her lips as she met his gaze in the window. "Well," she returned, "you do have a Gold Card." There were cowboy boots in every shape and size—ostrich skin, lizard, brightly colored leather....

"The cards are traceable," he said in no uncertain terms.

Hearing the twinge of guilt in his voice, she had to fight not to laugh. "But they're looking for Bonnie and Clyde, not William Heironymous Berdovitch." In the window, she could see his tongue dart out and catch an edge of his mustache.

"My name is not Heironymous."

Maybe the *H* was for Hunk. Even in reflection he was as handsome as sin. "Well, whatever your name is, I think it's lousy of you to expect me to walk around barefoot. Why, you should have seen how that nice woman looked at me in the gas station!"

Was it her imagination or was the man really considering buying her a pair of outrageously priced boots? The thought made her want to take a quick step backward, into his arms. She decided he liked her far more than he was letting on and turned around and scrutinized him.

"The cops have mug shots of you and me, not Bonnie and Clyde," he finally said. "For all we know, the cops think Clyde's an alias for Bill." His eyes narrowed, as if to impart the seriousness of the situation to her. "I've only got about a hundred dollars and we're going to need it. We've got to get settled somewhere and start making phone calls."

That more or less answered her questions about how much money he had. She stared down at her toes. Just as she glanced up again and batted her eyelashes, his hand clamped down on her shoulder.

"C'mon." He gently pushed her down the sidewalk.

She chuckled. "Don't tell me. You're going to wrap my feet in newspaper and bind them with wire." His lips parted and she thought he was going to assure her that he wasn't such an ogre.

"There's a secondhand store," he said.

"I've never bought anything in a thrift store before," she couldn't help but say.

He sighed. "Pretend it's Neiman-Marcus."

"That would take some imagination," she muttered glumly as they crossed the threshold. The store smelled of insecticide. Her eyes flitted uncertainly over the jumbled racks. Empty wire hangers stuck out from between the clothes like elbows held akimbo. Her hand shot to her heart. "That's a Betsy Johnson dress!"

And it was a good ten yards away! She'd have to hurry! Years of cruising department stores had taught her to recognize a steal. She wasn't above snatching real prizes from the hands of the competition, either. She glanced around. She and Bill were the only customers.

"A Betsy Johnson," she murmured in amazement. The path of her life might not have led in any clear direction, but she knew the path between herself and the dress was clear. Her shopping instincts were as well honed as Wild Bill's hunting knife.

Bill groaned. "The last thing you need is a dress."

She beelined for it. She'd nearly reached it when a pair of perfectly good black biker shorts leapt into her hands. And there were scarves, walking shorts, tank tops....

Her heart started racing so fast that she could really have been in Neiman's—or making love to Bill again. She gathered everything she wanted, then glanced at her partner in crime. He was picking over the sneakers. She hoped he was joking. Her flouncy floral sundress would look ridiculous with them.

When her eyes landed on the cowboy boots, they stuck like glue. If they were too small would she take them? How much too big before she put her foot down and said no? She decided they just *had* to fit. They were of scuffed red lizard skin with black uppers and green stitching.

Bill held up a running shoe. "What size do you wear?"

He hadn't even noticed the high tops, she thought with pique. Didn't he care how she looked? "Eight," she called, grabbing a floppy straw hat as she passed it. "Silk," she continued, reading the dress tag and hurrying toward Bill. There were no other customers, but she was still sure someone else was going to get those boots. "Bingo," she said, snatching them from the shelf.

She plopped into an armchair that was for sale, then grinned at the man behind the register. "Do you have a stocking?"

He looked at her as if she were out of her mind.

Dumb question. Even if the man had footies, he'd probably have withheld them given how dirty her feet were. Bill looked exasperated. She turned both boots upside down, shook them out, then peered inside, hoping nothing disgusting lived in the toes. Just as she shoved her foot into boot one, Bill leaned next to her.

"You know," he said, "we *are* running from the law."

His breath lingered beside her ear, and his lips stayed so close that her first impulse was to kiss him again. Every time he got that close, she couldn't have cared less about who they were running from. She just hoped the trek led back into his arms.

She smiled. "You're as much fun as a trip to the orthodontist."

"I wouldn't know," he shot back.

What he meant was that a lot of people couldn't afford orthodontists. "Your teeth aren't even crooked." She giggled. "Even if you *are* crooked in other ways. I mean—"

"I know what you mean." He put his hands on his hips and sounded resigned. "Please, Frannie, just try on the boots."

BILL GLANCED DOWN, saw one of Frannie's new red boots trailing along the pavement and wished she'd at least do him the courtesy of keeping her feet on the pegs.

"This is really Memphis?" she asked.

Hearing the excitement in her voice, Bill almost wanted to smile. He didn't, mostly because he was bone tired. They'd taken back roads, stopped exactly eleven times more than he'd meant to, including for dinner, and the muscles of his neck and back were bunched from hunching over the handlebars. The fact that Frannie's arms and legs had been wrapped around him all day didn't help. Especially since twenty-four hours ago he'd had her exactly where he wanted her—naked and handcuffed to his bed.

Now he was about to share a bed with her in the Paradise Motel. Driving beneath its neon sign, he realized only three of the letters were lit. *Not a good omen.* Bill blew out a sigh, parked around the corner from the motel office and killed the engine. "Yeah," he said. "It's Memphis. Near it, anyway."

But far enough away that seedy places like the Paradise dotted the terrain. He'd considered going to a truck stop, for Frannie's sake. There was one within spitting distance, with a high-rise hotel and a well lit, clean-looking diner, but this place would be less obvious in case the cops had picked up their scent.

Frannie's trailing boot suddenly stomped on the pavement. She swung her leg over the seat and her other boot stomped down. He smiled, thinking about the two pairs of socks she was wearing in order to make them fit. What some women wouldn't do for vanity's sake. He watched her whip off her helmet.

"You're getting good at that," he commented, thinking they'd sure stopped enough to give her practice, and wishing her thick blond mane didn't look quite so lusciously mussed and tangled as it cascaded down her back. He pulled off his own helmet, feeling the warm southern breeze ruffle his hair.

"I can't believe we finally get to rest!" She grinned and shifted the looped handles of her shopping bag from one wrist to the other.

"I was doing the driving," he said, his gaze dipping over her. There was no doubt about the fact that he wanted her, but during the long drive, he'd started to decide he actually liked her. Mostly because something so small as a second-hand hat made her eyes light up like Christmas. The shopping bag had thumped against his thigh ever since the thrift store, but she'd never lost her grip on it. It got heavier with each stop, too. In addition to the clothes he'd bought her, she'd thrown in free maps and tour guides. Now she rummaged in the bag and pulled one out.

"Is Graceland in Nashville or Memphis?"

Without taking his eyes off her, he threw his leg over the seat and grunted as he stretched his legs. Lord, did she really think they could take time out for a tour? He leaned against his bike. "Graceland?"

"Isn't that where Elvis lives?"

"Elvis is dead," he said flatly.

One of her broken fingernails stabbed the pamphlet. "Graceland *is* in Memphis!"

She looked so thrilled that he almost wished he could take her there. "C'mon, sweetheart. Let's just check in."

She shoved the pamphlet in the shopping bag again and glanced around the corner of the building at the motel's office. A sudden tug of longing suddenly threatened to push him right into her arms, and for the umpteenth time that day, he wondered how he was going to sleep in the same room with her. He'd considered getting two rooms, but they couldn't afford it. Keeping his hands off her was going to be impossible. Under the weak neon light, her blue eyes had become a bright enticing violet.

"Coming?" she asked.

He shoved himself off the bike and followed her.

"This place sure looks sleazy," she said, wavering uncertainly beside a bush.

The night breeze carried her scent. Beneath the shampoo and soap she'd used the previous night, there was something more alluring, musky. "Upset about staying in the Paradise?"

She flashed him a fleeting smile. "No, I've just never—"

"Been in a fleabag motel before." As anxious as he was to lie down, he leaned against the building. The day had been full of places she'd never seen and things she'd never done. He scrutinized her. "Why hasn't somebody like you done more? Didn't you all take summer vacations?" Something crossed her features that he couldn't quite read. Disappointment?

"New York every autumn," she said. "You know, fall fashions."

Bill nodded as if he understood perfectly.

"Then Nag's Head for two weeks every summer." She shrugged. "My father worked all the time, especially when I was little, and my mother was either hobnobbing, fundraising for charities, or taking to her bed with an imaginary ailment."

When she smiled, it was a little false. Maybe she was thinking that his childhood must have been worse. She'd be right, he thought grimly. Still, all day she'd been like a kid in a candy store and he couldn't figure it out. "You must have had a lot of friends. Cheerleaders are always popular."

Her soft chuckle sounded like sad music. "In high school."

She made it sound as if centuries had passed since that time. She glanced toward the ground and her heavy lids veiled her eyes, making her look mysterious. "Well, didn't your friends want to go anywhere?"

"Yeah," she said drolly. "To the mall."

"So, where is it you think you're headed now?" It was a loaded question, but he wanted to know. When she tilted her head, long shadows from the leaves in the eaves above danced on her cheeks. She merely shook her head as if to say she wasn't sure.

He rubbed his beard. "What about one step forward and one to the side?"

She squinted. "What?"

Still leaning against the building, he stretched out his hand and led her through the steps. When they landed her right in front of him, she giggled but didn't protest. Gliding his hands around her waist, he curled his head and kissed her.

It was a slow, easy kiss. He merely nudged open her lips with his and gently pressed his tongue against hers. With each touch, he wanted to build to a slow-burning fire. Not to the frenzied groping passion of their first encounter, but to what came after, when everything fell still and quiet, save for soft sighs and softer whimpers. He wanted to carefully kindle that flame, make each of his fluttering breaths stoke it, until it had the kind of heat that lasted.

"I don't think..." she began when he drew back.

"Sweetheart," he said, "I wish you'd just quit thinking." But she was contemplating the same thing he was—making love again. Her eyes said it even as her lips denied it. He wondered if she'd give in to her feelings once they were situated. It could sure complicate things, since he was beginning to like her.

"We'd better check in," she said, gently moving from his grasp.

"Whatever you say." He meant it, too. He was tough, but not enough that he could ignore her protests and take her once they were alone. He draped his arm across her shoulders as they walked toward the office. Just as he caught the smudged glass door and opened it for her, he moaned. "I parked the bike out of sight, figuring only one of us should come in."

Her eyes widened, as if to say that had been a good plan.

"I—" *Forgot because of how good you look. We started talking and I kissed you....* He shrugged. "Never mind."

She headed for the counter. Even though the proprietor was behind it, she examined the announcement bell as if she'd never seen one before, then rang it. It dinged merrily in the silence.

When the proprietor glanced up, Bill realized he was drunker than a skunk. *There's a piece of luck.* If pictures of him and Frannie started circulating, the man might not remember them.

"We'd like two rooms," Frannie said.

"One room," Bill corrected, realizing the proprietor hadn't heard Frannie. He lowered his voice. "We don't have the money." Against his better judgment, he'd spent over twenty dollars on Frannie's new wardrobe. Then he'd bought her disposable razors, a peel-off mask and a toothbrush.

The proprietor's head lolled on his neck, then rolled upward and righted itself. "You can't stay here if you—"

"We have money," Bill assured.

"Okay," Frannie said, her face coloring. "One room."

Bill felt her gaze drift over him. He was sure she'd never have kissed him if she'd known they were sleeping in the same room again.

"You have to pay up front," the proprietor said.

When the man exhaled, the scent of alcohol made Bill wince. He wished they'd gone to the truck stop. Drunks disgusted him. He dug in his pocket for the money.

"Oh!" Frannie suddenly exclaimed. "Do you have one of those beds that vibrates?"

Bill nearly choked. He brought out a wad of cash, slapped it on the counter and then stared at her. It wasn't that he minded having a bed vibrate, so long as he wasn't on it, but why would she request such a thing? Every time he thought he had a handle on her, the rug slipped out from under him.

"That'd be two dollars ex-tree."

"I've seen them in movies," Frannie explained in a pleading tone.

"You haven't lived until you've slept in a vibrating bed," Bill returned. He slid the cash across the counter. "Fine, we'll take the bed."

"I know you think it's dumb," Frannie said defensively, "but they only have them in places like this. This may be the only time I ever go to a sleazy motel."

"This is a well-respected establishment," the man slurred.

"That's exactly why we stopped," Bill said to appease him.

The man was still holding on to all of Bill's money and now he didn't look inclined to give it back. Not that Bill couldn't take it. The man was drunk and half his size. Still, the last thing he and Frannie needed was more trouble.

"Are y'all married?" the man finally asked.

Good going, Frannie. Now, he's going to give us a hard time. "Been married for more than a year." Bill suspected unmarried couples were the man's usual customers, but he held his tongue, put his arm around Frannie and hugged her close.

"You don't have rings," the man said after a long moment. "For all I know, you could be having an ex-tree marital affair."

Frannie gasped. "I wouldn't do that!"

Her side was pressed against his and Bill just wished they were having *some* kind of affair. And that the cops weren't after them. He felt as if he were slowly getting sucked into Frannie's view of things—where they were on an adventure that might include tours through Graceland. They weren't.

Fortunately, the proprietor pushed Bill's change across the counter with a key. "Room eight's around the corner. I guess y'all can sign in."

"We really are married." Bill wasn't sure why, but he didn't want the drunk old lout to think Frannie was loose.

"Actually—" Frannie shot Bill a mischievous smile "—we've got four kids and, well, you know how hard it is to get any time alone with kids in the house. Especially with all the cooking and cleaning...."

Bill bit back a smile and half listened to Frannie's ongoing monologue about the trials and tribulations of motherhood. She was a pretty funny lady. When she started talking about diapers—disposable versus hand wash—the proprietor shoved a pen toward Bill. When he started to write his name, he realized he'd have to use an alias. Clyde Calvert came to mind, but he sure couldn't use that.

"Little Scooter just gets into everything," Frannie was saying. "Why, I went to bed the other night and found four Matchbox cars underneath my pillow...."

Bill thought of the real Clyde—Clyde Barrow—and scrawled Mr. and Mrs. Heironymous Barrow into the book.

"And when Elsie skinned her knee..."

Bill watched her for a moment, wondering if she'd ever wanted kids. Her monologue was detailed enough that she seemed to have thought about them. "You about ready, Mrs. Barrow?"

She glanced down at the book. "Oh, Heironymous," she cooed. "I'm going to show you a night in paradise you'll never forget."

"SOME NIGHT in paradise," Bill commented dryly.

Frannie tried to ignore the one double bed and flipped through the television channels. "We've got to see if we're on the news or anything," she said, attempting to keep her voice brisk. "They've got cable. Maybe we can even get CNN. Are you going to call the cops?"

"I'm going to do it right now."

Frannie glanced at him, wishing she hadn't kissed him outside. Not that she didn't want him. But she didn't trust men who could turn as cold as he had this morning. The sparks they'd ignited were kindled with danger, too. Last night had been too fast, too volatile and too unpredictable. Besides which, William H. Berdovitch had *drifter* written all over him. And Frannie couldn't survive being left again.

She found the news, then turned around and surveyed the room, deciding it would have been spacious if Bill wasn't in it. When he sat on the bed and pulled the phone onto the mattress, the room shrank to the size of a pea.

How could the man's drawl sound so sexy when he was merely requesting numbers from information? The phone operator was probably waving at her girlfriends, indicating that they should listen in. *Am I really jealous of a mystery woman at Ma Bell?* she wondered as she glanced around. Worn brown carpet covered the floors and a print reproduction of a landscape hung above the headboard at a precarious angle. Through the thin curtains, she could see Bill's bike.

"What a rip-off!" she suddenly exclaimed. "He charged us an *ex-tree* two dollars and you have to use quarters!"

"Quiet," Bill said. "It's ringing."

She looked at him and their eyes locked. His expression was serious, but he winked and dug in his pocket. Just as he said hello, he slapped four quarters on the bedside table.

"I need to speak with someone about the Bonnie Smith and Clyde Calvert case," he said.

Forgetting her resolve to keep a physical distance, Frannie scooted next to him on the edge of the bed and watched his expression. Bill nodded and scribbled a string of numbers on a pad. Suddenly, Bill hung up.

"Why'd you do that?"

He pointed at the clock. "My three minutes were up. Frankly, I'm not sure how the newest tracing mechanisms work, but why chance it?" He picked up the phone and dialed again.

"Who are you calling now?"

"Reed Galveston," Bill said into the mouthpiece. "He's FBI."

Frannie edged closer. Then, unable to contain herself, she cozied right against him and Bill kindly tilted the earpiece in her direction. She kept her eyes on the clock.

What ensued wasn't good. It took four three-minute calls to establish that Reed Galveston wasn't available. Then, when Bill tried to explain their situation, it became clear that the police were no more enlightened than they had been the previous day.

"No," Bill said at one point. "I stayed at the home of William Berdovitch last night. It's *my* house. I am William Berdovitch."

"Five seconds," Frannie whispered, wondering if they could really be traced or not. She knew she should have been upset, but what she really felt was exhilaration at being involved in a manhunt.

"Myself and a woman named Frannie Anderson were wrongfully arrested yesterday," Bill was saying.

"Frances," Frannie added into the mouthpiece, her lips just a hair's breath from Bill's. "Frances Taylor Anderson of Pittsburgh." Her eyes flitted to the clock again. "One second!" she whispered urgently.

Bill cut the connection and scooted on the bed to make more room for her. His flabbergasted expression made him look years younger.

"I have a real respect for the law," he finally said. "But those guys are..." He finally settled on "dense." He shook his head. "A man named Reed Galveston is apparently in charge of the investigation and they couldn't even find him."

"Oh, no!" She tried to sound more appalled than she actually felt. Glancing at the TV, she saw a reporter interviewing the owner of a bicycle shop. Someone had driven a truck through his shop window. "I was hoping it would all be over, Bill."

She was lying. She hardly wanted to be hunted down, arrested or shot. But riding down meandering back roads with the wind blowing against her cheeks wasn't all bad. Neither was having Bill for her companion....

"Well, at least we know things can't get much worse."

Frannie's eyes suddenly widened and her arm flailed beside her. She grabbed Bill, somewhere in the proximity of his thigh. "They sure can," she croaked.

Because their mug shots were on TV.

And right beneath the pictures, the word *wanted* was flashing in glorious black and white.

BILL STARED into the darkness and tried to tell himself that his insomnia was due to the fact that he was on the run, the same way he had been ten long years ago. But he was honest these days. So, he admitted that how Frannie kept snoring and swinging her legs over his was driving him crazy. The way his fingers were itching to touch her, he could have had poison ivy. Only gliding his palms down the lengths of her legs would cure the burning itch.

Not that he would. They'd talked before they'd gone to sleep and if anything had convinced him she was serious about a hands-off policy, it was her businesslike tone. When she kept insisting he stay on the bed while she made it vibrate, he'd moved to kiss her, but she'd eluded his grasp. Didn't she want him?

He wondered. And he wondered whether Reed Galveston was going to be of any help. Probably not. Even though the man was FBI, he hadn't figured out what had happened yet. No, their best bet was to find the real Bonnie and Clyde, and turn them in. Maybe he and Frannie would get a reward in the bargain. Trouble was, Mexico was a big place, and they didn't have much to go on.

Unfortunately, Frannie wouldn't disguise herself. She'd threatened him with bloody murder when he'd suggested she dye her hair. He'd finally given up, gone to the bathroom and shaved off his beard and mustache. He'd had to use the whole pack of razors, too. Now, the jagged scar that wrapped around his chin and slashed toward his throat was in plain sight. Frannie had called it "sexy," which made him feel marginally better.

But if it was so sexy, why was the woman sleeping in secondhand gym shorts? He heard something outside and tensed. *Just a passing car.* Headlights beamed through the thin curtains, then made an arching pass across the wall. He relaxed. *If the man at the front desk recognized us, the cops would be here by now. He probably didn't see the news. Or else he was too drunk to notice.*

Bill reached down, gingerly moved Frannie's leg off his thigh, then scooted further toward his side of the bed. He was nearly out of space. It was just no use. For hours, she'd been cuddling. And he'd been scooting.

Within seconds, her snuggle radar spotted him again. She flung her leg over both his again and rubbed her cheek against his chest as if convinced it were her pillow. He lifted her knee and carefully replaced it on the lumpy mattress.

One more scoot would land him on the floor. So, he got up, circled the bed and got back in on the other side.

The Paradise, he decided, was sheer hell.

Chapter Seven

Bill woke wishing he hadn't dreamed of Frannie. Their past lovemaking kept haunting him like a ghost that appeared, disappeared, then hovered persistently. He suddenly realized that Frannie wasn't next to him.

"Frannie?" The shower wasn't running and terror seized him. Had she gone outside without disguising herself? Had the cops gotten her? Lord, their faces had probably flashed on every TV in the country.

He got out of bed, stepping right into his boots. He'd unsnapped his jeans for comfort and as he stomped toward the bathroom, he zipped and resnapped. Then he pounded on the door. "You in there?"

No answer. He flung open the door. The tub was wet, the air smelled of soap and her dirty clothes, gym shorts included, were in a pile on the floor. His pack was open on the counter and his brush was now on the sink's lip. Wherever she'd gone, she'd gotten ready. Didn't she realize people were looking for them?

And why hadn't he bought himself a secondhand shirt? He shrugged into the black T-shirt she'd worn the previous day, figuring her dirty clothes would smell sweeter than his. Then he turned on the tap and plunged his face beneath it. He came up sputtering and stared in the mirror.

A virtual stranger stared back—a man who'd seen one too many a knife fight and who could vouch for the fact that ice water on bare skin woke a man faster than if it had been filtered through a thick mat of hair.

He turned off the water, snapped a towel from a rack and dried his tingling, clean-shaven face as he headed toward the bed again. Suddenly his hand shot to his pocket. Had she taken his bike? Maybe she was really was Bonnie Smith and she had—

No, the keys to his Triumph were in the pocket. So were his money and credit cards. Had he really thought she could remove the items without his knowing? Hell, he thought, as he scanned the dresser for the room key, he'd been awake all night. Her eyes hadn't so much as fluttered with REM movements that he didn't notice. But where could she have gone without money?

His chest constricted. Yesterday, he'd gotten a taste of something he hadn't had for a long time—the feeling of what it was like to be battling the odds with someone next to him. And now she'd vanished.

"She took the room key," he muttered. He opened the window, so he could get back inside if he didn't find her. Then he went outside and headed down the sidewalk, trying to ignore the fact that Frannie's scent clung to the shirt he was wearing. If he took his bike and she returned, she'd think he'd left. *Unless she's gone for good.*

"I'm going to kill you, sweetheart," he whispered right before his gaze landed on a bank of newspaper machines.

His and Frannie's pictures were on the front page of the local rag. He sighed, shoved in a quarter and took out a paper. Then he stared at the truck stop in the distance, feeling a pang of gut-level loss. He realized that she was beautiful and funny and had the best set of legs he'd ever laid eyes on. What if she wasn't there?

"SO WHO'S GONNA up and vanish next?" Reed snarled, slamming down the phone. He leaned back in a swivel chair and surveyed the bank of telephones opposite him. Then he looked at Carly who was shoving pushpins in a map, marking all the locations where their suspects had been spotted.

"Who's missing now, boss?"

"Besides that deputy who was supposed to bring me coffee? Our suspects. And now Clarence."

Carly whirled around. "Larson's partner?"

Reed nodded. "Yep. He just up and flew the coop."

"What did Larson say?"

Reed rolled his eyes. "Says he's Clarence's partner, not his mother and that he doesn't know where Clarence went."

Carly chuckled. "Well, there's the guy with the coffee."

Reed's eyes narrowed as Tyler placed a foam cup on the desk. He peered into it, then glanced at the redheaded deputy. "Is there sugar in here?"

Tyler glanced uncertainly between Carly and Reed, as if he were well aware he needed to redeem himself.

"It's a simple yes or no," Reed prompted.

"Two sugars, sir."

Reed nodded curtly. "You've restored my faith in humanity." When Tyler grinned, Reed found himself smiling back. "Is that guy claiming to be Berdovitch gonna call back or not?" Reed suddenly continued. "I feel like a fool woman sitting by the phones."

"Looks to me like a *man's* sitting by the phones, boss."

Reed willed one to ring. "Well, those Larson contracts are as phony as this room. And who spent the night in that cabin? Maybe it was Berdovitch, in which case he'll sue the state of West Virginia."

"You think he was wrongfully arrested?"

Reed shot a wry glance at Tyler's retreating back. "Hard to say since the escapees prints were destroyed. Except for the ones on the blouse from the cabin, which do us no good."

"Clyde Calvert could have stayed in his cabin," Carly pointed out. "And now now he's using Berdovitch's identity."

Reed shook his head. "So where's Frances Anderson? I mean, she answers Bonnie Smith's description, was driving a classic white Caddy and never made her destination."

"Her father's the one who's gonna sue."

Reed snorted. "We're supposed to wait seven days on missing persons. But this woman's lawyer daddy pulls out his contacts. Then, as worried as he was, he never calls again."

Carly shrugged. "Well, the woman's thirty and her folks sounded overprotective and inclined toward hysteria."

"So you figure she lied and wasn't headed to the New River Raft Inn at all?"

Carly nodded. "And I say more power to her."

"I don't mind if she's having a good time," Reed barked. "I only want to know where."

"AND I'VE JUST GOT to have this!" Frannie lifted the plastic paperweight, peered inside at the miniature model of Graceland and then shook the souvenir. "I didn't know it snowed in Tennessee!" she said to the salesclerk, whose name was Irma.

Irma chuckled. "It doesn't much, honey. That's just the way they make those paperweights."

"Well, I'll take it." As Frannie placed it next to the register, Irma started ringing up her purchases. She'd found T-shirts, clay replicas of the Tennessee state bird and tree, sunglasses and a baseball cap for Wild Bill's disguise. She'd also gotten foundation, a blow dryer and a backpack.

"For your boyfriend?" Irma asked conversationally, as she packaged one of the two I Love Memphis shirts.

"My husband." Frannie felt a twinge of guilt.

"Newly married?"

Frannie smiled. It was definitely fun to try on new personalities and disguises. Yesterday she'd been a biker chick. Today...she glanced in the mirror above the rack of sunglasses and nearly chortled. In her floppy hat and sundress, she looked like someone's crazy aunt. And now she was married. "Just since last June," she finally said.

Irma took Frannie's money. "It's best when the passion's still fresh."

Frannie's smile faltered. Passion? She'd slept miserably. Every time she'd snuggled up to Bill, he'd scooted away. All night she'd kept wishing he'd hold her again—and that he wasn't an ex-convict. Jail experience hardly sounded promising; it definitely went in Frannie's minus column. Just thinking about it had turned her into a quivering bundle of nerves by six in the morning. So she'd gone shopping.

"You'll find those magazines just around the corner," Irma said as she handed Frannie a bag. "Free guides and maps, too."

With a wave, Frannie headed for the newsstand where she grabbed all the available free tourist information and a copy of *Modern Bride*. She scanned the racks, wondering what Bill read. *Hunting and Fishing?*

Why was she so darn desperate to buy the right thing and please him? "Motorcycles," she murmured. There was a whole section. But which one? When she realized the man at the register had started to watch her, her temper flared. She looked odd, but not like a shoplifter. *What if he recognizes me from the news?*

She quickly snatched two motorcycle magazines and one about guns for extra measure, then moseyed to the counter in a way she hoped didn't look suspicious. She plopped Bill's magazines down with hers. The clerk merely stared at her.

She should never have come to a public place, she thought. She could almost hear sirens, bloodhounds and gunshots. "The ones on top are for my husband," she said in her best tough girl voice. "If I don't get back soon, he'll come looking for me."

"*Guns and Ammo*," the man said. "I subscribe myself."

So, why was he squinting at her? she thought in panic.

"Oh!" He handed Frannie her bag. "Minnie Pearl!"

"Pardon?" she croaked, leaning on the counter for support.

"You came down to Memphis to be the next Minnie Pearl! Is that right?"

He'd said "down to Memphis." Did he know where she was from? *Probably just my accent.* After a moment's shock, Frannie giggled. "Minnie Pearl. How'd you guess?"

"You've got the price tag on your hat." The man grinned. "It's just that most Minnie wanna-bes go to Nashville."

Price tag? She'd shoved her hair beneath the hat and tied a bright blue scarf around the brim in lieu of the missing band. Her hand shot past the trailing end of the scarf. Sure enough, a price tag was dangling from the side. It hadn't been intentional. As she headed toward the diner, she heard the man call, "Good luck, Minnie!"

She was still smiling when she slid onto a stool at the crowded coffee counter, even if she felt a bit guilty. She should have left Bill a note.

As she dug in her bag for her new sunglasses, she decided she'd take Bill a nice breakfast. She glanced at the glasses, chuckling softly. They were of light blue plastic; two replica Elvises played red electric guitars at the tops of each lens. Shoving them on her nose, she glanced from her menu through the diner's window. In the distance, she could see the Paradise. Should she appease her rumbling stomach or go back? *I'll eat fast.*

"What'll ya have?"

When she heard the waitress's drawl, Frannie grinned. It was as syrupy as the molasses in the containers on the counter. "Pancakes—" Suddenly raw energy zinged along her nerves. She felt hungrier than she ever had in her life. "With bacon, two scrambled eggs, OJ, hash browns, and two biscuits. Large coffee and double the order. One's to go."

The waitress glanced up, looking impressed.

"After shopping," Frannie explained, "ordering food's my only real talent." Just as the waitress headed for the cook's station, Frannie felt someone lean beside her.

"I figure you're not bad at hoarding your money, either."

Frannie flushed and swiveled around on her stool. It was Bill, all right. His lips looked as tempting as when she'd left the room and his changeable brown eyes were still rimmed by those thick, sandy lashes. She could imagine his beard bristling against her cheeks even though it had been replaced by a solidly square jaw on which a heavy morning shadow was now visible. The scar was irresistible. He'd said he'd gotten in a fight in jail, which had merely served to make him all the more interesting. He was truly a man outside her experience.

"Well?" he finally said.

Frannie gulped, wishing he'd quit scrutinizing her outfit with that horrified expression. "When we got arrested, I managed to hold on to a little money," she said, keeping her voice low.

"I'm sure you'll tell me exactly how much once we're outside," he returned, placing his hand beneath her elbow.

Just how much *had* she spent? She wasn't accustomed to calculating. She tried to ignore the roughness of his palm against her bare skin and the forcefulness of his grip. When she attempted to squirm away, he hauled her to her feet. A hunger pang reminded her of breakfast. "But I just ordered!" She glanced at the woman who'd waited on her, hoping for support.

"Want it to go?" the waitress asked Bill.

"It's my food," Frannie said haughtily. "I should certainly have some say in where I partake of it." Why did she sound so defensive? She glanced around and realized that patrons were starting to glance in their direction.

"You should be shot for pulling a fool stunt like this," Bill whispered. More loudly, he said, "Please pack it up." When the waitress was gone, he brought his stubbly cheek right against Frannie's. "What were you thinking?"

Frannie jerked her face away and glared at him. "I was only trying to be nice and let you sleep."

"Oh, please," Bill said.

She watched in horror as his gaze drifted down toward the floor. He shut his eyes as if he couldn't believe what he was seeing.

He snorted. "You went shopping?"

Only shopping could have taken her mind off the fact that she'd spent the night next to him. She mustered a congenial smile. "I bought you some stuff," she ventured brightly.

"What I need," he said flatly, "is gas."

Her face fell. She hadn't thought of that. "Motorcycles don't take that much. Do they? I mean, I didn't think—"

"Well, start thinking." His lips parted in astonishment. "And the price of the gas wasn't the point."

Frannie was just about to ask what the point was when the waitress plopped a large brown bag on the counter. "Keep the change," Frannie said, sliding a ten across the counter.

She may have made a good first impression, but now the waitress's hands shot to her hips. "The bill's twelve."

Frannie sucked in a deep breath, trying to hold down her temper. She arched a brow in Bill's direction. "Might I please borrow my arm, so that I may reach into my pocket?''

His grip relaxed, but only momentarily.

''Hey,'' the waitress suddenly said as she pocketed her tip. ''I know who you remind me of!''

Thank heavens the woman was talking about Bill. If they were caught, it wouldn't be because of *her* disguise. Still, Frannie didn't exactly want Bill to be recognized, either. She watched him raise a brow noncommittally.

''That guy the cops are looking for,'' the waitress said. ''Clyde Calvert. I mean, he looked shorter on the news and he's got a beard.''

''Think I should turn myself in and take the reward?'' Bill asked with a chuckle.

The waitress glanced quickly at Frannie, then looked through her as if she were insignificant. ''Only if you take me out,'' the woman said.

Frannie had to fight not to reach into the woman's apron pocket and retrieve her tip. Bill was still grinning at Miss Come-on, as if to say he and Frannie wouldn't be an item for long. The image of Mr. Suave popped into Frannie's mind and she pursed her lips. One of these days, she was going to find a man who would fulfill all her fantasies of living the high life. And if he couldn't make love to her the way Bill had, she would survive. When all this was over, she would forget about Wild Bill Heironymous Berdovitch and—

He grabbed the food bag and firmly gripped her elbow again. She barely had enough time to snatch up her shopping bags before he yanked her off her stool and rustled her into the hallway of the truck stop's minimall. Just as they reached the door, she caught sight of a decorative box shaped like a duck. She glanced fleetingly at Bill.

''Don't even think it,'' he said tersely.

"Of course not," she shot back. "In fact, you keep telling me not to think at all!" *At least when you're kissing me.* Her voice had started rising. She tried to squelch her anger, but she kept thinking of Bill and the woman at the truck stop dancing in a honky-tonk. "That's probably how you think women should be—thoughtless and willing!"

He ignored her tirade until they reached the parking lot. "I can't believe I risked exposure and being plowed down by Mack trucks to come and get *you*."

"Believe me, I was having a fine time until you arrived."

He stopped in his tracks, but didn't release her arm. "Don't you get it?"

She got it all right. They were on the run. Still, if she didn't have some fun now, she felt as if she never would again. Real life loomed right outside the edges of the picture. When she didn't respond, Bill yanked her forward again. As much as he was manhandling her, she might as well have still been wearing handcuffs, she thought dryly. Not that he seemed motivated by her safety. He was merely afraid she'd be caught and that the trail would lead to him.

"Watch out for that gas line," he said gruffly, steering her over one of the hoses that ran between the pumps and a semi.

"Well, you don't have to be so rough!" No sooner had she shrugged off his grip than his fingers curled around her elbow again. He all but shoved her toward the Paradise, peering into her shopping bag all the while.

"While you were buying that stuff, didn't you happen to notice that our pictures are on the front page of the local paper?"

Her heart skipped a beat, then warm color flooded her cheeks. Too many thoughts and feelings were bombarding her at once. She was afraid of getting caught. She was sorry because going shopping hadn't been wise. And she was starting to wonder if Wild Bill hadn't been truly concerned about her. With every step, the grim set of his mouth was relaxing. He still looked furious, but she was sure she wasn't imagining the relief in his eyes. "Well, I don't usually read the papers...."

"Sweetheart, don't you think you should start concerning yourself with them?"

"It's all right," she ventured gently. "I was disguised."

As relieved as he looked, he still shook his head as if she were simply beyond words. As they headed down the last strip of dusty road to the Paradise, his grasp loosened. His hand remained beneath her elbow, but his fingers now grazed her skin, so lightly that they could have been the breeze.

"A sundress with spaghetti straps and a hat is hardly a disguise," he finally said. "And you can't ride on a bike in a dress. You'll show off—" He stopped in midsentence.

"No, I won't!" The dress was short, cool and comfortable, printed with blue and pink wildflowers. Without thinking, she came to a dead halt and lifted her skirt, hoping to prove to him that she was a practical woman.

He stared at her upper thighs for what felt like a century.

"Biker shorts," she explained, wishing she wasn't starting to blush again. Even when she straightened her hemline, it remained a good six inches above her knees because the dress was a mini. "And I have on these sunglasses- and—"

He jerked her toward the Paradise again. "Please, let's not even discuss those."

He was starting to really annoy her. She'd thought her Elvis glasses were kind of cute and campy. "And I have a hat, so you can't see my hair."

"That floppy straw hat?" He groaned. "I could see you from a mile away. You look like your name should be Lulu."

"Someone said I should be the next Minnie Pearl." It wasn't exactly true, but somehow it made her feel better.

"Now, that's what the world really needs," Bill said cynically. "Another Minnie Pearl." He squinted at her and frowned. "Just how many people did you chat with this morning?"

Pretty much anyone who'd looked the least bit interesting, she thought. "Well, you were the one they recognized."

"Almost recognized," he corrected. "And that waitress wouldn't have, if I hadn't had to go looking for you."

"So why did you?" She was really starting to wonder. He could easily have hopped on his bike and left her to fend for herself, she thought as they passed beneath the Paradise's broken neon sign. But he hadn't. Was he the kind of man who wouldn't leave a woman in a pinch? If so, it was a darn shame he could be so difficult to get along with. When it came to men, in her book the only quality above well employed was staying power.

"Good question," he finally said. After a moment, he shifted the food bag on his hip. "Did you invite some of these new friends of yours for breakfast or what?"

She dug in her dress pocket for the room key. "Maybe one or two."

"It feels as if there's enough food in here to feed an army."

"We'll need our sustenance for the day ahead," she returned in a practical tone.

He looked her up and down. "We sure will."

WHY WOULDN'T THE MAN lighten up? Even the rush of the cool air-conditioning didn't improve Frannie's mood. She seated herself daintily on the edge of the bed, laid out her breakfast, placed her packages beside her feet and opened

Modern Bride. She tried to read, but with every breath, she was acutely aware that Bill was on the other side of the bed.

Her eyes kept straying toward him and then she would glare down at wedding gowns again. "Here," she finally said. "I got you some." She dug in her bag, pulled out his magazines and tossed them across the mattress.

He made a sound that resembled a grunt. *"Guns and Ammo?"*

She realized he was looking at her as if she had no handle on his character at all. Which she didn't. "I thought you might like guns." Instead, he looked a little offended. When he shifted his weight on the bed and picked up the second one, his eyes widened, giving him away before he could hide his interest.

"But the motorcycle ones are okay?" she asked, hating the hopeful catch in her voice.

He opened one. "I'll read them."

Ha! He didn't read it. He devoured it. "And for someone who was mad about me buying breakfast, you certainly seem to be enjoying that, too," she couldn't help but say.

"Can a man eat in peace?"

She watched him wolf down half his eggs in a single bite and sniffed. "Not if a woman can't." As she averted her gaze and leafed through the bridal gown ads, she could feel Bill's eyes boring into her. His ocular activity seemed centered between her eyes and breasts, occasionally doing a leg dip. Her mouth went dry. She wished he'd quit staring. And yet she was glad he was.

"Just what have I done to disturb your peace?" he finally asked.

His mere presence set her teeth on edge. She lifted her gaze and watched him polish off his biscuits. "Well, you do seem to have awakened on the wrong side of the bed."

He chuckled dryly. "In the Paradise Motel, I don't think there is a right side of the bed, sweetheart."

She shrugged and slowly turned a page.

"We're in serious trouble," he continued. "And you don't even seem to be aware of it."

Her head snapped up so quickly that the trailing end of the blue scarf on her hat jerked over her shoulder. "I am fully aware of our circumstances."

He dusted off his hands above his plate, then pointed. "Frannie, you're reading *Modern Bride.*"

She shot him an overly sweet smile. "And you're reading that horrible thing about motorcycles."

His mouth suddenly quirked playfully. "That's different."

Her lips parted as if to say, "Is that so?" She gulped down the remainder of her juice and glanced at her magazine again. "Minigowns are coming back for the summer wedding," she said, as if he might actually be interested.

He chuckled softly. "Minis?" He leaned and stared down at the pictures with genuine attention.

"I bet you were reading Victoria's Secret catalogs by age four," she couldn't help but say. He really did seem hot-blooded. The type to be quick with a flirtatious smile—at least when it came to waitresses in truck stops.

"And sweetheart," he drawled, right before reading a piece of ad copy, "you'll want to mix and match your honeymoon wardrobe."

She giggled and wished she hadn't. She sounded like an overly excited teenager! "And wherever you go, don't forget that a bottle of bubbly and strawberries makes for the perfect romantic night!" she found herself trilling.

She glanced at Bill. His eyes suddenly narrowed and she was sure he was going to remind her that they were in danger. Instead, his mouth curled at the corners and he shook his head as if to say he wasn't going to waste his breath. He shoved his empty plate and plastic cutlery into the paper bag, collected hers, then crumpled the bag and tossed it into the wastebasket.

"Basket," Frannie said.

"So, do I get a cheer?" he asked as he rose from the bed.

"Two bits, four bits, six bits, a dollar," Frannie said. "All for Wild Bill, stand up and holler."

He burst out laughing. "Good. Now, can I trust you to sit right here while I take a quick shower? For all we know that woman at the diner changed her mind, decided I was Clyde Calvert and called the cops."

That woman at the diner. Maybe he wasn't as interested in her as he'd looked. "Or the guy in the motel office recognized you."

"Or you."

"Maybe."

Bill shook his head. "He would have called by now."

"Unless he only now got his morning paper."

"Maybe you're paying more attention than I think you are."

When Frannie glanced down, her gaze landed on just the kind of gown she wanted someday. It was white and traditional, with a long train and a bodice covered with lace and pearls. *Bill didn't leave me. He came after me.* "Oh, I'm paying attention," she assured, fixing her gaze on his.

"Speaking of money, how much have you got?"

This time, she decided she'd better not lie. "About sixty dollars."

"How much did you spend this morning?" He glanced toward her shopping bag.

Eighty? "Oh..." She gulped hard. "About ten or fifteen."

His shoulders shook with laughter. "Sweetheart, breakfast was nearly twenty with the way you tip."

She decided it was in her best interest to look at the wedding gown again. "Well, I had to get some things we needed—maps, makeup so you can cover your tattoo if you want."

"I'll bet that's what you were thinking about when you bought that makeup."

"So okay, it was an afterthought." Forget the gown, she thought. There was something wrong with every man who came down the pike. This one didn't talk unless he was giving her a hard time. His lovemaking, of course, went in the check-plus column.

"I have a map," he said.

"But these are—" She leaned down, pulled out a handful and fanned them across the mattress.

"Tour guides," he said. "Is it just me or are you hell-bent on turning this nightmare into some kind of vacation?"

She glanced down at the booklets. The one about Graceland had been $11.50. *Day Tours of Tennessee* was $5.99. There was no way she'd spent only eighty dollars. She pulled her remaining money from her pocket. While she counted, she thought of all the shopping trips she'd taken with her mother and of the ensuing game of hiding the packages in the trunk of the car until Dad was out of sight. Not that Jack Anderson had really minded. In fact, he'd made a show of leaving the house, so they could transfer the goods from the garage to the closets. Wild Bill Berdovitch was another matter.

She'd spent far more than she'd thought. The T-shirts and pack were nearly twenty each. The hair dryer was fifteen. With a sinking heart, she realized that getting her mind off Bill had left her broke. *And since I'm broke, we'll have to stay together.* Had that been part of her motivation? "I've got four dollars and forty-two cents." She waited for him to throw a fit. He merely surveyed her as if he were a world champion chess player and she was a piece on the board.

She found herself hoping she was a queen instead of a pawn. "I could return stuff," she offered.

"And risk being recognized?" He shrugged as if to say it didn't matter. "Would you please tell me why you want this to be a vacation?"

"Just go take a shower," she suddenly snapped. "We're on the run, remember? And you're not ready yet."

He sighed. "You promise not to move?"

"Oh, you know me," she crooned. "I have *Modern Bride,* so wild horses couldn't drag me away from this bed."

His gaze drifted over the tour guides again. "It's really not a vacation," he said levelly.

She frowned down at the gown a final time, then watched him head for the shower, wishing she could figure him out. He could be flirtatious and passionate but he could be downright mean on occasion. When she heard the shower, it was impossible not to think about him, stripped and wet, with fat glistening droplets sliding down his chest.

She tried to concentrate on all the nice things she'd bought for him. And about how unimpressed he'd been with her outfit. She'd thought he'd tell her she looked cute. Or maybe get a good chuckle out of the ensemble, but he hadn't.

After a long moment, she sniffed. She dug into her bag and began to arrange her new purchases on the bed. Out of habit, she mulled over what she would keep and what she would return. But she was leaving!

She made a special pile for Bill. His magazines formed the base of the pyramid, then his I Love Memphis shirt, makeup, baseball cap and sunglasses. He'd looked so serious when he'd told her to stay on the bed that she almost felt guilty when she got off and placed his gifts in a neat stack on the dresser.

There. He can take them or not. It's entirely up to him. That done, she filled her new backpack with the second-hand clothes that weren't on the bathroom floor and with the items she'd just bought. At the last minute, she pulled her I Love Memphis T-shirt on over her dress, since she might get chilly on the back of the bike.

After she'd packed, she pulled her arms through the pack's straps and adjusted them for maximum comfort. Then she sat up straight and folded her hands in her lap. When Bill returned, she meant to look like the consummate ready traveller. He would understand that she was all dressed and ready to go and just waiting for him.

She unfolded her hands and then tapped her fingertips on her knee. The shower was still running. Bill was naked and alone and there was no lock on the bathroom door. She wanted to rip off her pack, rummage around for her new nail file and polish and fix her manicure. It would get her mind off Bill, but it would ruin the impression.

She was counting sheep when she heard the terrible metallic crunch.

Her eyes shot to the window and she jumped to her feet. It was Wild Bill's bike! Through the filmy curtains, she could see a man get out of a station wagon. The window was open, so she could hear him slam his door.

He'd run over Bill's bike! Their only mode of transportation! The thought flashed through her mind that Bill knew how to steal cars... but she wasn't sure whether that was good or bad.

She was just about to scream through the window when she remembered how Bill looked at his motorcycle. It was on a par with the surreptitious glances she'd seen directed at her breasts. It was a look of pure masculine adoration. She was pretty sure that old Triumphs were a big deal in the motorcycle world. She fought the urge to race across the room, upset his pyramid of presents and double-check in a motorcycle magazine. No, she definitely didn't want to be the bearer of bad tidings.

Her eyes shot toward the bathroom. She didn't want to call him out of the shower, either. She imagined him opening the door with nothing on but water droplets.

At least it wasn't a hit-and-run. The driver of the station wagon was standing over the motorcycle, staring down and shaking his head. He looked wimpy and honest and was wearing a business suit. She'd wait and let Bill go out and trade insurance company numbers and—

They couldn't call the cops!

She plopped on the bed again, glancing between the bathroom and the window, as if watching a tennis match. What were they supposed to do? Walk to Mexico?

And Bill might blame it all on her. If the man tried to leave, she'd stop him. Otherwise, she'd let Bill discover the damage for himself.

Chapter Eight

"My bike."

Bill stood on the sidewalk and stared. His mind raced back to minutes ago, when things had been fine. Except for the fact that the cops were chasing them and he still had an itch for his running partner that he couldn't scratch.

Minutes ago he'd hacked off the legs of his jeans in deference to the heat and shrugged into the clean I Love Memphis shirt Frannie had bought him, even though clothes with hearts on them were hardly his style. The his-and-hers shirts made him and Frannie look like a couple, too, but he didn't mind. He'd been mulling over how his one smile at the waitress had obviously made Frannie furious and how her jealousy had made him feel as relieved as he had when he'd found her.

"My bike," he said again. He grabbed the bill of his red baseball cap, readjusted it and continued staring through his new sunglasses at the pile of metal that had once been his pride and joy. He wanted to lunge at the man next to it, maybe even kill him, but it wouldn't be a fair fight. The fellow was short, of slight build, and dressed in a gray suit.

"I'm so sorry," the man began. "I..." He winced and waited for a response.

Bill turned to Frannie. In spite of his anger, he had to admit that she looked downright adorable. Her hair was stuffed beneath the floppy hat and the trailing blue scarf just touched the line of one of her high cheekbones. Her lush lips were painted a flirty red. Miles of leg were showing, since the hem of her dress only hit her upper thighs. He was touched that she'd brought him presents, too. She'd done just fine on two of the three magazines and he would have chosen the imitation Ray Bans himself.

But his bike had been destroyed. And somehow, the fact that Frannie hadn't called him from the shower seemed more important than the jerk in the business suit. "You were right there," he finally said. "The window was open. How could you not have heard . . ."

She'd heard, all right. The sun had tinged her cheeks pink the previous day and now they turned a flaming guilty red. She glanced at the real culprit who straightened his tie and stared mournfully down at the pavement.

"You heard my bike get crunched and didn't bother to tell me?" He simply couldn't believe it.

She shrugged uncertainly.

Had he been that much of an ogre? Was she afraid of him? He squinted at her, wondering just what she was running from—or searching for. She was too easily led in new directions. Her planned vacation had been rerouted to an unknown destination in Mexico and she'd barely complained. Hell, maybe the Paradise had just become their last stop, he thought grimly.

"You told me not to get off the bed," she said defensively.

Lord, she could drive a man to distraction. Every time he looked at her, he wanted to haul her into his arms and kiss her again. And yet if she hadn't brought him bad luck, she'd brought him none at all. Without her, he wouldn't be in this jam. He could probably sleep nights, too.

"If you'd wanted to get off the bed," he finally said, "you would have."

"I knew you'd get mad and blame it all on me!" she burst out. "And he wasn't trying to escape."

Out of the corner of his eye, Bill could see the man's head wagging between him and Frannie. He sighed. "I'm not blaming you." But he'd been disappointed. She hadn't come running to him, which meant she didn't feel as if they were in this together.

"Right."

"I'm really not." He decided that if he had to say it another time, he would start. He glanced down and toed the curb with his boot.

"Really?"

When he glanced up, her hopeful expression made him feel guilty. He'd never even felt truly guilty about all the cars he'd stolen. He'd been young and foolish, with no real opportunities, and he'd paid his dues and done his time for it. With Frannie, he was lucky if he went a full hour without feeling as if he were Catholic and in a confessional.

She nodded. "See, you think it's all my fault."

She crossed her arms, which only served to accentuate her breasts. He imagined ripping off her oversize shirt and glasses and getting down to the basics—sundress and then skin. Even though they were in public, in broad daylight, and his Triumph was a mass of tangled metal, he desperately wanted to touch her. And hell, he felt guilty about that, too. He reached out and tugged her sleeve gently. "I am not blaming you. Okay?"

She stared him down through her sunglasses. Given the fact that plastic Elvises were gyrating their hips above her brows, he almost wanted to smile. When she crinkled her nose, the Elvises wiggled up and down.

"Please—" The man sounded far away. "Maybe we should—"

"Well, you shouldn't blame me," she continued. "I mean, I was doing exactly what I was supposed to."

"I said, I am not!" He'd had it. He grasped her arm forcefully and pulled her against his chest. The kiss he delivered was quick and wet. Sloppy enough to be effective but not so passionate that she'd realize he spent every spare moment thinking about her. He drew back.

When she gaped at him, he started telling himself the only reason he'd kissed her was to shut her up. He just wished he could see her eyes. They'd tell him whether she'd really minded the kiss or not. "End of conversation," he said.

"Let's hope so," she said from between her kiss-wet lips.

"If anyone's to be blamed, it's me," the man said quickly, sounding nervous.

"You said a mouthful there," Bill muttered. A second look revealed that the man had short, closely cropped brown hair and anxious brown eyes. He was leaning against the hood of his station wagon, as if for support. "Just relax," Bill said. "If I was going to kill you, I would have done it by now."

But what *was* he going to do? He couldn't call the cops or his insurance company. He didn't have the money to repair the bike. He should have made Frannie return her purchases. But how could he—when she'd looked so pleased with them? Now, they'd ripped off the tags. Heisting a car was out of the question. And if they stood here much longer, they were going to draw a crowd, which meant someone might recognize them.

"There's a garage up the road," the man said as if reading Bill's mind. "Can I drive you there?"

"Great!" Frannie exclaimed.

Somehow, Bill didn't want to burst her bubble. "Well, I don't know if..." Discussing his and Frannie's finances with the stranger didn't seem too bright. And what if the man recognized them? Bill glanced toward the newspaper machines on the corner. "Well," he added, "I'd hate to put you out."

Frannie was already loading the bike into the back of the station wagon, single-handedly. He strode toward her.

"Don't worry!" Frannie said, waving him away. "We'll get your bike fixed Bi—Heironymous."

And she'd almost called him Bill.

"We sure will...er...Heironymous," the man said. He got behind Frannie and heaved. "I'll pay all the costs, too."

"First piece of luck I've had all day." Bill wrestled the Triumph's fender from Frannie and finished shoving it inside, then he circled around to the passenger door. He opened it and nodded at Frannie to get in.

"No, you two go ahead and ride up front."

Was it his imagination or did she really sound like Joan of Arc? *What a martyr.* He'd assured her she wasn't responsible. Did she want it in blood? "Fine, sweetheart," he drawled. "You ride in back." He slid into the front seat.

She started to get in back, huffily saying, "Then I will."

He wrenched around. "Look, you're a grown-up. You can do whatever you want as long as it doesn't endanger someone else. Okay? I said you had nothing to do with what happened to the bike. It's you who feels guilty. Otherwise you wouldn't ask me a thousand times if I'm mad. And you wouldn't take it upon yourself to try to shove three hundred pounds of wrecked metal into this station wagon by yourself."

Her mouth set in a prissy little pout.

"And I may feel guilty about having said that, but it needed to be said."

She sniffed. "I'm sorry."

He groaned. "Don't be."

"Let's all just ride up front!" the man said brightly.

Bill started to get out so that Frannie could get in, but the man maneuvered her through the passenger door. She wound up in Bill's lap. "I know you're probably angry with me, Frannie, but would you quit shoving?" he said. Before he knew what was happening, she'd made him scoot all the way to the driver's seat. His long legs got pinned beneath the steering wheel. "What's your problem?"

"I do not have a problem," Frannie said succinctly. "But he has a—"

"Just shut up," the man growled, as he jumped into the passenger seat and slammed the door. "And drive."

All Bill was going to worry about today was keeping his hands off Frannie? He grabbed his door handle and jerked. *Intentionally jammed.* A terrified-looking Frannie hemmed in his right.

And Mr. Friendly was waving a .38 between the two of them.

"Drive," he repeated as he cocked the hammer of the pistol.

"Great," Bill muttered.

"I WANT THAT VIDEOTAPE," the man said for the ump-teenth time. "Where is it?"

Bill clenched his teeth, glanced at Frannie to make sure she was all right, then stared through the windshield at the setting sun. It was bright orange and strips of purple broke on either side of it. He'd been driving due north for hours. Tension was making his shoulders ache, and the road was starting to shimmer and waver like a mirage.

He no longer gave a damn about getting to Mexico. He just hoped he could get himself and Frannie out of this sit-uation alive. If he'd been less intent on how much he wanted her, he'd have realized the man's eyes were beadier than a rat's. Now it looked as if his overactive hormones might get them both killed. "You're sure they didn't say anything on the news about a tape?" Bill asked Frannie.

She shook her head. "We don't know anything about a tape!" she burst out. "I'm not Bonnie Smith, he's not Clyde

Calvert and we don't have the money. You saw Bill's credit cards.''

Right before he'd thrown them out the window, Bill thought. As soon as they'd hit the Interstate, the man riffled through their packs. He'd tossed items through the window one by one. Except for their cash, which he'd pocketed. All they had left were their sunglasses, the clothes and hats they were wearing and the Graceland paperweight, which had wound up beneath the seat along with some tour guides. He still had his checkbook, too. It was shoved in his boot.

Not that it would help. The Triumph, of course, was gone forever. He'd been forced to stop on an empty stretch outside Flora, Illinois. At gunpoint, he and Frannie had heaved what was left of the bike over a guardrail and into a culvert. Bill wasn't sure which was worse—watching his bike tumble into the weeds or watching Frannie lose her souvenirs.

He glanced at her again, then stared at the road. The farther north they went, the colder it got. He'd taken off his T-shirt, so she could drape it across her knees. In spite of the circumstances, her demeanor remained every bit as cool as the car. He couldn't help but admire her for it. The woman could sure handle herself in a crisis.

"So, who are you?" she asked.

"None of your business," the man said.

Frannie took off her hat, tightly rewound her hair in a knot, then put on the hat again. "Well then, would you mind telling me where we're going? And would you please get that weapon out of my face?"

Was Frannie in the line of fire? Bill's chest constricted and his head jerked toward their captor. If a bullet was discharged, it would hit the dashboard, which was still too close for comfort.

"Where?" Frannie demanded.

A grim smile touched the corners of Bill's mouth. Frannie was relentless. She'd been pursuing the conversation for hours, even though it went nowhere but in circles.

"Somewhere nice and quiet where you're going to tell me where that money and the tape are."

Frannie sighed. "But we don't know—"

Bill took a hand from the steering wheel, reached down and rested it on Frannie's thigh. "You're not going to get anywhere with him, sweetheart," he said softly. No matter how much he admired her for trying.

When her crystal blue eyes raised to his, he realized she was more frightened than she was letting on. He winked, trying to communicate more assurance than he actually felt. What was it about imminent danger that made you decide you liked someone? he wondered. As soon as he'd seen that gun pointed at Frannie, the same emotions he'd felt when she vanished from the Paradise washed over him—loss and a desire to protect.

His first thought had been that she wasn't going to get any souvenirs from Mexico. Then he decided that he'd wanted to take her to the Dakotas to see the badlands. Hell, maybe he still would. If they lived.

"Well, don't you have a boss or something?" Frannie prompted. "You know, he's going to be really mad when he finds out that you brought back the wrong people. Bonnie and Clyde are going out west, not north."

The gun zeroed in on Frannie. Bill's heart dropped to his feet.

"West?" the man asked in a murderous tone.

"Bonnie Smith and Clyde Calvert are from Texas," Frannie said, the merest hint of a waver in her voice. "Maybe they were headed home."

"They're right in this car." The man wrenched around so that his back was against the passenger side door and waved the pistol. "We've been watching you and we know everything the cops know. I just want you to tell me where you put the money."

"And the tape and Jason Morehead." Bill sighed and squinted through the windshield. A light rain had begun to fall and he turned on the wipers. Their rhythmic *tha-thump* sounded in the silence.

When he glanced at Frannie again, her eyes said, "Am I being too pushy?"

His said, "Might as well keep trying." Reasoning with the gun-wielding maniac hadn't rendered results. On the other hand, escape had been impossible. Bill had gone too fast, hoping to attract the law, since at this point cops were preferable to their traveling companion. He'd gone too slow for the same reason. He'd considered punching the gas and shoving the man out the door while at top speed, but he was too afraid the guy would grab hold of the first thing he could—which meant Frannie.

They'd stopped twice, but the gun had remained riveted on Bill. As many times as Frannie had requested stops the previous day, she hadn't asked yet. Bill kept expecting to see one of her pained-and-gotta-go expressions, but he didn't.

"We who?" she asked, starting in again. "Who are you and who are you working for?"

"You're below the speed limit." The man rested his free hand against the dashboard and narrowed his beady eyes. "Punch it up, buster."

Bill stomped on the accelerator and the station wagon leapt forward. He realized the drizzle had stopped just as suddenly as it had started. He slammed the wiper button. Thankfully, the annoying pass of the wipers ceased.

Beside him, Frannie whispered, "Wisconsin."

For the first time, her voice didn't catch with excitement as it usually did when she mentioned some new place she'd never visited. Deciding he'd just kill himself if something happened to her, Bill slid his palm beneath her flouncy hemline and hooked a finger under the tight rim of her biker shorts.

"We just crossed the state line," she said.

He nodded and started rubbing soft slow circles on her cool skin. In spite of his touch, goose bumps were rising on her thighs. He reached for the heater lever, realized it would go no higher, then double-checked to ensure that the vents were trained on her knees.

He realized the fight was going out of her. At the first opportunity he'd disarm the man. Bill was larger and no doubt a better street fighter. Trouble was, the man knew it. More often than not, he kept the gun pointed at Bill rather than Frannie.

"Where are we going?" she said again, this time with a hint of panic.

"Don't worry." Bill said it as if men with guns didn't disturb him in the least. Maybe they didn't. He'd had guns pointed his way more than once and he'd come out skin intact.

If Frannie wasn't next to him, he'd have made a move long before now. People didn't call him Wild Bill because he took it cautious. He was sure he could both drive and wrestle away the gun in such a way that the shots would hit the roof. He could push the guy through the door and onto the pavement, too. But he couldn't bring himself to risk Frannie's safety.

He felt her palm glide over the back of his hand. Her fingers fell in the gaps between his. It was as if she meant to hold his hand and wait for whatever was to come. She curled against his side and shut her eyes, clearly meaning to sleep through the rest of it.

"You're gonna be fine, sweetheart," he whispered.

She would be, too. Even if he had to risk life and limb to ensure it.

HOW LONG HAD SHE cuddled against Bill and dozed? Frannie wondered. An hour? Two maybe? More, judging by the sky.

Without moving her head, she glanced around the car's dark interior. The man's hand rested loosely on his knee and the pistol dangled from his fingertips. Should she grab it? Just imagining doing so, her hand flinched. Bill's responded immediately. He twined his fingers tightly through hers.

It was dark, but she could make out Bill's profile—the strong jaw, the high cheekbones, the prominent nose that was just a little crooked. She stared through the windshield, wondering how such a clear, starlit night could be so menacing. Only the callused softness of Bill's touch offered reassurance.

Her life had no direction? she thought in wonderment. They'd started taking back roads while she slept, and the countless hours of roadway had left her dazed. She felt as if she were a kid again and playing pin the tail on the donkey. She'd been blindfolded, spun in dizzying circles and was now flailing her arms, searching for the donkey. She'd never felt so lost. Since dark, each headlight of each car that whizzed past seemed to shine with the light of her possible salvation—only to continue on with a flash of fishtailing red taillights.

"Pull over," she said suddenly.

Bill squeezed her hand. "You need to stop, sweetheart?"

"We're not stopping," the man growled. "We're almost there." His arm flew upward and he aimed the gun right at Bill's head.

"I haven't stopped all day," Frannie said, her cool tone belying the fact that her pulse was pounding at her throat. During the long silence that ensued, she blinked the sleep from her eyes.

Bill squeezed her hand again. No wonder he'd been furious about her shopping trip. They were in serious danger. Bill was right. She'd been so caught up in wanting some time away from home that she'd latched on to this nightmare and tried to turn it into a vacation.

"I'm stopping now," Bill finally said levelly.

"Keep driving."

"I'm pulling over."

"It's okay for the guys to go, but not the girls?" Frannie's words sounded strained.

The man sighed, then waved the gun toward the shoulder. "Over there."

Following a previously established protocol, the man slid out and shook the gun between her and Bill. As Frannie climbed out, she felt Bill behind her, his body warm and comforting.

"Well," the man said. "Go ahead."

She gasped. "Here?" The three of them were a scant two feet from the car. The passenger door was still open and light from the weak dome fixture streamed out onto the grass. She tried to fight down her fury but couldn't. "This is an outrage," she said in a low tone.

Even the cretin who'd car-jacked them seemed to see the delicacy of the situation. Still pointing the gun at Bill, he dug in his pocket with his free hand and withdrew a handkerchief. "Get in front of me," he said to Bill. "Lie down flat, hands clasped around your neck."

Frannie's body froze in numb, cold fear. Was she about to witness a mobster-style execution? Murderous rage suddenly made her see red. She'd kill the man before he touched Bill.

"Here." The man lifted the handkerchief and pointed toward the weeds as Bill lay down. "You take this. Go to that bush. Keep the handkerchief in the air and wave it."

Her hands trembling, she took the white cloth and headed for the bush he'd indicated.

"And, lady," the man called, "I want to see that handkerchief at all times. If you so much as drop it, I'll shoot Clyde first. Then I'm gunning for you."

Frannie didn't doubt it. She crouched behind the bush and peered through the leaves. It was clear the man was afraid of Bill, but not of her—not really. Even so, she'd seen Bill in action and was positive he could have overtaken the man by now. So why hadn't he? She wondered if he'd been concerned about endangering her further, then winced, thinking she really did have to relieve herself.

But there wasn't time.

"Where's your hand, lady?" the man yelled.

She waved the handkerchief just above the bush's top leaves while her eyes scanned the ground. *Someone's on our side.*

She'd been hoping for a stick, but amidst the tin cans and rubbish, a frustrated motorist had tossed a piece of pipe. It looked like a car part, a section of a muffler or an exhaust pipe. She may have spent the morning shopping, but she was now determined to show Wild Bill what she was really made of. She only hoped she didn't get him killed.

"Hurry it up!"

"I didn't go all day!" She mustered her haughtiest yell as she gingerly picked up the pipe. "And I don't even have toilet paper!" She gulped and hung the handkerchief on the highest twig of the bush, where it fluttered in the breeze.

As she lay on her belly and started shimmying under the cover of the shrubs, she prayed that the wind wouldn't lift the handkerchief from the limb. Unfortunately, some of the plants she was hiding behind were too close to the ground. If the man looked, he would see her hat bobbing in the darkness.

She peered through a veil of foliage. She was almost there and the man was still glancing between Bill and the hanky. She raised to a crouch and tiptoed, cutting a wide circle around the car, so that she'd wind up behind the man. Could she hit him before he heard her?

As soon as she reached the car, she ducked behind the trunk and crept stealthily toward the back tire nearest him. She was so close that his huffing breath met her ears. She held her own, for fear he'd hear it.

Two more feet. Bill remained as still as a painting, seemingly unaware of her movements. The man was standing near Bill's feet, training the gun at his head. As Frannie inched forward, she silently swung the pipe high and right. If the gun went off when she struck him, the bullet would hit the bushes, not Bill. At least she hoped so.

A twig snapped.

The man's head turned sharply.

Frannie slammed the pipe down on his skull. Bill rolled to his feet and started punching, with rapid-fire blows that were apparently more effective than her pipe. The gun flew from the man's hand and skated across the ground. Frannie dived for it. By the time she whirled around and pointed it at their captor, he was lying on his side.

"Don't shoot me." He raised his hands but otherwise didn't move. "Just don't shoot me, lady."

"Trouble is," Bill drawled, "she just might. I've known her to be trigger-happy when circumstances warrant."

Frannie's heart flooded with relief. In the weak light from the car's dome, she could see Bill grinning at her. She smiled back, then glanced up and down the road, hoping no one passed and thought she and Bill were muggers.

"In fact—" Bill shoved his hands in the pockets of his cutoffs "—this lady asked you a number of questions. I think she deserves polite answers while you empty your pockets. Isn't that right, Frannie?"

She kept the gun aimed at the man and nodded. "Absolutely."

Bill starting taking the man's belongings. "So, who are you?"

Under the threat of death, the man got more talkative. Frannie just wished Bill had a jacket. His bare chest and cutoffs didn't suit the Wisconsin night. Not that he seemed to mind.

"I—I'm Clarence," the man finally said.

"Clarence Smithers? Langston Larson's partner?" Bill asked as he unfolded a paper against his chest.

He was on the ground, so the man nodded, as best he could.

"According to this map, we were apparently headed toward Larson's main headquarters, near Oshkosh," Bill said.

"Jason Morehead videotaped me and Larson taking the wood off your land. Larson says he taped you and Larson arguing about it, too. I don't even see why you're asking me. You were there."

Frannie rolled her eyes. The fool man still thought they were Bonnie and Clyde. "So there's proof that you two fouled up the fishing streams with the silt that came off your equipment?" Frannie prodded.

"It's a ten-thousand-dollar fine!" Clarence burst out. "Larson ain't paying it."

Bill's chuckle sounded lethal. Frannie decided she'd never want to get on his bad side.

"And you intended to?" Bill was saying.

"We shouldn't have logged your land in the first place," Clarence said in a pleading tone. "The contracts were phony. I admit it. I'm sorry you had to take on this new identity and that you're pretending to be this William Berdovitch character and—"

"One last time," Bill said tersely. "I *am* William Berdovitch."

The mortified look on Clarence's face told Frannie that he finally believed it. At this point, they had no reason to lie.

"So where are *they?*" Clarence croaked.

Bill shrugged. "Wherever they are, you'll be walking, buddy." With that, he headed for Frannie and took the gun.

When his fingers grazed her skin, a thrill trembled right through her body. As frightened as she'd been, only now did her knees start quivering. She mumbled a quick excuse, then fled back to the bush and relieved herself.

"Go ahead and get in the car, sweetheart," Bill said when she returned. "You drive."

Her smile faltered. Shopping and dining out were her forte. In the area of driving, she occasionally experienced difficulty. But now that Bill thought she was worth her salt, she didn't want to ruin the impression. Besides, she'd just brained a villain and been instrumental in an escape. "Fine," she said, feeling confident. As she slid in the car and scooted toward the wheel, Bill reached in and grabbed the I Love Memphis shirt she'd kept over her knees.

"Sorry, sweetheart," he whispered, "but I'll need yours, too."

She pulled it off, thinking she was going to freeze in her sundress. Bill shoved the pistol under his armpit, turned around to face Clarence and started ripping the shirts in strips. After that he made Clarence remove his suit jacket and then he tied the man to the guardrail. When he was done, Bill pocketed the bullets from the gun, then took the keys and locked the weapon in the trunk.

"How much money did he have?" Frannie suddenly called out.

"Fourteen bucks. He was using his cards. Altogether, we've got less than fifty." Bill slid in the passenger side, with Clarence's jacket dangling from his finger. "Much as I hate anything of his touching your skin," he said, "it oughtta keep you warm."

"You can't just leave me here!" Clarence screamed.

Frannie chuckled and slipped the jacket around her shoulders. "Wanna bet?" She started the car, stepped on the gas and squealed off the shoulder. This time heading due south.

"If you weren't driving, sweetheart," Bill drawled as he retrieved her Graceland paperweight and placed it on the dashboard, "I'd scoop you up like a dip of ice cream and smack my lips on that cold nose of yours." He burst out laughing and shook his head. "Well, that'll teach me not to mess with you."

She couldn't believed the pride that welled in her chest. After all, holding a man at gunpoint wasn't exactly admirable. And yet, by doing so, she felt like she'd stood up for a lot of things—things that had nothing at all to do with Clarence Smithers. Someone had ordered her around. She'd said no. And it felt good.

"Well, Bill, you're no slouch yourself."

"Maybe not," he shot back, "but I sure feel like slouching down."

He suddenly lay across the seat and rested his head right in her lap. Her thighs tingled and warmth curled in her belly, staving off the cold. "You drove all day and I dozed," she murmured. "Why don't you try to sleep?"

"That's just what I was thinking, sweetheart. Now that we've got a car, we can drive in shifts."

When he spoke, his breath whispered against her thighs. "Sounds good to me," she said, even though it didn't. Driving in shifts was reasonable, but she wouldn't be able to talk to him.

As if satisfied, he snuggled against her and yawned. She chuckled softly and gripped the wheel. "How can you be tired after an encounter like that?"

"It plumb wore me out."

His hair tickled her skin. Just below her biker shorts, the wavy, windblown locks curled in tendrils. The weight of his head pressed her abdomen . . . and lower. "You just sleep," she nearly whispered, trying to keep her voice even.

And he did. At least, she thought so. In the silence, his even breaths warmed her skin in waves. They were in the middle of nowhere and she'd never noticed so many stars. Whole new constellations seemed to have come into being since the last time she'd bothered to look. The clear night made the world seem larger than she remembered it, full of possibilities.

She could have been seventeen again. Everything could still be in front of her—right within her grasp. College, marriage, children, a career. All the wondering over which things would pan out and which wouldn't.

She glanced down at Bill, then cautiously took a hand from the wheel and grazed her fingers over his hair. When he didn't awaken, she ruffled the messy locks, then smoothed them. Finally, her hand rested gently on his head. Bill shifted and his lips wound up pressed hard against her thigh.

It had been a long time since she'd lived for the moment, she thought. And right now, with Bill in her lap and the stars above reminding her of life's possibilities, living for the moment felt good and right. Maybe she and Bill were just stars passing on a cool, clear night. And yet, she felt almost sure it wasn't true. Their meeting was too strange to be anything other than fated.

She found herself thinking of sadder fates, of her son. When she'd had Raymond, so many people had turned their backs on Frannie, including Joey Florence.

He'd had a future ahead of him that was every bit as bright as Frannie's own. That future had played out, too, as efficiently as a well-executed football play. Joey had gone on to play college ball, then been drafted into the pros. And no one had understood why Frannie had tried to ruin his career by wanting an early marriage. But she'd never expected Joey to marry her. She'd only hoped. And, for all that, she had lost her baby.... She glanced down at Bill again, wondering why men always left. And if Bill was the kind of man who stuck around.

As she drove, the hypnotic hours seemed to pass slowly. Mile markers on the road's shoulder fell down like dominoes, ticking away time. In the past, she had lost her son. She didn't know where her future was leading. In the present, she only had Bill. Her white suit and her father's Caddy had vanished, just like Bill's bike. But twining her fingers in his hair, everything felt fine. Somewhere between Illinois and Indiana, she felt sudden tears sting at her eyes. "When you ain't got nothin', you got nothin' to lose," she whispered.

Much later, she realized she'd gotten pointed east and followed the signs, meaning to double back through Tennessee and head toward Arkansas. But how? She was on the wrong darn stretch of Interstate. Wasn't she?

And then she saw a gap in the guardrails. The dirt road beyond led to the stretch of roadway opposite. She could see headlights beaming in the dawn light, shining in the direction she wanted to go. She pulled onto the makeshift byway, wondering if she was still in Tennessee or Kentucky. Or had she already reached Arkansas? Her geography wasn't too good, but it seemed as if she should have gone farther in the time she'd been driving.

"Where are we?" Bill asked sleepily, an hour later.

"In a ditch." She hit the gas again, but the tires only whirred in the culvert.

When Bill sat up, she was more than a little sorry to feel the weight of his head leave her lap. She'd tried not to move for so long that her thighs tingled with pinpricks. She took her foot off the pedal and looked at him. He was sleep rumpled, his hair wild from where she'd nestled her fingers in it.

He blinked. "It's morning."

"Sleep well?" she asked softly.

A sexy smile played on his lips and his eyes drifted toward her lap. It was clear he couldn't have cared less about the fact that they were stuck. "Real well."

She followed his gaze as he glanced around. The sun was still tinged with pink and the sky was more gray-white than blue. It was just light enough to see that they were in a gully between two mountains. The dirt road had led to what looked like a local necking spot.

While she was still gazing through the windshield, Bill leaned and traced a line on her thigh with his thumb. Her mouth went dry and her breath caught. And then he kissed her. His lips were so soft and sweet that her body went languid. By the time he drew back, she was as limp as a noodle.

He cradled her against him and nodded through the side window. "What's that?"

She tore her gaze from his lips. In the distance, a chimney peeked between the tops of the trees. "It looks like a cabin."

He chuckled. "Want me to carry you over the threshold?"

Chapter Nine

A foul-tempered Reed crossed the threshold of the interrogation room. "So, why were you tied to a guardrail in Wisconsin?"

"We just want to hear your side of the story," Carly cooed.

"Maybe you oughtta be the one playing bad cop," Reed whispered. He scrutinized Clarence Smithers who shifted uncomfortably on a metal chair and attempted to straighten his rumpled tie.

Carly placed a restraining hand on Reed's arm, as if she were desperate to protect Clarence from Reed. "Please, just tell us what you know."

Clarence sighed. "Like I told you an hour ago, I picked up two hitchhikers who said they were William Berdovitch and Frannie Anderson."

Reed rolled his eyes. "And they took your cash."

Clarence nodded. "My credit cards, too!"

"Go make sure no one's in the hall, Carly," Reed said in a menacing tone. "I'll get this guy to talk."

"Mr. Galveston," she murmured. "You were cited just last month for conduct unbecoming...."

"I thought they were Bonnie Smith and Clyde Calvert," Clarence suddenly said. Then a story tumbled out that was a tad more believable than the first. Clearly, Clarence had thought he'd found Bonnie and Clyde and he was after the money.

"So you were going to take them to Larson's headquarters?" Reed finally prompted.

"I don't even know who they really were," Clarence moaned. "I got the impression they knew a lot about Bonnie Smith and Clyde Calvert, though. Maybe they were trying to track them down."

"Gee, maybe you should have been a cop," Reed said sarcastically.

"The lady said she thought Bonnie and Clyde were headed west, maybe back to Texas," Clarence suddenly added.

Reed snorted. "So you took it upon yourself to hold a gun to their heads and drive them to headquarters, since Larson went there for a meeting this morning?"

"The reputation of our firm was at stake!" Clarence exclaimed.

"So you're not denying you had a weapon?" Reed asked.

"I demand to see a lawyer!" Clarence burst out.

"Back off him, boss," Carly said.

Clarence shot Carly an appreciative glance, as if sure she was his ally.

"If you thought they were Bonnie and Clyde, why didn't you tell us where they were?" Reed glanced at Carly. The helpful expression she'd plastered on her face made him want to chuckle. Clarence looked stymied.

"I—I—"

"You?" Carly prompted gently.

"I thought maybe we could work something out," Clarence said. "That I could help keep them out of jail. I mean that old man, wherever he is, is just too old to go to prison."

Reed blew out a sigh. "Since when did you become such a Good Samaritan?" He shook his head in astonishment. "Carly," he said, "let's let Mother Teresa stew a little more." He turned, strode toward the door and held it open for Carly.

"You're becoming quite the gentleman," she teased once they were in the hall.

"Guys like that bring it out in me."

"Afraid you're getting as mean as they are?"

Reed leaned against the wall next to a water fountain. "Maybe." Carly took a drink. "Well, we can proceed on the assumption that we've been chasing Berdovitch and Anderson. But if Larson ripped off Clyde Calvert and Bonnie Smith, why didn't they just call the cops?"

Carly shrugged. "They're country people. Maybe they don't trust us."

Hints of the lacy black bra Carly wore beneath her tank top rimmed an enticing valley of cleavage. Reed's mouth went dry. "Maybe they shouldn't."

She glanced up from the fountain. "Not trust cops? Why?"

"Never mind." He lifted his eyes from her breasts. "Let's just go find them."

"Which them?"

"All of them," Reed said. "Berdovitch and Anderson first. He didn't show up for work this morning and she never arrived at the inn. We'll let Clarence go, then follow him in case he knows where they're headed. They're holed up somewhere. I can feel it."

"SURE I CAN'T DO anything to help?" Frannie called.

Bill wriggled his back on the dolly and rolled out from beneath an old Impala they'd found in a shed. It wasn't painted, only primed, and he still wasn't sure he could make it run. He blew out a sigh and sat up.

Then he smiled. Frannie was standing in the doorway looking as pretty as a picture. Earlier, she'd taken a shower and a nap, then she'd come out, bringing him a sandwich and a bandanna she'd soaked in cool water.

"Brought you a soda," she said.

He nodded. "I'm hotter than hell and I could sure use it."

He watched her step around a pile of gardening tools and over a coffee can that was full of nails. The lady of the house was a good five times Frannie's girth, so Frannie's new, faded green housedress hung to her ankles. She'd put on a slip, for propriety's sake, but because a crack of afternoon sunlight was shining through the door behind her, Bill could almost see through the dress.

He suddenly gulped. He was fairly sure she wasn't wearing underwear. Probably not, since those of the female occupant wouldn't have fit, and Frannie would have wanted to wash out her own. He tried not to stare. One side of the dress was hanging lower than the other since she'd stuffed her pockets with the remaining travel brochures.

"Here you go," she said.

He fought the urge to run his hand from her ankle upward, and beneath the dress. He took the soda instead and gulped down half of it. "The condensation alone feels like air-conditioning," he said. But where their fingertips had touched felt hotter than the air. He wanted to pull her onto his lap but didn't. He was covered in grime from head to toe and she was as fresh as a daisy. She'd found hairpins and fixed her hair in a pile of braids that wrapped around her head, too. Her nails were painted bright pink, and because she'd filched a pair of sandals, her fresh pedicure was visible. And then there was the fact that she probably wasn't wearing panties.

"The things some women can do," he drawled.

She chuckled. "Think you can make the car run?"

He reached into his back pocket, found the bandanna and wiped it across his forehead. "Yeah."

She found an old bucket, upturned it and sat down. She hiked the hem of the dress, spread her legs slightly and stuffed all the excess material between them. Then, she tugged a pamphlet from her pocket and started fanning herself.

"It really is hot in here," she commented.

She had no idea how hot. "Hotter by the minute," he said, the soda doing nothing to ease the dryness of his throat. "Why don't you go back inside the house?" He wasn't going to get a bit of work done when he could stare at her instead. "You could snoop some more."

She grinned impishly. "Judging by the mail, we're really in Arkansas, in the home of Vi and Woodrow Silverwood. They have no TV or radio or phone, but they do have a washer. The dryer's on the blink." She giggled. "I know all there is to know, so I came out to help you work."

He found himself smiling at her lazily. In the hazy light of the shed, she looked like the proverbial farmer's daughter. "Know much about transmissions?"

"I'm a walking encyclopedia."

His eyes drifted from her face to her feet and back up again. "If encyclopedia's looked like you—" his voice turned husky in midsentence "—guess I would have made better grades in school."

She shifted her rump on the uncomfortable-looking bucket and grinned mischievously. "You would have studied so hard...."

"All night long, sweetheart."

Still smiling, she quit fanning herself and plopped the pamphlet in her lap. Then she whipped the rest of them from her pocket and started leafing through them. "I couldn't find the keys to the car," she said absently.

He shrugged and took another sip of soda. "I can hot-wire it."

She shot him a hundred-watt smile. It made him feel as if he'd been elected president, not reminded her that he'd been a car thief.

"It's a good thing I didn't get stuck with an accountant," she said drolly.

He smiled back at her. "How do you know you didn't?"

She squinted at him. "What *do* you do?"

He wiggled his brows.

She sighed. "I refuse to ask again."

He scooted on the dolly and leaned his back against the car's passenger side door. "What are you studying in school, anyway?"

She shot him a coy glance, then wiggled her brows as if she weren't going to tell him. "Accounting," she admitted after a moment.

He threw his head back and laughed. He started to tell her that she was the least likely accountant he'd ever met, but then decided it wasn't wise. Still, she could blow over a hundred dollars and remain convinced she'd merely spent twenty. "So that's why you've got accountants on your mind," he finally said. "Just whose money are you planning to tally up?"

"Gee, I don't know. Maybe that rich husband's. You know, the one I was supposed to snag on my white-water rafting vacation."

"Ah, Mr. Suave." Not only would she probably make a lousy accountant, but Mr. Suave hadn't looked right for Frannie, as far as Bill was concerned. Even from a distance, the guy had looked spineless and self-absorbed. But then what did Bill know about guys? Zilch. "Were you really looking for a husband?"

She laughed. "A girl can hope."

"Ever been married?" Sadness suddenly touched her eyes and he was almost sorry he'd asked.

"No, but why is it me who's always answering the questions?"

He stretched out his legs and crossed them at the ankles. The way she was scrutinizing him made him self-conscious. If she went for Mr. Suaves, he didn't have a prayer. His cutoffs were filthy and he'd stripped off his shirt. There were black smudges on his pectorals. Still, he was pretty sure she liked looking at his bare chest. He hoped so, anyway.

"So, what is it you want to know about my life?" he finally asked, thinking he might not mind telling her.

"Everything," she said softly.

His gaze shot to her eyes. As compelled as he felt to touch her sexually, her eyes suddenly seemed too soft, too kind. And he hated pity. He shrugged. "My mother ran off with a guy when I was four or five. Left me with a father who was dead drunk all the time and couldn't hold a job." It was the shorthand version, but it would have to do.

To his surprise, she didn't offer any comment, but simply fanned herself with one of the tour guides. After a moment, she glanced up. "Stealing cars must have looked like a pretty good deal, huh?"

He found himself smiling in relief. Someday, maybe he'd tell her the nitty-gritty. She clearly wasn't the type to wring his hand and weep all over him, which drove him crazy. After all, it was the distant past. "Made more money than I do now," he teased.

Her head shot up and she stared at him expectantly.

There was no shame in how he made his living, but he merely pursed his lips and shook his head. His tongue reached for his mustache out of habit, but then he realized it was gone. Teasing her had its benefits. Her mouth turned pouty and her nose crinkled, making her look more cute than pretty.

She suddenly looked down at her dress. "This is truly hideous on me, isn't it?"

It was, but it was what was in it that counted. "It's all right," he said playfully, letting his gaze drift over her again. "In its way."

"Well, I've picked out an outfit for you, too," she assured, a hint of haughtiness creeping into her voice.

He chuckled. "I can't wait."

She sighed. "Maybe when we leave, I'll buy something new."

He rested the cool glass against his knee and wondered if the police had made any headway in figuring out the whole mess. For all they knew, Bonnie and Clyde had been found. Maybe the police were still looking for him and Frannie—but to apologize. "We'll be lucky if the rest of the cash buys us a full tank of gas." And if he could get the car running. Even if he could have gotten the station wagon out of that ditch, it wouldn't have done them any good. Clarence had probably reported it stolen by now.

She narrowed her eyes thoughtfully. "I think we should siphon some from another car. We'll need money for food."

Bill burst out laughing. "And I thought I was the one who was supposed to have the criminal mind."

"I wouldn't mind making use of Clarence's credit cards," she said slowly.

He gasped. "I'll just bet you mean to run up a big tab on our friend Clarence."

She sniffed. "That man pointed a gun at me! And he made us drive for hours and—"

"That hardly justifies credit card fraud." Her face fell, as if she just now realized that using Clarence's cards was illegal.

"Under the circumstances, I don't think I'd get in trouble."

It was clear from the gleam in her bright blue eyes that paying Clarence back for their day of terror was high on her priority list. She was contemplating the prospect with real relish. "As a first-time offender," he finally admitted, "you'd probably just get a year or two probation."

She suddenly chuckled. "Unless I didn't get caught. Probation seems a small price to pay for what he did to us. I could just see his face when he opens his bills!"

"What am I gonna do with you?" He smiled lopsidedly and shook his head, thinking of the million things he wanted to do. Like making love to her again. If she hadn't looked so tired this morning, he would have tried. Instead, he'd put her to bed alone like a gentleman, with nothing more than a chaste kiss. Now he wished he hadn't. He couldn't look at her without imagining unbraiding all that soft, thick hair.

"You could tell me how to climb the old ropes before I even got to prison," she suddenly continued.

"Don't even joke about it, sweetheart." He drank down the mix of melted ice and soda in his glass, then set the glass next to the dolly. "I guess I better try to get this thing running."

"Well, I do need to check my casserole."

His stomach rumbled. "Casserole?" He watched her nod and turn the page of a pamphlet. There was something distinctly domestic in the moment—him working on a car, her cooking a casserole—and he was shocked to feel himself responding. *It could be a good life, buddy.*

"There was tons of stuff in Vi and Woodrow's fridge," she continued.

"Which means they didn't go far," he returned, feeling a tad anxious. He laid down on the dolly again and decided he'd very definitely rather look at her than the undersides of a car.

"Woodrow's due back tomorrow evening, so Vi went to visit Jancy in Little Rock until then. Jancy's her sister."

Bill chuckled and leaned up on an elbow. The way Frannie discussed the cabin's inhabitants, he was half convinced she'd known them for years. "You're a wealth of information."

"There's a note on the fridge," she said in a preoccupied voice. "And I found the Interstate."

She'd gotten awful darn interested in her pamphlets, he thought. She wasn't so much as looking at him. "You did?"

"It's just over the ridge. The dirt road in front of the house leads right to it."

Something in her tone made him do a double take. She started riffling through the tour guides, as if she had a purpose. She found the one she wanted and rapidly turned the pages.

"Sanctuary," she suddenly said breathlessly.

He squinted. "What?"

"They said they were going to Sanctuary in Mexico."

He nodded. "Yeah, we know that."

Now she stared right at him, a grin splitting her face from ear to ear. "Sanctuary is an historic landmark. It's a chapel in San Miguel. It's right over the border from Texas."

What in the world was she talking about? Bill sat up on the dolly again. "They're going to a church?"

"Sanctuary," she said emphatically.

Her smile was so breathtakingly beautiful that for a long moment, he could merely grin back. "Well, sweetheart," he finally drawled, "it's a good thing I insisted we get all those tour guides."

She sent him a long, censuring look. "You certainly did not."

"I just knew they'd come in handy," he returned. He lay down quickly, kicked himself off and rolled beneath the car. "Don't you have a casserole to check, honey?" he called in his best man-just-home-from-work tone.

From under the car, he could see her shapely calves and ankles as she headed for the door of the shed. Soft, bubbly laughter trailed behind her like one of her scarves.

"Men," he heard her say.

"IT SURE BEAT bologna on white bread." Bill tossed his napkin beside his plate and stretched his arms over his head.

Frannie fought down a blush at the reminder of their first night together, but let her gaze drift over Bill's chest. It was nearly midnight, but she'd held dinner until Bill could get the car running and take a shower. She smiled sleepily. "I'm not sure how well a tuna fish and potato chip casserole goes with noodles and vegetables."

"It was the presentation that was stellar," Bill returned. "And I think my third helping was better than my second."

He did have an appetite. And not just for casserole. "It was a humble meal,' she commented, "but you get the basic idea."

"Basic idea?"

It was romantic, but she wasn't going to say so. She'd shoved the dining table next to the window, turned off the overhead lights and lit candles. They were decidedly Christmasy—red with green holly—but they flickered in the night breeze and caught the gold of Bill's hair and eyes. She'd made a centerpiece of wildflowers.

Bill had passed on the overalls she'd laid out for him and found a pair of painter's pants. He hadn't bothered with a shirt. She glanced down, hoping her sundress and shorts would line dry overnight. "Think we'll find them in San Miguel?" she finally asked, realizing that he was staring at her intently.

"Who?"

He looked as if his mind had been a thousand miles away. What was he thinking? she wondered. Maybe what she was. That she wanted him, pure and simple. In the shed, she hadn't been able to keep her eyes off him. Sweat had made the muscles of his bare chest glisten as if he were a professional weight lifter whose body had just been oiled.

Her mouth went dry. "Clyde Calvert and Bonnie Smith," she said raspily. "Do you think they'll be at that church?"

He stared back at her, his golden eyes steady and unflinching. Then they softened and the candlelight caught their irascible gleam. His tongue darted out and he licked his lower lip, as if his mouth had become as dry as hers. His powerful shoulder lifted slightly in a shrug. "That's tomorrow," he said softly.

Tonight was on his mind. Her eyes flitted toward the hallway that led to the two bedrooms. She wanted him and she could have him. He wanted her, too.

"What do you say we leave these dishes until tomorrow?" he drawled. "We can do them before we leave."

He leaned back in his chair and her eyes darted to where the loose painter's pants hung on his hips. "We?" she managed. When she glanced up, she realized he'd caught her gaze—and where it was directed.

"Jailhouse training," he said, a gruff huskiness in his voice. "A guy learns to clean up after himself."

"I guess more guys could use a stint in prison." She watched his mouth quirk. His low, throaty chuckle floated to her end of the table on the breeze. He rose and started collecting the dishes.

"Here..." She began to gather her own and blew out the candles. The second she'd done so, she wished she hadn't. They were in the dark now...and he was so close, right beside her. She cleared her throat. "I'll help you."

He leaned over and kissed her then—not passionately, but with a sweet, quick brush of his lips. It was so natural and deep, like birth and death and all the things that made the world go around. When he drew away, she felt bereft.

"Thanks, sweetheart," he said as they headed toward the illuminated kitchen.

"Anytime."

As he finished tidying up, she leaned in the doorway and watched the muscles of his back ripple. The pants hung low on his hips and somehow, all that expanse of bare back made him look naked. Glancing over his shoulder, through the kitchen window, she became more conscious than ever of how alone they were. The cabin was utterly still. Outside, the lush mountains rose up all around them. If it wasn't for the inhabitants of the cabin, they could stay here for a lifetime and no one would ever know.

"I'll take the guest room," she said as Bill turned around. It was the room farthest from the kitchen. Given the items in it—dusty catcher's mitts and models of sailboats—it looked as if it had probably belonged to a son who had left home. She'd stood in it long moments after her nap, thinking of her son and of the future he had never lived to see.

Bill crossed the room and lightly placed a hand on her shoulder. He gazed into her eyes. "I was hoping you'd sleep with me."

"I know," she nearly whispered.

"I'll walk you down," he said simply.

He was too much of a man to protest. But she'd made love to him before. She knew the depth of passion inside him. And knowing that, she felt suddenly cherished. Bill protected women, respected them.

When they reached the hallway, he casually draped his arm around her shoulders. The way his chest warmed her side and how the closeness of his breath feathered against her skin made her wish she'd flicked on the hall light. The farther they got from the kitchen, the darker it got.

"This looks like it," she said. She'd tried to sound brightly perky, but her voice was rough with desire. She leaned against the doorjamb and gazed up at him. In the dim light, shadows played across his face and his eyes looked almost black. When he leaned his elbow against the wall next to her, she instinctively backed up, then realized there was nowhere to go.

"I've seen the way you look at me," he said gently. "I know you want me."

"You don't waste time in getting to the point," she murmured, hoping he wouldn't push too hard. She hadn't known him long, but the list of his good qualities lengthened by the second. She didn't want to muddy the waters by having sex with him. She wanted to know whether he could love her. And whether he would stay.

"Life's too short to waste time," he whispered, leaning even closer. His lips grazed her cheek and fluttered down her neck.

"I just don't know" was all she could think of to say. It was what she always said. There probably wasn't a soul within miles and yet, like him, she felt compelled to whisper.

"We've been together before," he said in a low tone. He reached down, found her hand, then lifted it and cradled it against his chest.

The way he held her hand was so romantic that her insides started quivering. Her legs suddenly felt as if they couldn't support her. Even if their lovemaking was like the first time—stormy and dangerously passionate and without any real love—she wanted him. "But that was different," she finally managed to say, her voice sounding throaty to her own ears.

"Why?"

Because you're not the man I thought you were when I first saw you. You seem to be infinitely more—and I have to know if you are. "Because I didn't know you then."

He sighed softly. "True."

If they made love again, maybe it would be different for him too, she realized. "I just think I'd like to sleep on it."

Her voice was as flimsy as her dress. It wavered with a yes as surely as leaves waved in response to the breeze outside.

"Just wish you were sleeping on it next to me," he said.

His breath fanned against her cheek. The hand above her, where he'd been leaning against the wall, dropped down. His fingers traced over her braids and his free arm circled around her waist and he drew her against him with nothing more than the softest pressure of his fingertips.

His mouth found hers but the kiss wasn't demanding. It was as gentle as the night, his lips grazing hers, his tongue slowly probing open her lips. A low-building heat curled in her belly and started to rise, like a trail of ascending smoke. Only arching toward him could appease the ache at the core of her.

He deepened the kiss ever so slowly, drawing his lips back, then pressing them against hers just a little more, every touch almost imperceptibly taking her to another level of response. It was such a leisurely, languid kiss that she barely noticed what was happening to her.

Then she felt it all at once—the muscles of her behind tightening and urging her forward, the tingles that washed over her skin in a relentless tide. The way her belly felt full and warm. Her breasts had peaked, the tips cresting into tight, hard nubs against the scratchy lace cups of the slip she was wearing.

Somehow, as if by magic, she was just close enough to him and just far enough away that those aroused tips gently grazed his bare chest. A soft, cooing whimper rose in her throat and he captured it with his mouth. Her body strained toward his, but he held back, not coming any closer. He began to move his upper body, so slowly and rhythmically that she might not have noticed—except for the fact that his movements were sending her into a sweet, blissful agony.

In a heartbeat, her dress and slip became as insubstantial as air. As he rocked his strong, powerful shoulders, her loose full breasts swayed against the hardness of his chest and, each time, the constricted tips rubbed against him with a persuasive friction.

Before she could think it through, one of her hands circled his waist and the other pressed flat against his bare belly. His lips drew away, but not so far that they didn't touch. His tongue—so warm and wild now—began to flick between her lips with the rhythm of each of his touches.

And when he brushed his chest against her nipples just as the spear of his tongue licked at her lips, there was no doubt that the slow, hot friction was intentional. One of his shoulders dipped and his hard male nipple grazed against her own. Then his other shoulder dipped. His arm tightened around her waist and his palm pressed against the small of her back.

She moaned against his lips, then inhaled a quick sharp breath. Somehow, things had gone so far, so fast, that she knew she couldn't or wouldn't stop now.

He licked her upper, then her lower lip, his tongue feeling as hot as fire. Suddenly, he grunted. At the sound, her heart thudded. She arched toward him, but he kept her at bay, so that his erection grazed her, too. Her loose cotton dress and the silk of the slip were no barrier. The cloth merely draped around him.

He was caught between her legs but barely brushing her, and she felt nearly mindless with what he was doing to her. With a rhythm that threatened to shatter her, he continued to flick his tongue between her lips.

She leaned back her head and sighed against his shoulder. He broke the kiss and gazed down into her eyes.

''You'd best get on into bed, sweetheart,'' he whispered, his voice ragged.

She'd never felt so torn in her life. There was no one here. No eyes upon them. No one to judge her or care what she did.

"I just—" she began, her own voice sounding dry and raspy. "Just feel like my life has been so..." Her breath caught. He leaned farther back, just perceptibly, but she could still feel the male part of him against her. "...so directionless," she said on a shaky sigh. "I'm tired of not knowing where I'm..."

"I know, sweetheart."

In the darkness, she could see him watching her. His eyes caressed her breasts as surely as if he were still touching them. He lifted both hands and traced his fingers down the line of her neck to her chest. When he reached her breasts, the hands fanned outward, fingers splayed. He cupped her, feeling the weight of her breasts in his hands. Then his palms slid over her belly. His hands finally settled on her waist.

"What is it that got you so turned around?" he asked, the pads of both his thumbs rubbing her stomach through her dress.

"My... my son," she whispered.

He tilted his head.

"I got pregnant when I was seventeen," she said softly. "My boyfriend had a—a pro ball career in front of him." She squinted at Bill in the darkness, glad she was telling him, but wishing he was holding her more tightly. "He ditched me," she finally continued.

"What a jerk," Bill whispered, raising his hand to her forehead and brushing the tendrils of her hair.

Her physical ache for him was slowly subsiding. She leaned back and gazed at him. As rough and tough as he could be, he had a gentle streak that ran deeper and wider than she would have ever suspected.

"So, you have a kid," he said.

She realized that he'd misunderstood. Did he think she'd been trying to hide the fact that she was a single mother? He didn't seem displeased that she might be, which surprised her. The mention of children had sure made Joey Florence turn tail and run. "Bill," she said tentatively. "I lost my son."

His sudden intake of breath was audible.

"Crib death," she said. "He was three months old." Even as she said it, she realized her eyes weren't tearing. That was a first. Maybe she was finally ready, after all these years, to start fresh. And it helped that Bill's arms tightened around her, not with desire, but in comfort. She smiled wanly. "I'd just turned eighteen. I talk to him, sometimes," she said. "I mean, in my head. And I think about what he'd look like now. He'd be thirteen and even though I don't know—not really—I have a clear picture of him, growing up in my mind." She glanced down. "Do you think that's silly?"

"Ah, sweetheart," Bill said. "Not at all." After a long moment, he continued. "You must have had a lot of friends. Parents who supported you."

She half chuckled, half moaned. "The girlfriends in my circle were appalled. The captain of the team had ditched me and I refused to have an abortion. My parents love me and I love them, but they're well-off, overly concerned with social stigma, and I was an only child. I'd been accepted to four different universities—all really good schools. Nobody wanted me to have a baby."

"What was his name?"

She felt her eyes sting. "Raymond."

"Well, I would have wanted you to have Raymond, Frannie," Bill said, his voice so low that she barely heard it.

"Bad things happen to good people," she said, trying to sound strong as her hands glided over his strong back.

"C'mere." Bill pulled her even closer and into his comforting embrace. And then he hugged her tight. "I'll tell you something else," he whispered.

She smiled against his shoulder. Who would have guessed that the man could be so kind? "Hmm?"

"It looks like good things happen to bad people, too."

She wasn't sure, but thought she heard a hint of playfulness in his voice. "How's that?"

"Well, mean old me's got pretty old you in his arms."

She leaned back and shook her head. "You're not a bad person, Bill."

He smiled, a crooked half smile. "No, I'm not, sweetheart." He took both her hands and stepped back a pace. "C'mon."

Her chest constricted. Had he been nice only because he thought that might make her want to make love with him? If he had, she decided, it was probably working.

"Get in bed with me," he said. "We'll just sleep."

"What?"

"I just want to hold you."

Once again, his honesty took her by surprise. The man may have once been a criminal, but when it came to his feelings or voicing his needs, he could be entirely on the level. "You just want to hold me?" She realized no man had ever said that to her before.

"Yeah." Bill chuckled throatily. "I want to lie on my back and have you use my chest for your pillow."

Nothing had ever sounded better to her in her life. He looped his arm casually around her shoulder.

"You know something?" she asked as they headed back down the hall and toward the room with the double bed.

"Hmm?"

"You can be a real sweetheart, yourself."

He chuckled. "Why? Because I sometimes want to hold a woman without having sex with her?"

She grinned in the darkness. "Yeah."

He flashed her a sleepy-looking smile. "Sometimes, it's good for the man, too, you know."

But it wasn't.

Frannie had been around long enough to know that much. Some men took what they wanted and then left.

Some had a sixth sense about when a woman needed something, too. They vanished just as soon as their internal radar told them something would be required of them.

But Wild Bill Berdovitch was as solid as a rock.

And her fantasy man—that elusive Mr. Suave she'd always thought she wanted—was, in reality, not a man at all.

Once they were lying on the bed—clothed, with him on his back and her snuggled in his arms and with the night breeze drifting through the window—she whispered, "Bill?"

"Hmm?"

"Do you ever think about settling down? I mean, getting married and having kids?"

His shoulders shook with laughter. "Just go to sleep, Frannie," he whispered in a singsong voice.

It had been an obviously leading question, but he hadn't said he wasn't interested. She smiled against his bare shoulder. "Just wondering," she murmured.

"I'll just bet you were," he whispered.

JUST HOW SERIOUS WAS HE when it came to Frannie? Bill found himself wondering the next morning, as he finished a note of explanation for the inhabitants of the cabin. He'd come close to telling her that she was the most interesting woman he'd ever met.

Of course, maybe it was just the circumstances, he reminded himself. After all, it wasn't every day that he made a jailbreak with a drop-dead gorgeous woman. And yet, the little she'd said about the death of her son had made his heart ache for her. Over breakfast, she'd told him about how protective her parents had become. He'd told her some of his own nitty-gritty details, too.

He'd lusted after women who looked like her all his life—rich girls who represented everything he wasn't. Opposites attracted and he was drawn to the type like a magnet. He'd had women like that, too. But he'd never really sympathized with them. Or felt like he was falling in love with them.

Frannie was different. She'd made him feel—deep in his gut—that a life like hers wasn't necessarily all it was cracked up to be. It was in her eyes when they were touched by sadness or in how easily she became excited over the little things. It was in the falseness of her smile when she feared she was being too much trouble, too. And in the way she sometimes tried too hard to please.

"I found a camera!"

"And I fixed the dryer," he said. He turned around just as she bounded into the small, ramshackle living room, waving her prize in the air and unwinding the long shoulder strap that had been stuffed inside the case. The flouncy hem of her sundress waved back and forth as she skipped toward him. She stopped, placed a hand casually on his shoulder and stared down. Her eyes widened as she took in the note he'd written and the check. She gasped. "A check for four thousand dollars?"

Even he knew the car wasn't worth that much. He shrugged. "It might be the only car they have," he explained a little defensively. "I mean, we didn't even find a working TV."

Frannie glanced down at the camera in her hand and then slowly put it on the table. She looked so guilty that he burst out laughing. "Don't worry," he said, whipping out his checkbook again, "I'll buy it for you."

She tried to contain her devilish grin and failed.

He poised his pen over a new check. "How much do you think I ought to spend?"

He watched her glance between him and the checkbook. "Two thousand?" she finally teased.

Even though he substantially decreased the amount before he started writing, it was definitely the most extravagant gesture of his lifetime. He'd grown up poor and squirreled away most of what he made. He realized that she was gaping at him and bit back a smile.

"Are those checks going to bounce?" she suddenly demanded, her eyes narrowing.

He surveyed the check he'd written for the car, then the one he'd written for the camera and tried to look shocked. "And I thought you trusted me."

"You have that much in checking?"

He nodded. "Sure do, sweetheart." He glanced down at the table. "Well, I did."

"This is it, Bill." She whirled around in a graceful circle so that her skirt flared right before she seated herself at the table. "We've slept in the same bed three times and I have a right to know what you do for a living."

He burst out laughing. Gentleness and kindness seemed to be Frannie's top priority, but she clearly hadn't given up on finding a man who'd be a good provider. Once she heard his professional prospects, he half suspected she'd start trying to march him toward an altar.

"If you don't tell me," she threatened, "I'm not going anywhere." She crossed her arms over her chest.

"I'm a lawyer."

She gasped. "What? You mean, you really did straighten out in prison and become a lawyer?"

He nodded.

She looked shocked to her toes. "You prosecute people?"

Her jaw suddenly dropped and she stared at him wide-eyed, as if it occurred to her that he might send her to jail. "Not quite, sweetheart. I get them off the hook."

Relief flooded her features. "You're a defense attorney?"

He nodded. "Want to know what the *H* is for?"

Her incredulous expression was relaxing into what looked like happiness. "What?"

"Howard," he said. "Can we go now, sweetheart?"

She giggled. "Sure." As she stood up, her giggles gave way to real laughter. She sagged against him. "If I use Clarence's cards, do you think you could keep me out of jail when all this is over?"

"Like I said—" he flashed her a grin "—you might get probation."

"With an attorney like you," she trilled, slapping her thigh, "I bet I get off with nothing more than a slap on the wrist."

And a wedding ring. The way Frannie looked at things, she might just use Clarence's cards to buy him a tux. He imagined himself getting married at a historic church in San Miguel. And at that moment—watching how the morning light caught her hair as she slung her new camera over her shoulder—he decided it might be fine with him.

But he'd never considered marrying anybody before. And he didn't quite know what to make of it.

Chapter Ten

"What in the world do you make of this?" Reed muttered, picking up a stack of pamphlets and fanning himself. He realized that the Silverwoods and the local Arkansas boys were watching him expectantly. "Turn this cabin upside down," he bellowed. "Find out what they ate, what they wore and what they took."

"They ain't taken a thing," Vi Silverwood boomed in a voice that matched Reed's for volume. "'Cept the car and the camera. They fixed my dryer, too. I'll bet those kids were even trying to call for help, but didn't find my phone. Woodrow made a special cabinet for it in the bedroom."

Reed chuckled. The lady of the house didn't seem the least bit cowed by his overbearing manner. She clearly felt her age and girth gave her the leverage to bellow back at him and he'd liked her immediately. "You really think they left you all that money for a car that didn't run and a camera?"

Woodrow Silverwood ran his thumbs beneath the straps of his overalls. "But the car did run. I don't know how he fixed it. Every feller in this county's been underneath it at one time or another."

Reed sighed. "If there's one thing William Berdovitch knows his way around, it's a car."

Carly sidled up beside Reed, just as she clicked off her cellular phone. "He spent five years in Moundsville because of it, too."

"Poor fellow," Vi said. "I was hoping his checks wouldn't bounce. The car was no good and I never did use that camera, anyway." She smiled at her husband. "We've always said real life's more interestin' than pictures."

"I can't guarantee it, ma'am, but I think they'll clear," Reed said. He hoped so, for Vi's sake, except that it would mean he was chasing good guys. And, as far as Reed was concerned, good guys weren't terribly exciting.

"They found another check about a mile down the road, boss," Carly said.

They'd found Clarence's car and a motorcycle, too. The wrecked Triumph was registered to William Berdovitch. Tyler had finally admitted that Frances Anderson was a name given by the woman he'd arrested. He'd been sure it was an alias. They were close to finding their suspects and Carly's dark eyes were lit up with the thrill of the chase. They looked so wicked that Reed wished it was him she was pursuing. "Where'd they leave it?"

"Under a windshield wiper," Carly said. "There was a check for fifty dollars and a note saying they siphoned off some gas. The owner said it couldn't have been more than a couple of gallons."

"Fifty bucks for a couple of gallons of gas?" he repeated.

"You sure them two are outlaws?" Woodrow asked, pulling out a dining room chair and seating himself. Before Reed or Carly could answer, he continued, "You know, Vi, I do like where those youngins put the table. It's real nice here by the window."

"I've been thinking of movin' it," Vi said, "but I couldn't ask you to haul something so heavy. They must've read my mind."

If Clyde Calvert and Bonnie Smith were anything like William Berdovitch and Frances Anderson, they were probably making just as many friends, Reed thought. His suspects had breezed through and left a bundle of money to folks who could use it. According to the inhabitants, the cabin was cleaner than they'd left it, too.

Vi seated herself across from her husband. "I might as well heat up that leftover casserole for dinner later," she said. "Looks like she's a good cook."

"That'd be fine." Woodrow winked. "Those kids got out the Christmas candles, too."

"And she picked wildflowers," Carly said, leaning to touch the top of a bright bouquet that had been left in a water glass in the center of the table.

"Please tell me my fugitives aren't saints," Reed muttered. He was still holding out hope that Clyde Calvert and Bonnie Smith might be more worthy adversaries. He looked at Carly and held up the handful of pamphlets. "I just don't get it."

Carly's eyes narrowed. "You'd think they were on vacation, not running from the law."

"One of them even drew circles around points of interest," Reed said, trying to sound more disgusted than he actually felt, so Carly wouldn't think he was going soft. "In different colored pens." He rolled his eyes. "Now, isn't that sweet?"

Carly's mouth quirked. "Oh, I don't know, boss, I've always wanted to go to Graceland, myself."

He shoved the pamphlets in her hands. "Find out if they went to any of those places."

Carly frowned. "It's just a shame they didn't leave any information about where they *were* going."

"Finding them'll be simple enough," Reed assured.

Carly tossed her mane of dark curls over her shoulder. "Did you get ESP in your sleep or something last night, boss?"

No. He'd gotten dreams about Carly. They were racy enough that even he'd blush if he mentioned them on poker night. She'd sure never hear about them—not even if they wound up married, which they wouldn't, of course. He was ancient and decrepit and she was too nice a girl to get messed up with the likes of him. Besides which, he had no intention of even asking her on a date. *A date.* He told himself he hadn't been on one since drive-ins went out of vogue and boys wore short pants. "All we've got to do is follow the checks," he finally said.

"I should have thought of that," Carly said apologetically.

They had to find the couple who had stayed here since they seemed to know where Bonnie and Clyde had gone. Besides which, William Berdovitch had assaulted a deputy and stolen Clarence Smithers's car, which meant the fool—who'd obviously turned his life around—could get disbarred. "So, why didn't you?" he finally said.

"With a macho man like you around, what girl could concentrate?" Carly asked drolly.

"You falling for me?"

"It's that boss-secretary thing," she explained.

His eyebrows shot up. He had tried with all his might to treat her like an equal. "You're not my secretary."

Carly laughed. "I'll remind you of that next time you tell me to get your coffee."

His mouth dropped open in astonishment. "I have never once told you to get my—"

"We've determined that they slept in the same bed, Mr. Galveston," an Arkansas deputy drawled, walking into the room.

Reed whirled around. He started to tell the deputy he was busy, but then he realized he'd just been flirting with Carly. Wasn't he?

"They slept in the same bed?" Carly asked.

"The sheets are hanging on the line out back." The deputy tried to keep a straight face and failed. "The note of explanation was signed by Frannie. According to her, the line-dry will make them smell fresher."

"How's that for a first date?" Reed muttered. "Guess being on the lam did the trick."

"Hey, boss," Carly said with a smile, "I saw that man's mug shot. I know what I'd do if I was handcuffed to him." She shoved the tour guides in her back pocket and headed out to the hall.

"Jealous, Mr. Galveston?" Vi asked.

Reed wanted to say that he'd seen Frances Anderson's mug shot, too, and that he wouldn't mind being handcuffed to *her*. But it would have been a lie. The only woman he wanted was Carly. He leaned close to Vi Silverwood. "If you tell her, I swear I'll kill you."

"You ain't ever killed a flea," Vi boomed. "And if you don't do something besides look at her, young man, you'll wind up being the best man instead of the groom."

Groom? Reed stood to his full height, wondering if anyone besides Vi Silverwood had ever had the nerve to call him "young man."

"Figure Frances and William will get hitched, Vi?" Woodrow asked. He turned to Reed. "Vi has a sixth sense when it comes to marriage. She even predicted Lowell and Louann up the hollow. And they used to fight like cats and dogs."

Vi chuckled wryly. "Still do," she remarked.

Reed started to say he wished he'd discussed his nuptial game plan with Mrs. Silverwood before he'd married his first wife. Instead, he said, "Will they?"

"Why sure," she said, leaning her elbows on the table. "They're getting married. The way they burned those Christmas candles right down to the nubs tells the whole story."

"Is that so?" Reed murmured.

"The only real question is whether or not you and Carly'll beat 'em to the altar," Vi said with a grin.

"And I thought we were just trying to beat them to Bonnie and Clyde," Reed teased.

"Mark my words," Vi said, "every last one of you is gonna wind up in a church."

"BUT WHY WOULD THEY GO to a church?" Frannie wondered aloud. She adjusted her floppy hat and stared nervously toward the interior of the gas station where Bill was determining whether or not they could use Clarence's credit cards to buy gas. To appease her anxiety, she glanced from Bill to her replacement copy of *Modern Bride*. Then she leaned forward and turned up the radio which was tuned to an oldies station. It was no use. Her eyes darted toward the plate glass window again.

It looked as if Bill was signing the credit card receipt. They were really thieves now—so why didn't she feel guilty? She tried to tell herself that any woman in her shoes—flat broke and wrongfully arrested with a wonderful man— might do the exact same thing. But maybe not. She stared down at an ad for a sexy white peignoir and admitted that what she really felt was fear. Was her time with Wild Bill about to come to a dead end?

It just couldn't—not yet. They were in the heart of Texas, headed toward San Antonio. Later, the police could find them. Maybe she and Bill really would go to jail. For all she knew, she couldn't leave the state of Pennsylvania if she was put on probation, either. And Bill lived in West Virginia. *Please, let me stay with this man awhile longer.*

He'd held her all night long and kissed her awake. They'd sung along with the radio as if they were kids out joyriding. Bill had used a few of their remaining dollars to buy her some film and she'd taken countless pictures. Bill had started stopping at scenic overlooks of his own accord.

Yes, they were in trouble. They could be recognized at any moment. The police were probably still hunting for them. And yet she couldn't bring herself to care. When Bill hadn't bothered to call them again, she hadn't reminded him. Was he becoming as unconcerned about being caught as she was? If they'd really wanted to, couldn't they have straightened out this mess by now?

"A church," she murmured, as she turned a page of the magazine. "Why would armed robbers head for a church?"

"Isn't that where Butch Cassidy and the Sundance Kid wound up?" Bill asked through the window.

Frannie's attention had been riveted on a beaded gown with sweetheart neckline and lengthy train—her dream gown. When she glanced up, whatever passed between her and Bill's eyes said that it was done—they'd become outlaws, for real. They had a full tank of gas, compliments of Clarence. "Hmm?"

"Didn't they wind up at some Mexican church?"

Frannie smiled. "Bolivia, I think. And wherever it was, they had a shoot-out." She was trying to feel guilty, but she just couldn't. Bill looked so good that she wanted to reach out and pull him right through the car window. Even though he'd thrown on a denim work shirt at the Silverwoods', he'd left it unbuttoned. "You look so good, I'm almost sorry I didn't do more than kiss you good-morning."

"Well, sweetheart," he drawled, leaning in the window frame and resting his elbows on the ledge, "when you're more than almost sorry, you just let me know."

She already was. He'd turned around the baseball cap she'd bought him so that the bill was in back and while his friendly smile made her feel special, the scar on his chin added a hint of danger to his good looks. All night, he'd rocked and cradled her, then he'd merely lain still, letting her press her face against his chest. "You're waiting until you're sure I've got that crazy-in-love feeling before you make your move?" she teased.

A horn honked behind them and he glanced in the direction of the car that had pulled in. "That can't-live-without-you feeling?" He opened his door and got behind the wheel.

He slid something between his seat and the door, but she couldn't see what. "That's the one."

In a quick, lithe movement, he leaned across the seat and pulled her right into his lap. "Well, Frannie..."

She flung her arms around his neck and thought of how Kim Basinger had been handcuffed to Richard Gere in the Movie *No Mercy*. And how Meg Ryan had been attached to her real-life husband Dennis Quaid in *D.O.A.* Her own adventure with Wild Bill Berdovitch felt every bit as fantastic. "Well what?" she asked breathlessly.

"That crazy-in-love feeling is always nice—" Bill flashed her a wicked grin "—but I'll sure settle for less."

"You will?"

"With the right woman."

She wanted to point out that there was a car behind them, but couldn't bring herself to do so. Not when Wild Bill's mouth was just an excruciating inch from her own and his breath teased her lips. "What's that mean?" *Am I the right kind of woman?*

"Nothing all that complicated," he said right before his mouth smacked hers. His wet, sloppy kiss was more flirtatiously fun than romantic, so Frannie giggled and squirmed away. Not that Bill let her go.

When the driver behind them honked a third time, Bill drew back. His hand slid down her side and he playfully swatted her backside.

"Ouch!" she exclaimed, even though the love tap had become an instant caress. She scooted toward the passenger side.

"Now, Frannie," Bill chided as he turned the key over in the ignition, "the only pain you're feeling is one of unsatisfied longing."

She chuckled. "For what?"

"Me, sweetheart."

Nothing could have been more true. When she drew in a deep, satisfied breath, even the gasoline smelled good. She hadn't minded watching Bill pump it, either. There was something decidedly sexy about a guy wielding a gas hose. As soon as he turned onto the road, Bill reached in the space between his door and his seat. He pulled out a United States atlas.

"An atlas?"

"It's a present."

"I wish I hadn't forgotten half my books," Frannie said, thinking of all the pamphlets on the Silverwoods' dining table. When Bill had announced he was a lawyer, she'd been so shocked that she'd left some of them behind. She turned down the radio and took the atlas. "I don't know why I get such a kick out of looking at stuff like this," she said, leafing through it.

Bill shrugged. "Maybe you ought to be a travel agent instead of an accountant."

"I never thought of that." She scooted nearer to Bill but stopped before she was next to him.

As if sensing her hesitation, he lifted a hand from the steering wheel and opened his arm in invitation. "C'mere."

She slid against his side. His arm relaxed and settled comfortably across her shoulders. She turned back to the first pages of the atlas, wondering if she really would make a good travel agent. She loved to look at maps and pictures of faraway places and she could be personable. Mostly, she'd decided to be an accountant because her father always needed one.

When she turned to the two facing pages that showed the entire United States, she smiled. Bill had marked out their route with a red pen. Small connecting arrows began in West Virginia, meandered to Memphis, then turned north to Wisconsin. There was an arrow pointing southwest again. "You marked it for me," she said softly, feeling genuinely touched.

He glanced down. "Yeah."

She sighed and placed the atlas next to her on the old vinyl seat. "What could be better than this?"

"Hmm?"

She glanced through the windshield at the Texas landscape, wondering if it was wise to tell him everything she was feeling, but knowing she had nothing to lose. She shrugged. "Driving down the road on a fabulous early afternoon, with the wind blowing in your face through the open windows, listening to good, old songs on the radio when you know all the words...."

He nodded. "I think we did the chorus to 'Born to Run' together in a decent attempt at harmony."

She giggled. Somehow, all the singing they'd done had freed her up. It was better than a primal scream. She felt young and unfettered, as if the world was at her command. It seemed impossible that deputies, cops and the FBI were somewhere behind them, in pursuit. She swallowed and forced herself to forge onward. "...Curling up against a guy you really like."

His hand tightened around her shoulder. "So, you like me, huh?"

It wasn't really a question, and they both already knew the answer. "It would be strange if I didn't, after all that's happened..." *Between us.*

He smiled and steered around a bend in the road, his fingertips barely touching the wheel. "I liked last night."

"Last night..." She'd felt more at peace with herself than she had for years. *But why not say it all, Frannie? There's love to be found, maybe not with this man, but somewhere. All people have to do is reach for it. All I have to do is reach for it.* "Bill, you're going to think this is crazy, but—"

"What could be crazier than the past couple of days?"

She drew in another deep breath, pulling in the woodsy scent of his skin. "What I was trying to say..."

He glanced down at her and squinted. "Hmm?"

"I—I think—"

"You can tell me anything, sweetheart." His eyes narrowed even further, then he glanced back through the windshield, as if realizing he needed to keep his attention on the road. "Believe me, I've heard and seen it all."

Somehow, the way he touched her convinced her of that. She'd never had a man hold her with such surety and acceptance. "I think I could fall in love with you," she said in a rush. *Did I really say that?*

Maybe she hadn't. He gave no indication of having heard her—unless his hand really did tense on the wheel and his fingers really did quiver against her bare shoulder. She glanced quickly down into the lap of her sundress.

Well, she could live with rejection. She was thirty years old and a full-grown woman. In just two weeks, after her last round of finals, she would find a job, maybe as a travel agent. And from now on, what she would care about was voicing her own feelings. At least she'd said her share. "I honestly think I could fall in love with you," she repeated. She glanced up, stared straight through the windshield for a long moment, then forced herself to look at him again.

When his lips parted, just slightly, her heart nearly dropped to her feet. And when they slowly curled into a smile, she wanted to kiss him. Then his eyes fixed on hers and melted her heart.

"Ah, sweetheart," he said softly, "you mean you haven't already?"

Her heart was hammering against her ribs and even though she remained motionless against his side, she couldn't catch her breath. She tried to calm her nerves. "Let's just say I'm thinking about it,' she managed to say.

He glanced in the rearview mirror and through the windshield before ducking his head to kiss her. His lips were as wetly gentle as dew kissing morning grass and as full of promise as morning sunshine that announced a perfect day ahead. When the car started veering toward the shoulder, he drew back and turned the wheel.

"Know what I like about you?" he asked.

She took off her hat, tossed it on top of the atlas and rubbed her head against his chest. She shook her head. "What?"

"You'll always be changing."

She glanced up.

"Somehow you don't seem like the exact same woman I met just days ago. You're searching for the right direction in which to take in your life. It's why you read maps and—" he chuckled softly "—only you could turn something like this into a vacation."

"Oh? Don't tell me you're on vacation now?" He was, whether he'd admit it or not. He was stopping for the overlooks and buying the film. She watched his expression turn suddenly serious. "Did I say something wrong?"

"No, sweetheart," he assured, pulling her closer.

"There's something wrong and you didn't tell me," she said. His lips puckered, looking kissable, and he blew out a sigh. Sudden panic made her sit up straight. "What is it?"

"Along with the atlas, I picked up a paper," Bill said gently. "They're looking for us."

She reached out her hand and grabbed the dashboard for support. "Who? I mean, I know Clarence and the police..." She watched in horror as Bill reached between his seat and the door again and pulled out a newspaper.

"They've identified us as who we really are—as William Berdovitch and Frances Anderson," he said.

She gasped, barely glancing down at the paper. *What could be wrong with that?* She thought of her parents, ensconced in their borrowed cabin in North Carolina. She was fairly sure they wouldn't have seen a paper, since her father refused to read them on his vacations. But if they had, they would be worried sick. "Why, Bill that's wonderful. Isn't it?"

He sighed. "They think we're still driving Clarence's car. At least, that's what they thought at the time the article was written."

"Well, we have a new car," Frannie murmured, glancing down at the seat. Yellow foam peeked back at her from an oval shaped rip in the vinyl. Somehow, it looked like an eye gazing back at her. She glanced at Bill again. "If they know it's us, then we can go..."

The unspoken word hung in the air.

"Home," he finally said.

Her lips parted in protest. Outside, the countless miles of Texas were passing. Right next to her was the sexiest, most decent man she'd ever met. "But I'm not sure I want to go home, Bill," she nearly whispered.

"I don't want to, either," he said. "But we can't anyway. We've still got no choice."

She looked down at the paper, then stared at him. "Why not?"

"We're suspected of auto theft—"

She drew in an indignant breath. "Excuse me?"

"Clarence's car," he explained. "And I'm facing an assault and battery charge because of the deputy."

"He told you to hit him!" she exclaimed.

"That's hardly an excuse," Bill muttered, sounding furious with himself.

"My parents," she said. "They're on a camping trip...my mother never pays attention to the news, anyway. But what if they saw me, somehow?" She gasped. "If I'm really under suspicion, they'll track down my parents to ask them questions."

"If they did, your parents would have gone home," Bill said reasonably. "We'll call them."

She nodded. The deep timbre of his voice alone was enough to set her at ease. "I'm sure there's no phone at the cabin where they're staying. My father likes to really get away from it all. They're just so overly protective that I'm afraid—" Bill's arm tightened around her shoulders again and she sank against his chest.

"Things'll work out, Frannie."

Something in his tone made her believe him. She stared through the windshield, watching how the guardrails and mile markers seemed to flatten against the asphalt as they passed. When Bill took the next exit, she said, "I think you took a wrong turn."

His mouth quirked. "With you in the car, no turn could be a wrong turn."

"How can you joke at a time like this?" She glanced at him and when their eyes met, unspoken words seemed to pass between them. Frannie, who'd been so intent on ignoring what was happening to them was now playing straight man, while Bill was determined to make the best of a bad situation.

"There's not a whole lot left to do but joke," he said after a moment.

"Oh, I could think of a few things."

He leaned over and kissed her again. Because he kept one eye on the road, he merely caught the corner of her mouth. "I bet you could, sweetheart," he said huskily.

She grinned. "Where are we going?"

"To a place I saw in one of those books of yours."

"I've got to call my parents," she reminded him. "And the police are looking for us."

"They've *been* looking for us," he returned, still sounding like the voice of reason. "So far, between your new hairdo and hat and my clean shave, no one's stopped us yet. Besides—" He winked at her. "Maybe *I've* been looking for you all my life."

Was he really serious about her? Either way, apparently Bill was ready to throw caution to the wind. With each mile they'd driven, they'd seemed to go deeper into something Frannie couldn't quite define. What had begun as a white-water getaway with an itinerary of lobster lunches and cocktail parties had turned into something far more significant. "So, where are you taking me?"

"Don't worry, sweetheart." He glanced down at her and chuckled. "You'd drawn a thousand circles around this place, all done in different colored pens."

"YOU HAVE NO LUGGAGE?" the clerk asked uncertainly.

Bill tightened his grip reassuringly around Frannie's hand and returned the clerk's gaze. He'd already parked the car, backing it into a space in one of the many numbered garages, so that no one could read the plates, and Frannie's folks weren't home, which was a good sign. Still, the clerk, whose name tag said Lisa, was so watchful that Bill was getting nervous.

He forced himself to grin. Beneath his palm, he could feel Frannie's pulse thudding out of control. "No. No luggage," he said, as if coming to a fancy resort without suitcases should have been commonplace.

Lisa glanced toward the wide glass front of the hotel anxiously. "Er...may our valet park your car, then?"

"We already parked," Frannie trilled brightly.

Lisa's eyes narrowed. Bill wondered if she was really squinting at them, trying to place them, or whether he was imagining it. Frannie readjusted her hand and twined her fingers through his. She leaned forward conspiratorially. What was she up to?

"Frankly," Frannie said. "We don't want anyone to know we're here."

"I—I need to get the imprint of your credit card," Lisa said.

Frannie raised her free hand and put *Modern Bride* on the counter. She tapped the top of the magazine lightly with her fingernails. When Frannie glanced downward, Lisa followed her gaze. "We're getting married," Frannie whispered.

A slight smile touched at Lisa's lips.

"My—my father..."

"Doesn't want you to?" Lisa asked.

When the clerk's wide eyes shot to Bill, he felt as if they were twin spotlights and that he was on display. The twentyish woman looked him over, clearly trying to decide if Frannie's father had reason to distrust him. He shrugged sheepishly and grinned back.

"No offense," Lisa said, "but I'm eighteen and you both look..."

"I know!" A hint of a wail crept into Frannie's voice. "But my father wants me to marry one of his hotshot employees—the one he's grooming to take over his law firm. And he's been having someone follow me. Bill's a mechanic, you know, and my father just thinks..."

"He's not good enough?" Lisa finished, leaning over the counter. "That's terrible. My husband installs cable and my father thought the same thing. I think he expected me to marry the president.''

"Yeah." Bill tried to look angry, but not too angry. "We've been together for over five years, but he still hasn't warmed to me."

"We're in love and we're going to get married," Frannie vowed. She glanced at Bill. "One way or another."

Lisa's eyes widened. "You're eloping?"

"Driving to Mexico tomorrow," Bill said.

"It's a beautiful little church..." Frannie leafed through *Modern Bride* until her remaining pamphlets fell out. "See," she continued, pointing. "It's an historic landmark in San Miguel and it's called Sanctuary..."

"I know!" Lisa giggled. "It's the first church across the border."

Lady Luck was smiling on them, Bill thought. "You've been there?"

"I got married there," Lisa said, a slight hint of pink staining her cheeks. "And I was only seventeen."

Frannie disentangled her hand from his, leaned both her elbows on the counter and blew out a heartfelt sigh. "I wish we could have gotten married when we were seventeen," she said wistfully, real sadness touching her eyes as if she'd just thought of Raymond.

"But then we'd be an old married couple now," Bill said, hauling Frannie against his side and planting a smack on her cheek. "Instead of newlyweds."

Lisa glanced around nervously. Then she glanced at her computer screen and started typing. "One of our two bridal suits is open," she said a little breathlessly. "I mean they're really separate bungalows, with their own pools and everything. Outdoor Jacuzzi. I'm working a double shift, so if you check out by ten tomorrow, I'll be here. I could take the imprint of your card, but—" she glanced up and grinned wickedly "—I'll put it in a special place...."

"Special place?" Bill asked, deciding this was too good to be true.

Lisa shrugged. "You know, in a drawer or something. That way if your father comes, he won't be able to find you. I mean, in case another clerk is helping him." Her face suddenly fell. "The bridal bungalows are awfully expensive."

"The card's good," Bill assured. The man at the gas station had run the one Bill had chosen through his machine. Apparently, Clarence hadn't reported the cards stolen. At least he hadn't a few hours ago.

Lisa started typing again. After a moment, she took the imprint of Clarence's card, returned the card to Bill and tossed the paperwork in a drawer. She glanced up and smiled. "Just hang out in the lobby for a half hour or so, then you can catch a shuttle out front to take you there."

"They're really separate bungalows?" Frannie asked.

She sounded so thrilled that Bill was almost convinced they were getting married. He wondered how much of her excitement was real and how much was for Lisa's benefit.

"Very remote," Lisa said. "And with lots of complimentary stuff. That's why we need the half hour."

"This place is just beautiful," Frannie said when they turned away from the counter.

His gaze followed hers through the glass front of the hotel. The resort overlooked Big Bend National Park, which contained the closest thing to badlands that could be found in Texas. From where they were, he could see breathtaking desert and interesting rock formations.

"Ideal for a honeymoon," he finally said, a tinge of irony in his voice.

"We could change," Frannie said breathlessly. "Explore the place, then have a romantic dinner and—"

Frannie's gaze shot to his and she flushed. Everything in her eyes said she'd just realized she'd gotten carried away.

They weren't eloping, there would be no honeymoon and they were headed toward Sanctuary—to find Bonnie and Clyde, not a preacher.

"There's just one problem," he found himself saying gently.

Her eyes wavered uncertainly, as if she expected him to say that he didn't love her. "What?"

He smiled and put his arm around her. "We don't have anything to change into."

The relief that crossed her features did his heart good. So did the wicked glint that sparked in her eyes. He hoped it meant she was thinking what he was—that maybe they could change into nothing at all. "Unless it's our birthday suits," he ventured.

"Is today your birthday or something?" she asked innocently.

"Impossible," he returned, steering her toward the shops in the lobby. "Around you, I feel younger by the second."

"Don't get too young," she shot back. "I like my men mature."

"But young at heart, I hope."

"No." She chuckled. "Wild at heart."

"Ah, sweetheart." He pulled her against him and kissed her right in the middle of the lobby. "They didn't start calling me Wild Bill because I was tame."

Chapter Eleven

"We probably shouldn't," Frannie whispered as she pulled Bill inside one of the lobby's many boutiques.

"Shouldn't what?" he asked.

She glanced around, deciding that the Alpine Resort and Spa was just the sort of place she would have chosen for her honeymoon. Beyond the ultramodern high-rise hotel were small cottages with landscaped grounds that overlooked the desert. Accustomed to northeastern vegetation, she found herself gawking at the profusion of stark cacti and brightly colored desert flowers. "Shop," she finally said, her eyes darting over the clothes for sale.

"Since we are, what are we looking for?"

"A pair of trunks," she said, riffling through the racks. "Just in case a bathing suit's preferable to your birthday suit."

When he rubbed his chin, as if considering, she couldn't help but imagine how his stubble might make her bare skin tingle. He quickly reached past her and snatched a pair of bikini trunks from the rack.

"You wouldn't really wear those," she managed to say shakily. "Would you?" The men's bikinis amounted to nothing more than a handful of leopard print silk. When she thought about them soaking wet and clinging to Wild Bill, she felt downright faint. "I had you figured more for the cutoff jeans type."

He grinned mischievously. "Or the big baggy trunks that hide it all?"

"Don't you think those are a little tacky?"

He leaned against the rack. "Tacky as hell, sweetheart, but that's not the point."

She wouldn't ask what the point was.

"C'mon." He grinned as if he were thoroughly enjoying her discomfort. "I'd feel like Tarzan."

"Sorry, Bill," she managed to say, "but I doubt there's a jungle in the bridal suite."

He leaned close. "The jungle's a state of mind."

Or body, she thought.

"Still," he continued, "I refuse to be Tarzan, unless you'll be Jane."

"Don't forget, underneath it all, you're really a Howard," she returned. Except "Howard" just didn't suit Wild Bill—not even as a middle name. And yet she'd hardly been sorry to find that her rough-and-tumble ex-con had a little Howard in him, after all.

She watched as he turned in the aisle, scanned the women's suits and pulled out the female component to the suit he'd chosen for himself. "You can wear whatever you want, but I am not wearing that," she assured.

"It's our honeymoon," he protested.

But it wasn't. No matter how much Frannie was beginning to wish it was.

"And you wouldn't believe how many of those his-and-hers sets we sell!" a salesclerk suddenly piped in helpfully.

"Who in the world buys them?" Frannie couldn't help but ask.

Clarence Smithers, she found herself thinking not twenty minutes later as Bill took out Clarence's card. She glanced over their purchases. They were buying a pair of baggy trunks and the leopard bikinis for Bill, as well as a new pair of jeans and a shirt. For her, they'd compromised. She'd gotten a two-piece suit sans the leopard print. Bill had co-ordinated the quintessential tourist outfit for her, too—a light, flouncy white muslin dress with a new straw hat and sandals with ribbons that tied around her calves. The outfit made her feel nearly sure they were headed for Venice, where they would float down a canal while their gondola driver sang love songs. Since blue plastic eyewear didn't quite do her new ensemble justice, Bill had found oversize sun-glasses of the sort Jackie O. had made famous, to replace her Elvis glasses.

"And this," Bill said.

Frannie stepped back a pace as seeming miles of filmy white floated over her shoulder. When the peignoir set landed on the counter, her heart suddenly ached. Instead of protesting, she reached out and touched it.

"I'll get the box," the clerk said, circling the counter and heading toward the back of the store.

The gown was a tube of pearl-colored silk covered with thick ornamental lace and supported by two whisper-thin straps. The matching robe consisted of many layers of white illusion lace, and the sleeves were tied to the bodice with the same pink silk ribbons that had been threaded through the cuffs. The gown was every bit as beautiful as it was compli-cated-looking.

"I—" Frannie paused, wondering whether she should say anything or not. The gown was clearly meant for a bride. Wild Bill, one-hundred-percent male that he was, probably just hadn't noticed. Or maybe he had and the choice was intentional. Heaven knew, he'd seen ones like it in the copy of *Modern Bride* she'd been reading. When his fingers traced up the length of her arm and curled around her neck, she leaned against the counter for support.

"You what?" he finally prompted.

Her fingers drifted over the gown. "It's...well, it's really a bride's..."

He arched his brows as if he didn't have the faintest idea what she was talking about. "I chose it for comfort's sake."

"Whose?" she couldn't help but ask, her voice growing husky.

He chuckled. "Mine probably."

She didn't know which she felt more, relief or disappointment. "It looks about as comfortable as a corset," she remarked, hoping he didn't realize how much she longed to wear such a gown. *On the right night, with the right man...*

"But sweetheart," he whispered in her ear, "I don't think it was meant to be worn for long."

"At least we have luggage now," Bill commented moments later as he held open the door for her. He glanced down at the shopping bags.

Frannie crossed the threshold and looked at him. "Have we gone too far this time?"

He maneuvered her toward a fountain in the center of the lobby and she seated herself on the tile ledge. Behind her, she could hear the tinkling of the water as it fell from tier to tier. Her side warmed as he sat down next to her. Maybe he hadn't heard her, she thought. Or maybe he hadn't understood what she'd meant.

"Do you want to stop?" he asked softly.

She drew in a deep breath. "One thing's just..."

"Led to another," he finished.

She glanced around, as if the landscape beyond the windows might contain the words in her heart. "I mean, when it all started, I was supposed to be going on vacation...."

"And then we got arrested and were handcuffed together."

She nodded. *And then we made love.* "And then we took off on your motorcycle, but Clarence ran over it."

He smiled. "Rising to the occasion, we escaped and stole his car."

"And his credit cards," Frannie said a little glumly. "I mean taking his car and cards...well, that's real theft."

Bill sighed. "Especially since we just used the cards again."

"Yeah." Frannie nodded. "Not that the man actually deserves fair treatment," she added. The rise and fall of Bill's chest against her side was so rhythmic that he might have been asleep. With the peignoir set nestled in the bag at their feet, she couldn't help but wonder if she would wake beside him. What would it mean to him if she did?

"So, do you want to stop?" he asked.

She raised her brows, considering. "Using Clarence's cards?"

"Sweetheart, that's not what we're talking about."

She looked at him again and drew in a breath deep enough that it brought his scent with it. "Then what are we—"

He put his arms around her and snuggled her against his shoulder. "We're talking about the fact that every step of the way, I've wanted you just a little more."

Her eyes widened, as if to say, *You have?* She watched his tongue dart out and touch his upper lip. He shifted on the tile ledge and pulled her so close she was nearly in his lap. He ran his hand beneath her hair, caught it in fistfuls and let it drop.

"You know how you said you kind of don't want to go home?" he asked.

Between the man's near proximity and the subject of the conversation, Frannie felt so panicky she wanted to flee. His breath made those age-old pinpricks tingle along her skin. The chills told her she was cold, but everywhere he touched, she was warm. Her breasts began to ache, wanting his touch. Inadvertently, she glanced down, only to see that the signs of her arousal were visible. "Yeah," she finally managed. "Sometimes, I wish we could just..."

"Keep going?"

She nodded slowly. "I don't want to escape my life. I know more about what I want now than I ever have." She flashed him a quick smile. "I'll finish school and then I'm going to try to open my own travel agency."

She waited and hoped that Bill didn't say something stupid like "good luck." When he didn't, she continued, "And I want to keep—" In touch? That was all wrong.

"To maybe—" The real words were beyond words, sleeping in the depths of her consciousness. *To keep going—to explore you like a whole new world, to touch the rugged terrain of your face, the planes of your body and the valleys. To leave my mark on those places I've touched—on your heart...*

She felt his palm glide up her back and under her hair. When his fingers settled, all the nerves at the nape of her neck seemed to meet in a tangled, throbbing mass where skin met skin. "To—"

"Frannie," Bill murmured softly. "I know what you want."

MARRIAGE, Bill thought two hours later as he seated himself on the bed and started unbuttoning his denim shirt. That's what Frannie wanted. He stared at the interconnecting door between the two bedrooms.

The all-white master bedroom was on the other side. So was Frannie, since she'd gone there to change into her suit. The bridal bungalow really was remote, isolated from the rest of the resort complex and surrounded by high walls of exotic plants and flowering trees. As soon as they'd arrived, they'd eaten outdoors, on a patio overlooking a small pool and separate whirlpool. Indoors, the hotel had left a complimentary arrangement of fresh flowers, a fruit plate and champagne. Beside the beds were baskets of tastefully hidden condoms, lotions and body oils.

Every time Bill thought of those oils, he imagined his palms gliding down Frannie's naked skin. When he'd seen the white canopied bed in the master bedroom he'd imagined the sheets rumpled and Frannie lying across the mattress, even though the bed was so well made that a quarter would have bounced on it.

Right now, she was stepping into her lavender string bikini, too. His vision of her undressing was so vivid that he might have just been given the gift of X-ray vision. Her floral print dress was dropping to her feet and puddling there, like a pool of blue and pink silk flowers. When she unhooked her lacy bra in front, her breasts burst free and swayed slightly.

And suddenly he was rolling his callused thumbs across the darkened tips...capturing them in soft pinches... bending to lick them while his fingers slid inside the lace of her panties....

How the hell had he wound up in the second bedroom? And what were two bedrooms doing in a bridal suite, anyway? He had half a mind to undress and head next door. But he knew the kind of relationship she wanted. Was he ready to give it? Committing to her would be crazy, wouldn't it? He'd quit doing impulsive things after his stint in Moundsville and yet just looking at her filled him with all that crazy energy.

He stood abruptly, unzipped his pants and stepped out of them. He wanted her. But did he want more from her than what he'd get just today or tonight or even tomorrow? Maybe. He'd wanted her to wear that white peignoir... and to make love to her as if she really was his bride.

She'd said she wanted to keep going—until when?

"Until the cops show up," he muttered as he stepped out of a pair of Woodrow Silverwood's boxers.

A knock sounded on the door and he glanced toward it again.

"You ready?" she yelled.

"Stark naked," he called, glancing down at his erection which was thankfully beginning to subside. "So I guess it's up to you to decide." He stared at the door for long moments, wondering whether it was going to open or not.

It didn't.

He could open it anyway. He was fairly certain she wouldn't turn him down, either.

"I'll be in the living room," she called.

Too bad. "Be right out." He reached behind him and grabbed the swim trunks they'd bought. Then he tossed them aside and picked up the bikinis. When he'd first showed them to her, he'd only meant to tease her. Still, their pool, which was surrounded by cacti and tropical flowers, was isolated.

He held the bikinis between his thumb and forefinger and turned them one way and another, thinking they'd sure leave nothing to her imagination. Then he decisively stepped into them.

"Well, sweetheart," he whispered, as he headed toward the door to the living room, "I hope it's a smile I see on your face."

FRANNIE SMILED and stared across the bubbling water of the whirlpool at him. "Just look at that sunset."

He smiled back lazily, feeling the cool water eddy around his chest. Over her shoulder, the sky had burst into color and all that was left of the sun was a golden red ball of burning fire. It sank behind a sheer rock face in the distance. "That old sunset?"

"I think it's beautiful."

"You put it to shame, sweetheart."

He watched as her feet floated upward, rose through the bubbling water and surfaced. When she wiggled her toes at him, he reached forward swiftly, grabbed them, then curled his palms around her insteps. Awareness pricked his lower body.

He let one of his palms glide from her foot to her ankle. Then the other slid from her foot to her calf. As he floated toward her, his behind bumping the shallow tile bottom of the Jacuzzi, he found handholds all the way from her calves to her thighs. By the time his thumbs rested high on her thighs, next to the triangular lavender swath of her bottoms, he was wishing he hadn't worn his fool bikini.

Or that she hadn't worn hers. The bottoms exposed most of her delectable backside. And as he'd moved toward her, floating between her legs, her thighs had parted. His thumbs now grazed the lavender bottoms, while his eyes drifted over her top. The amount of fabric over her breasts made the bottoms look generous.

"This is better," he murmured, crossing his legs, Indian style, beneath her and letting her thighs float around his waist.

"Very nice," she whispered as his arms circled her hips.

He leaned forward and kissed her gently, barely parting her lips and flicking his tongue against hers, until they began to sink. When the waterline hit his shoulders, he sat up again, pulling her with him. He glanced downward, at the two triangles that covered her nipples. The fabric was so tight that he actually saw the tips of her breasts turn hard and bead. Goose bumps suddenly rose along her arms. He gazed into her eyes.

"It's getting chilly out here," she said huskily.

It wasn't, but he nodded. "Maybe we should go in," he suggested softly.

Her hands, which had circled his waist, came around front, then crept up his stomach, grazed over his nipples and rounded over his shoulders, leaving a trail of fire.

"I'm about ready," she said.

To go in or to make love? He sure hoped it was the latter. "Me too." But instead of moving, he merely continued to gaze at her. When he kissed her again, her legs locked behind his back. She was floating right above him, nearly weightless in the water, so close that he began to feel the most intimate part of her graze across his lap.

"Maybe we should call it an early night," she murmured.

Was she going to sleep? He nearly groaned. "I was kind of hoping we could make it a late night," he whispered in her ear.

As if to convince her, he kissed down the column of her throat and didn't stop until he'd nibbled her breasts through her suit. He caught a hard, constricted tip between his teeth and tugged ever so lightly, hoping he could make her feel even half the longing and desire that he felt for her.

"Bill," she whispered in a strangled voice.

He glanced up.

"Let's go in."

He stood, feeling the cooler evening air hitting his body, and held out his hand. She took it, her blue eyes full of need.

"Your room or mine?" he asked once they were inside.

They hadn't even bothered to dry off. She turned around in his arms to face him, droplets of water still on her cheeks. Her hand strayed from his shoulders to his abdomen. He covered it with his own and slowly guided it downward over his wet suit, until she was cupping him.

"I'm not a gentle man," he suddenly said, guiding her hand upward again. So, why was he inclined to be gentle with her?

"You're gentler than you think," she nearly whispered.

If he was, he'd become so because of her.

"Wait here," she said softly. When she reached on her tiptoes and kissed his cheek, he somehow felt as if his heart would break. He was used to women. And when he wanted them, he took them. But this . . .

His hand pressed against his heart as she walked slowly into the master bedroom and shut the door. Still seeing the vision of her, his palm rubbed over his chest hairs.

"Please come back," he whispered.

FRANNIE OPENED THE DOOR with trembling fingers. She didn't know whether or not donning the peignoir was the right thing to do, but she had. She could barely even process the way her body felt—warm and cold, wet and dry, aroused and calm.

And Bill was merely staring at her.

Had she done the wrong thing? Would he indulge the fantasy that this was their wedding night? And what about the future? Would he indulge her deepest fantasies and then leave her?

"Maybe you've made a gentle man of me," he finally said.

She drew in a shaky breath as he crossed the living room and took her in his arms. As his lips claimed hers, he began walking toward the bed. He didn't stop until the backs of her knees hit the mattress and buckled over it, and until she was lying on her back with the full weight of him covering her.

While her hands molded around the contours of his back, he began to touch her through the layers of transparent lace, until he dipped his fingers under the hem of her gown. "You look so beautiful," he said.

"I don't like you because you're gentle," she found herself whispering as his kisses rained down on her breasts, his lips touching her through the fabric.

"Hmm?" he asked, drawing back and sliding his palms from her thighs all the way up her sides.

"I—I like that you're a little tough." She ran her hands through his hair, letting the coarse damp strands fall through her fingers. "I feel I can say anything. You . . ."

"Won't make judgments."

She nodded. In every area of his life, this man seemed to accept things. He could make conversation in bed and touching a woman was something he did as naturally as breathing.

"Sweetheart?" he said after a moment.

"Hmm?"

"Could we possibly talk about this later?"

"We sure can."

He moaned softly, as if she'd just said words he'd waited an eternity to hear. And this time, when his lips claimed hers, there was no going back. The kisses seemed to race forward, like a story that would have no end. It was a love story written on the wind and every word seemed to be about longing and commitment and passion.

She felt a thrill of exhilaration so strong it seemed to lift her body. She felt as if they really were floating—just the two of them rising through the air, drifting high above the earth. Somewhere, along the way, her gown left her body so naturally that it was as if the clothes had never been there. His fingers slid between her legs, rubbing quickening circles around the melting core of her, until she arched against him, fisting her hands in his hair.

"I want to be so gentle," he whispered, leaning away and ripping the foil from a condom.

Her lips parted, her mouth, so wetly kissed, went dry, but she couldn't take her eyes from him. When his lips touched hers again, he was entering her and her moans began running together like one long throaty-sounding song. Reality broke apart, as if all her sensations were passing through a kaleidoscope. There were cops somewhere. A bridal gown. But everything was in bits and pieces. All she knew was that she hoped Bill would never leave her. "Say you won't leave me," she whispered.

"I'll never leave you," he moaned against her mouth.

It was all she wanted to hear. She clung to him until she crested again and until he buried himself deep within her and exploded. Then she pulled him close, resting his head between her breasts.

"Wait, Frannie," he whispered breathlessly.

She knew he had to get up, but wished with all her heart that he didn't.

He blew out a long, shaky sigh. "I hate to have to tell you this," he said softly.

Her heart was still hammering against her ribs. She felt as if she'd gone to another world and hadn't quite yet returned. Her body was no longer her own. It belonged to Bill Berdovitch and she still wanted to beg him to stay with her. "Hmm?"

"It broke," he said.

Not the condom. She gasped, as much in shock as for breath.

"I'm healthy," he said quickly.

"You sure know how to take the romance out of a moment," she managed to say.

He rolled over and lay on his back, pulling her into his arms. "Actually, it is romantic," he whispered after a few more breath-catching moments had passed.

How a broken condom could be romantic, Frannie didn't know. All she knew was that the skin of his chest was hot beneath her fingertips. "I can't believe I'm not hysterical," she finally whispered back. "But right now I couldn't care less. I just want to lie in here and talk all night."

"And what will you do tomorrow?"

Worry. Her smile curled against his chest. "The usual," she said. "Run from the law."

"Here's the romantic part," he said.

"Which is?"

"Well, Frannie—" his arm tightened around her shoulders "—if we can beat the cops to the church, do you want to get married?"

Her heart, which had almost slowed, started pounding hard again. Was he serious or was he teasing her? It was crazy, but she wanted to. Heaven knew, she wanted to. But not because their protection had failed and she might be pregnant. Not because of something she'd foolishly said in the heat of passion. Still, Bill had seemed to know how much she'd needed his response. *I'll never leave you.*

"A marriage proposal," he finally said. "I thought it was romantic."

"Don't kid about stuff like that, Bill," she whispered.

He shifted his weight so that he could look into her eyes. "I'm serious."

She still couldn't quite believe it. Marrying him under the circumstances would be crazy. "I—I . . . can I sleep on it?"

His soft laughter filled the air. "Not yet," he said right before he kissed her.

Chapter Twelve

"Ah, let me dream," Bill murmured, vaguely groping at his chest. Who was trying to wake him? And why did his chest feel funny? *Frannie.* She was curled on top of him like a purring cat. His fingers weren't twined in his chest hairs, as he'd thought, but in her blond locks. They'd talked long into the night and made love as if their lives depended on it. At some point, they'd snuggled beneath the covers. Now he realized that his muscles ached, but that it was a good kind of ache.

He felt her eyelashes flutter against his skin and tilted his head. Had a rap sounded on the sliding glass door?

"Is someone outside?" Frannie whispered groggily.

"I'll find out." He rose from bed, pulling the white spread with him for cover and hoped it wasn't the police. His vision for the morning hardly included an interrogation. As his bare feet padded over the thick, white carpeting, he decided he was going to have breakfast in bed and Frannie for dessert. At least he hoped so. Sudden panic seized him. *I proposed to her last night!* Had it been on impulse, because of their lovemaking—or did he really love her?

There was someone outside. Whoever it was knocked insistently on the glass. Bill lifted the curtain an inch and peeked out. "Lisa?"

He turned and glanced at Frannie. When she sat up, the sheet dropped to her waist. Under the white canopy, with the filmy peignoir rumpled by the bed's footboard, she looked like a bride on the morning after. "I don't know about you, sweetheart, but the last thing I want is company."

"You'd better find out what she wants." Frannie craned around and glanced at the bedside clock. "Did we oversleep?"

"No." Bill shook his head, shoved the curtains aside and waved at Lisa. Then he headed toward the lock. He opened the sliding door, stepped onto the patio and squinted against the midmorning sun, pressing the spread against his belly.

"Her father!" Lisa exclaimed in a breathless, loud whisper.

"What?" Frannie called. "What would my fa—"

Bill glanced over his shoulder. "Your father," he said emphatically.

Frannie's eyes widened. She hopped out of bed, with the sheet wound around her like a toga and headed toward the shopping bag that contained her new clothes.

"Get dressed!" Lisa said, shooing Bill inside the room. "Don't worry, I won't watch." She obediently shut her eyes.

"What did he say?" Frannie asked.

Lisa remained mum, as if talking with her eyes shut was a skill she lacked.

Bill ran into the adjoining room and grabbed some clothes. He stepped into his new jeans as he headed back toward Frannie. On his way, he swooped down and snatched her bra from the floor. Just as he started to toss it in her direction, she looked at him helplessly, then glanced down. Her fingers were already flying up the bodice of her new white muslin sundress, fastening the buttons. Not knowing what to do with her bra, he stuffed it into his back pocket, then riffled through the shopping bag, ripped the band from around the collar of his new white shirt and tugged it on.

"You can look now," Bill said.

As soon as Lisa's eyes blinked open again, words tumbled from her lips. "It's got to be him," she continued. "A man and woman just showed up at the front desk. I didn't hear everything they said, but they wanted to know if people answering your description had registered at the hotel."

"What did the guy look like?" Bill asked.

"I only saw him from the back. Tall, black hair. He was with the woman—and a cop, too!" Lisa glanced at Frannie. "Is that him?"

Bill watched Frannie frown as she barreled out of the second bedroom and returned, tossing items into the bag. Lisa had been so kind that she clearly didn't want to lie to her anymore.

"Probably," she finally said, her eyes darting to the corners of the room and over the French provincial style dresser as if she might have forgotten something.

"The woman couldn't be your mother," Lisa said. "I got a better look at her. She was too young. Kind of short with long dark hair."

"Your sister," Bill said to Frannie. "Maybe it was your sister."

Frannie shot him a long, penetrating glance, as if to say he was lying unnecessarily.

"Anyway," Lisa continued, "I didn't register you in the computer yet, so it'll probably take them a while to find the paperwork. Still, you'd better leave."

Frannie grabbed the two shopping bags with their things and turned to Bill. "Ready?"

Someone started pounding on the front door.

Bill froze. Frannie stared at him wide-eyed. He nodded toward the sliding door.

"Go," Lisa whispered. "I'll stave them off."

"Thanks." Frannie picked up the shopping bags and tiptoed onto the patio.

"Open up," a man yelled. "This is the police and you're surrounded."

No, we're not, Bill thought as he and Frannie all but dived behind the wall of exotic plants that enclosed the bridal bungalow. As they crept through the flower beds, heading toward the front door and in the direction of their parking lot, Frannie tugged at Bill's sleeve. He glanced at her, relieved her of one of their two shopping bags, then followed her gaze through the foliage. Sure enough, a uniformed policeman was standing by the door, next to a petite brunette.

A tall, dark-haired man who looked meaner than a snake put his hands on his hips and stared at the door. "See this door?" he boomed. "I want to see it broken down!"

The three officials backed up and then ran shoulders first toward the door. Just as it gave, Bill grabbed Frannie's hand and darted across the road toward the next bungalow, Frannie's shopping bag thudding against his thigh.

Cops, he thought grimly.

Two unmarked cars were coming from both directions.

A siren suddenly screamed in the silent morning air. It seemed to split right through the orange sun, like a sharp knife halving a cantaloupe.

An arm swung through the window of one of the cars and planted a flashing dome light on the roof.

Tires squealed close by. Bill tightened his grip on Frannie's hand. Just as he turned toward the sound, a bright red Jeep convertible with a roll bar shot from the driveway opposite. As the driver squealed around and screeched to a halt next to him and Frannie, the passenger door swung open. A deeply tanned twenty-something woman in a wet one-piece swimsuit and white jacket screamed, "Get in!"

Frannie clutched her shopping bag and lunged inside the Jeep, pulling him with her.

"Hang on!" the woman yelled.

"There's not much choice," he muttered. As the woman backed right into the driveway she'd just exited, Frannie wound up stretched right across his lap, with her shopping bag scrunched between them. She planted a hand on top of her head, so her hat wouldn't blow away. Even though they were headed over a landscaped lawn, the woman kept driving. The Jeep bounced around man-size cacti. Bill could only hope they hadn't been rescued by another Clarence Smithers. He didn't check the speedometer, but the woman had just gone from zero to about fifty.

"I'm a lifeguard," she yelled over the wind when she hit the pavement.

"The way you drive, the life you should be saving is your own!" Frannie yelled back.

She threw her head back and laughed. "Lisa told me everything! Which parking lot?"

"Number two," Bill yelled.

It seemed as if less than a minute passed before she'd braked behind the Impala.

"The minivan took a half hour," Bill said in awe, once Frannie was next to him in the seat of the Silverwoods' car. His shoulders started to shake with laughter as he turned the key over in the ignition. "I think she missed her calling."

Frannie snuggled next to him and threw an arm around his neck. "Which was?"

"Grand theft auto," he said wryly.

Either his words or the fact that she'd both escaped the police and survived the Jeep ride made Frannie laugh so hard that her eyes teared. His darted between cars, checking for police cruisers. The sweet sound of Frannie's laughter seemed to take the edge off the situation. Only when he hit an expressway, did she calm down.

"You okay, sweetheart?" he asked, putting his arm around her. There was such a long silence that he started to worry. "Frannie?"

Her gaze raised slowly to his. "Did you mean what you said last night? Do you really want to marry me?"

He quickly glanced in the rearview mirror and through the windshield, then he cranked down the window, so that the fast-blowing wind swept into the car. He'd felt a little panicky, there was no denying that. He gazed into her eyes. "Yeah."

"Even though it's crazy?"

He grinned as she grabbed a fistful of her blowing hair and twisted it behind her neck. "No, Frannie. I want to do it *because* it's crazy." He'd lived on the straight and narrow for a long time. But she'd made him realize that even upstanding citizens were occasionally allowed to take a walk on the wild side.

She tilted her head and surveyed him from beneath her light-colored lashes. "Aren't you scared that things won't work out?"

He rested his fingertips lightly on the wheel and took a curve. He nodded. "Sure." Suddenly, he grinned. "But on the road of life, we've got to take the chance."

"I just—I..."

If anything convinced him he really did want to marry her, it was the way his heart sank when he thought she might say no. Where else was he going to find a woman he wanted so much? When he'd passed through the gates at Moundsville, on his way to the outside, he'd felt more free than he ever had in his life. Now, he felt even freer—and he wasn't alone.

"I just don't want you marrying me because I might be pregnant."

His lips parted in surprise. It had crossed his mind, but he'd been thinking that he wanted a baby. Hell, he wanted a whole family to call his own. "It's not—"

"You know about...Raymond," she said.

He gently stroked her shoulder, rubbing the callused pad of his thumb over her soft skin. He'd felt the depth of her loss as surely as if he'd experienced it himself, he thought. "It's all right if you don't want to have other children," he forced himself to say gently. He wanted kids, but not if he couldn't have her. It was a sacrifice he was willing to make, as hard as it would be.

She turned in the seat, to get a better look at him. "I'm ready to go on..." Her voice trailed off. "I want babies," she said suddenly. "I want to try again." Her voice caught. "And I want a family and a real man—one who doesn't desert me. But I don't want you marrying me because of something I said in bed or because of the past."

"Then it's a good thing we're driving into the future, sweetheart," he said glancing through the windshield again.

"Mrs. Wild Bill." She strained upward and kissed his cheek. "I like the sound of that. I'm in love with you, Bill."

He knew he should be watching the road, but he looked at her. He was shocked to find that his eyes were suddenly stinging with tears. And he'd never cried in his life. "You saying yes, Frannie?"

She blew out a long breath and then kissed him again, this time catching the corner of his mouth. "Yeah, I sure am."

"I love you, too," he nearly whispered. He took his foot off the gas and glanced toward the shoulder, intending to pull over and kiss her soundly.

"Stop and I'll kill you!" she exclaimed, her voice catching with excitement.

"Seeing as I'm now your fiancé, killing me wouldn't be in your best interest, sweetheart." He punched the accelerator harder than necessary, making the old Impala lurch forward again. "Mind telling me why I can't pull over and kiss my bride-to-be?"

She giggled. "I've got a willing groom in the car. So, what do you think?"

He chuckled. "Guess you want to make damn sure you get me to the altar."

"I HAVE NOW SEEN IT ALL," Reed boomed, glaring down at the floor. He watched as the uniformed man donned gloves, picked up the pair of men's leopard print bikinis and dropped them into a plastic evidence bag. Reed glanced at Carly, a sudden smile curling his lips. "Cover your eyes, Carly."

"Afraid I might be imagining what you'd look like in them, boss?" she returned.

He didn't know whether he was more flattered or appalled and he fought against the urge to gape at her. "What's gotten into you?" he muttered. Without waiting for her response, he turned toward the clerk who'd identified herself as Lisa Diane Mooney. "Contrary to what you believe, William Berdovitch and Frances Anderson are wanted fugitives. If you do not divulge all information concerning where they're headed, you—Lisa Diane Mooney—will become an accessory to their crimes." He glared at Lisa, who sank into an armchair as if her legs could no longer support her.

"They're eloping," she said in a weak voice. "And you're her father. I—"

Reed felt Carly sidle up next to him and watched as Lisa's eyes gained a steely expression. "You?" he asked.

"I—I think you're just awful!" the young woman burst out. "You want her to marry that jerk in your law firm and—and she's in love with Bill!"

"Lisa." Carly whipped out her badge. "We're both FBI."

"You are not," Lisa snapped. "You probably borrowed those badges from law enforcement friends or something like that!" Her eyes wavered uncertainly between Carly and Reed. "That's really low, in my opinion."

"Ma'am," the uniformed man chimed in. "They're tell
ing you the truth."

"And you're going to wind up in jail if you don't help
us," Reed said in his most threatening tone.

Lisa's hand shot to her belly, as if she might be sick
"I—I can't go to jail," she murmured.

Good, Reed thought. She was beginning to believe them
"You're a nice-looking kid," he said, trying to soune
soothing. "But judges and juries just look at the facts."

"Not jail!" Lisa wailed. "I—I just can't."

"Why's that?" Carly asked sympathetically.

"I'm pregnant!" Lisa exclaimed.

"Congratulations," Carly said breathlessly. "You mus
have just found out."

Reed's eyes shot to his partner. She was grinning and he
eyes were all lit up. No, Carly wasn't playing good cop. Sh
was genuinely excited. "Carly," he muttered in exaspera
tion, "are we chasing bad guys or what?"

She stomped on the white carpeting and whirled around.
Her eyes—shining with excitement just the second be
fore—flashed with fury. She looked as if she hated his guts.

"You can be a real jerk, Galveston," she growled.

Had she really called him Galveston? He leaned close and
peered deep into her eyes, feeling as if he were looking at a
complete stranger. "Excuse me, Miss Sharp?"

"You don't care about anything but your fool job," she
said huffily. "And you don't have a romantic bone in you
body. I've seen the way you look at me." She brought he
face so close that they were nose to nose. "Don't look sc
shocked," she bit out. "You're so out of touch with your
self that you don't even *know* how you look at me!"

"The hell I don't." Reed met the fire of her gaze with the
intensity of his own.

"Oh, dear," Lisa murmured from her armchair.

"Oh, dear," Carly echoed in a strangled voice.

"Sanctuary," Lisa piped in, as if she thought that Reed and Carly's argument might come to blows. "They went to a church called Sanctuary."

Reed barely heard the word. A hair couldn't pass between his nose and Carly's. She thought he wasn't aware of his own desire? Reed clamped his hand on her back and jerked her forward, so that his lips slammed down on hers. He kissed her quick and hard, then released her.

"Now," he said, "may we please continue our pursuit?"

Carly was so breathless that she might have been on the run herself. Her eyes were as wide and round as her just-kissed mouth. "Whatever you say, boss," she croaked.

Reed nodded. "Good."

"There's one thing I can say about you," she said. "I guess you'll do anything to catch your man."

"Or woman," he returned, his gaze drifting from her eyes over her figure. For the first time in his life, he wished he wasn't working. But he was. He glanced around as the uniformed cop entered from the adjoining room. Outside, he could hear the guys from the unmarked cars talking on their radios. "Sanctuary." His gaze returned to Carly's. "Let's get a move on."

"SANCTUARY." Frannie's eyes riveted on the old church. It was beautiful and quaint, with Spanish architecture and white stucco. It looked like a safe haven nestled on dusty ground that must have once held a town. "Maybe we should hide the car."

Bill nodded and steered toward some bushes and trees. He turned behind the outcropping and suddenly slammed on the brakes.

"The Cadillac," Frannie said in a hushed voice. "Bonnie and Clyde's Cadillac." She glanced at Bill. "So much for getting married," she said glumly.

"Don't you worry," Bill said as he turned off the motor. "We're getting married—even if I have to hold a gun on the preacher."

She chuckled and scooted out of the car on his side. "For the first time in my life—" she glanced toward the open door of the church "—I sure wish I *had* a gun."

When Bill slung his arm protectively around her shoulders and headed toward the front door, she found herself hoping they really could get married, somehow. Instead, heaven only knew what was about to happen. "What if they're really crooks?" she whispered as they ascended the steps. Her grip tightened around his waist. "Bill, they could shoot us. A half-million dollars is a lot of money."

"I can take care of us, sweetheart," he whispered.

She followed his lead, creeping inside the dimly lit church and tiptoeing behind a pew. Then she squinted toward the altar—and couldn't believe what she saw. She stared at Bill, slack-jawed. He maneuvered her into the center aisle and started walking down it.

Frannie could only stare. It had to be Bonnie and Clyde. They were the same people she'd seen in the gas station. The couple, who could have been the spitting image of herself and Bill, at least from a distance, were standing at the altar. A preacher was speaking to them in low tones and Jason Morehead, who was wearing old overalls, was standing behind Clyde. He had his cane in one hand and a shotgun in the other. The yellow duffel that was presumably full of the cash was nestled next to his feet. So was a videotape.

"I do," Bonnie said with firm resolve.

They were close enough that when the preacher began speaking again, Frannie realized it was in Spanish. She didn't understand the words, but got the general gist. Clyde looked a little stiff in his suit and Bonnie was wearing a simple white dress that was similar to Frannie's own. She gasped. "They're getting married," she said aloud.

The preacher glanced up, Bonnie and Clyde spun around and Jason Morehead slowly raised the shotgun. "And you ain't gonna stop 'em," Jason said.

"Please," Bonnie called.

"Bonnie," Clyde said, "it's not the cops. It's that couple they were chasing instead of us."

Bonnie's hand shot to her heart. She headed toward Frannie and Bill, but Clyde caught her hand and hauled her back toward the altar.

"All I've got to do is say I do," he said. He turned toward the man who was performing the ceremony. "I do," he said quickly.

Bonnie barely seemed to notice. "I'm so sorry," she rambled. "Jason—" she glanced at the old man "—he made a videotape that proves Larson robbed us and dumped oil in our creek, but it won't be admissible in court. And if we're going to get in trouble, we wanted to—" Her eyes shot to Clyde's. "Well, before we turned ourselves in, we wanted to be in it together as husband and wife. My parents and my grandparents were married in this church, so... And when Jason pulled the gun on Larson, we just didn't know what to do and—"

"He robbed y'all, Bonnie," Jason said in heartfelt protest.

"I know, Jason," Bonnie said soothingly. She glanced at Frannie. "Please, just let us get married," she begged.

"Honey," Clyde said, "we *are* married."

Frannie gawked as the man settled his lips on Bonnie's. Glancing over him, she realized that the tattoo on his hand said Bonnie.

"Bonnie and Clyde." In his happiness, Jason inadvertently lowered the gun. "Them's their real names, so you just knew they had to get hitched."

Frannie let herself be pulled forward when Bill headed toward the altar.

"Don't you get too close," Jason suddenly threatened raising the gun again.

"Mind standing guard while we tie the knot?" Bill asked

Frannie glanced at the preacher who didn't seem the leas bit concerned about performing shotgun weddings. The she looked at Clyde and Bonnie, who were still wrapped i the most romantic kiss she'd ever witnessed. She realize that Jason's eyes were flitting between her and Bill. His dis trustful expression faded by degrees and was replaced by smile. Was she really about to marry Bill? Would it even b legal?

"Don't mind if I do," the old codger said with a wink "As ancient as I am, I ain't good for much except being best man." He chuckled. "Clyde," he continued loudly "why don't you take that there bride of yours to the pews?"

Clyde broke the kiss and Bonnie laughed softly. She pu her arm around her new husband and sidled in front o Frannie and Bill. "Y'all are getting married?" she asked.

Frannie smiled at Bonnie. Up close, they didn't look at al that much alike. Bonnie was older, with tiny laugh line around eyes that were a lighter blue than Frannie's. "Yeah," Frannie murmured. "I think so."

"Know so," Bill said.

Bonnie placed her bouquet in Frannie's hands and gentl pushed Clyde toward the front pew.

As soon as Frannie and Bill stepped up to the preacher, h riffled back through the pages of his prayer book and starte speaking in Spanish all over again. When Frannie looked u at Bill, she realized he'd been watching her face. His eye said that he was equally clueless about what the preache was saying, but that it didn't matter.

Never taking her eyes from Bill's, Frannie listened to th soft rolling Spanish *r*'s and the lilting cadence of th preacher's words. No, what he was saying didn't matter Because he was talking about lifelong commitment and th universal gift of love and about how Frannie had found a man she loved who would never leave her. She finally tore her eyes from Bill's and looked at the official who was marrying them, committing each line of his face to memory, never wanting to forget it.

After long moments, the preacher lifted his gaze. His kind brown eyes watched hers expectantly.

There was no doubt in her mind about what she was supposed to say. "I do," she whispered.

A slight smile touched the preacher's lips and he continued speaking again, this time to Bill.

"Hold it right there!" someone yelled.

Frannie's heart sank as she turned toward the voice. *Just let Bill say, "I do!"*

"Move a muscle and I'll kill you," Jason growled.

"Clarence," Frannie murmured.

The man was standing in the aisle with his hands on his hips. "I want the money and that tape," he said, sounding murderous.

"Too bad," Jason said with a chuckle, as he raised the shotgun and pointed it at Clarence's heart. "Now, come up here, sit in the pew like a regular wedding guest and shut your trap."

Frannie watched nervously as Clarence eyed the gun, the tape and the money bag and slunk toward the front pews. He took a seat across the aisle from Bonnie and Clyde, looking none too happy about it.

The preacher smiled pleasantly at Clarence, with all the serenity of a man who lived close to God, and then calmly began speaking again. Frannie's eyes fixed on Bill's when the vows were finished.

"I do," he said softly.

"We're married," she whispered.

"We sure are, sweetheart." Bill's voice caught with emotion.

"You'd best kiss that bride, boy," Jason said. "'Cause it looks like we've got some more wedding guests."

Frannie didn't bother to turn around. She flung her arms around Bill's neck and felt her feet leave the floor as he lifted her into his embrace. His lips claimed hers, feeling softer and sweeter than they ever had. "Ah, Bill," she murmured simply, right before he deepened the kiss. When his tongue flicked against hers, her hands drifted downward and she realized her bra was still in his back pocket. Chuckling against his lips as her arms circled his neck again, she couldn't have cared less about what strange circumstances had brought them to an altar in San Miguel or about who was chasing them.

"Reed Galveston," a man barked. "FBI."

"FBI," a woman yelled. "Special Agent Carly Sharp. Drop the weapon, turn around and put your hands on the altar rail, where we can see them."

Frannie's eyes opened slightly, so she could see the action, but she didn't quit kissing Bill. Not even when Jason laid down his shotgun and she realized that the FBI agents had their pistols drawn. She wasn't about to turn away—not when her husband was kissing her. As his lips nuzzled hers, she felt a hand pry her fingers from Bill's neck. Cold metal cuffs clamped around her wrist. A second later, just as she leaned back, she heard another click. She and Bill were joined together at the wrists again.

The woman who'd cuffed them held up a badge that said Carly Sharp.

"Carly," the man who'd identified himself as Reed Galveston said, "I can't believe you cuffed those two together!"

Carly merely chuckled. She winked at Bill and Frannie. "It's something special the FBI does for newlyweds," she explained.

"Oh, fine," Reed said huffily, cuffing Bonnie and Clyde together.

Just at that moment, Clarence lunged from the pew and slid across the floor on his belly. He looked comical until he grabbed the shotgun on the floor and pointed it at Reed Galveston.

"You shoot that man," Carly warned, "and I will kill you."

"It ain't even loaded," Jason said helpfully.

Frannie blew out a shaky sigh of relief and leaned against Bill. "What a day," she whispered, watching the agents secure Clarence Smithers.

"Best day of my life," Bill said softly.

"I could think of a better ending for it," Frannie said wryly once they were ensconced in the back seat of Reed and Carly's cruiser.

"What could be better that this, sweetheart?" Bill kissed her again, then raised their joined wrists, so that they could wave goodbye to Bonnie, Clyde and Jason who were in another car. The siren of the car that contained Clarence whooped once, then fell silent.

"A real honeymoon," Frannie said, snuggling close to Bill. And not going to jail, she thought, wondering about what lay ahead.

"Hmm." He smiled down at her and then ducked and nuzzled his face in her hair.

"Why did you kiss me?" Carly snapped from the front seat.

Frannie poked Bill in the ribs, to indicate that something interesting was happening between the law enforcement officers.

"Look, Carly," Reed said, "do you want to go on a date? I mean, I think I'm too darn old for you...." He glanced over his shoulder. "Don't you two felons listen to this!"

Frannie's eyes met Bill's and they both stared at each other. She tried to fight her grin, but when Bill nuzzled his cheek against hers again, it tugged at the corners of her mouth.

"How old are you, anyway?" Carly said in a fit of pique.

"Forty-two."

"Old as you are, boss," Carly said, "maybe I should just fix you up some vitamin E and a hot water bottle."

Reed sighed. "Please, just yes or no."

"Yes, you old fool," Carly finally said. "What did you think I was going to say?"

Frannie smiled as she looked at the couple. Bill playfully pulled her across his lap and settled his lips on hers. "Guess we really did drive right into our future," he whispered.

"And you know what?" she asked between kisses.

He licked her lower lip. "What?"

She could see the path of their lives stretching into eternity. "We're never going to stop."

He deepened the kiss, every touch of his lips the assurance that wherever the road ahead might lead, they would always travel it together.

Epilogue

Bill reached beneath the table reserved for counsel and defendants, then laced his fingers through Frannie's. He glanced from her eyes down the row at Bonnie, Clyde and Jason. Behind him, he could feel Reed Galveston breathing down his neck. His gaze returned to Frannie. In her tasteful cream suit, she looked as if the most criminal thing she'd be capable of was undertipping at a fancy restaurant.

He winked at her as Judge Kindsdale shuffled his papers and prepared to announce their fate. Not that Bill was worried. Galveston had gathered enough information to put both Clarence Smithers and Langston Larson behind bars and he had painstakingly helped put together a case that would exonerate not only Bill and Frannie, but Bonnie, Clyde and Jason as well. On the stand, the deputies who'd released Bill and Frannie, Tyler and Kent, had sworn that the mess was their fault—even if the twinkle in their eyes said they felt single-handedly responsible for the sea of nuptial bliss that had washed over the participants in the case.

Between Bill and Frannie's father's connections and the unusual circumstances of the case, they'd gotten the court date in just six weeks, too. And, of course, Judge George Kindsdale was one of Bill's favorite fishing buddies. Bill was hardly above calling in a favor to keep his wife out of jail, and it didn't look as if he were going to be disbarred, either.

Frannie leaned close and Bill ducked his head so he could hear her. "Did you notice the ring on Carly Sharp's finger when she testified?" Frannie whispered. "It looked like an engagement ring."

The courtroom was dead quiet and Bill hoped he could manage not to laugh out loud. "Must have been some date," he whispered back.

Frannie flushed and glanced down at her own ring finger. After the fact, he'd bought her an engagement ring and wedding rings for them both. Even though her many rings had been returned, his were the only ones she was wearing. "Couldn't hold a candle to one of ours," she assured him with a smile.

"Now, now, you guys," Carly said from behind them in a stage whisper. "It's not a competition."

Reed chuckled as if the quiet in the courtroom didn't faze him in the least. "Let's hope not," he said in a low voice. "Because she's wearing me out as it is."

"Yeah," Bill said over his shoulder, "but you love it."

"I think George—I mean, Judge Kindsdale is going to say something," Frannie said in a hush-hush tone.

As curious as he was, Bill couldn't manage to tear his gaze away from his wife's. It was strange how things were turning out. During the long wait in the hallway before the hearing, he and Reed and Clyde had gotten to talking about trout fishing, and Bill was sure they were all going to wind up as friends. After all, they lived nearby. While they'd talked, he'd overheard Frannie asking Bonnie and Carly if they wanted to go shopping sometime, if they stayed out of jail.

Frannie's parents, who were right behind Reed and Carly in the courtroom, hadn't even been aware of what had transpired until after the fact. Apparently, they'd checked on Frannie and called the police when she hadn't arrived at her initial destination. Later, they'd called the resort again and a rushed clerk—thinking she'd made an error—had assured them that Frannie had arrived safe and sound. They'd finished out their vacation and had a wonderful time.

When they'd realized Frannie was married, they'd both looked markedly relieved and agreeable to having Frannie move into Bill's house in Charleston. Frannie's father—thrilled to have another lawyer in the family—had wrung Bill's hand so long that Bill had been convinced the man meant to take it with him.

Right behind Jack and Alice Anderson, Mickey and Darrell were fidgeting next to their parents. Both boys had apologized profusely for holding Frannie at gunpoint. Nevertheless, it was clear they didn't feel too guilty. Sheriff Jackson—out of embarrassment or a kind heart or both—had allowed the boys to keep their rewards. Darrell had stopped down the hall, right before court time, to finalize the papers for the license tags to his new car.

Bill's prized Triumph was up and running, too, thanks to Galveston's skill as a law officer. He'd picked up and bagged every piece of the motorcycle when he'd found it in the culvert. As soon as he'd gotten the parts, Bill had put all his mechanical abilities to use and fixed the bike. It was as good as new. And, because of all the publicity the case had generated for the Alpine Resort and Spa, Lisa Mooney had actually gotten a promotion. Frannie had written the Silverwoods, thanking them again.

In spite of all the excitement, once they'd been released on bail, Frannie had returned to her last week of exams and aced every one of them. She'd graduated with honors. And after the ceremony, Bill had taken her to her present. At first, she'd just stood in the middle of the office space with a puzzled expression while he told her that he'd taken out a five-year lease and meant to give her operating capital.

And then she'd noticed the posters. He'd had prints of getaway islands and sunny beaches framed in brass for her. Unless George Kindsdale suddenly went crazy and sent them to jail, Frannie's travel agency would open within the week. Bill had enrolled her in travel business courses and, for the time being, Frannie was going to hire a licensed agent.

"Counsel?"

Yes, the past six weeks had completely convinced Bill that marrying Frannie was the best thing he'd ever done. He couldn't imagine waking without her next to him and—

"Mr. Berdovitch?" George Kindsdale said pointedly.

Bill suddenly decided that he and Frannie should put off opening the travel agency for an extra week, so that they could take a proper honeymoon.

"Bill?"

His eyes shot toward the judge. "Huh, George?" he asked. Then he realized he was still in court and winced. "I mean, Judge Kindsdale."

"Didn't you hear a word he said?" Jason Morehead chuckled.

Frannie grinned. "We're free! No jail! No probation! You're still a lawyer!"

Bill blinked, then threw his head back and laughed. All around them, people were standing up and shaking hands. Jack Anderson's hand clamped down on his shoulder. "Good presentation of the case, son."

Bill murmured his thanks and finally managed to extract his wife from the crowd. "C'mon."

"Where?" she asked breathlessly as he steered her down the aisle and out of the courtroom. "Carly and Bonnie and I were thinking we all might want to grab lunch...."

He draped his arm around her shoulders. "We're going down this hall and then we'll come right back."

She grinned up at him. "You know," she said, her eyes shining with female appreciation, "you look great in a suit."

He chuckled. "Hides the tattoo."

"I like your tattoo," she said, tilting her head to survey his face. "Your beard, too."

"Anytime you want me to grow it back," he said, stopping in front of a glass door and then opening it for her, "you just let me know."

Frannie's eyes shifted to the lettering on the glass. "Licenses?" Her eyes widened. "But we're legally married, aren't we, Bill?"

He shrugged. "To tell you the truth, sweetheart, I'd have to look it up."

She didn't say a word, just kept gaping at him, slack-jawed. She looked as if the fact that they might not be legal had stricken sheer terror into her heart. "Don't worry," he said softly. "We're going to do it again, either way." He smiled. "Nothing against Spanish, Frannie, but I'd kind of like to hear the ceremony in words I understand. And I know you still want that long white dress with the ten-foot train. It's in April's *Modern Bride*." He smiled. "Remember? You dog-eared the page in two different copies of the magazine."

She blew out a shaky breath. "We have to be married," she said levelly. "Really married." Her tongue darted out and she nervously licked her lips. "You'll do it again?"

When he nodded, relief flooded her face. Didn't she know how much he loved her? He hauled her close and kissed her hard.

She flung her arms around his neck. "Remember what happened back at the hotel?"

"I made love to you like crazy," he said.

"And the condom..." she whispered.

He drew back an inch and squinted at her. "Huh?"

"Bill, I'm pregnant."

He stared at her in shock. Was he really going to be a father? In a strange way, the child Frannie had lost was already a part of Bill's life. They spoke of Raymond sometimes, as if he'd belonged to them both. He and Frannie were going to share it all—both joy and heartbreak. And now, they were going to try again, and have a family together. His mouth was still hanging open in surprise when it settled on hers again.

Somewhere in the room, a man cleared his throat loudly. "Excuse me."

Bill kept Frannie pressed against him and glanced toward the counter. A wiry man with glasses flushed slightly, straightened his tie and stared back, clearly trying to suppress a smile.

"Maybe you two ought to head straight for Mexico," the man finally said.

Frannie giggled. "Mexico?"

The man laughed. "Around here, it takes us a few days to process the papers. But if you catch a plane for Mexico, you could be on the honeymoon by tonight."

Bill ducked and kissed Frannie's nose. "Want to go to Mexico?"

"This time, let's get married here," she returned, "In English." She lowered her voice. "And before I'm so pregnant that I can't wear that gown."

Bill couldn't really see, but he felt the eyes of the clerk riveted on them.

"This time?" the man asked.

"We got married in Mexico a few weeks back," Frannie returned, her eyes still on Bill's.

"But we have to do it again," Bill said grinning. "Because now we're pregnant."

"You're marrying her again?"

The man had sounded thoroughly confused. Bill stared deeply into Frannie's eyes and brushed his lips against hers. "I'd marry her a thousand times."

"You would?" she whispered.

He didn't bother with the words, but merely nuzzled her lips apart, for a kiss that meant every day of every minute of the rest of his life.

HARLEQUIN®
AMERICAN ◆ ROMANCE®

Once in a while, there's a man so special, a story so different,
that your pulse races, your blood rushes. We call this

AMERICAN ROMANCE
heartbeat

Trevor d'Laine is one such man, and LOVE BITES is one
such book.

Kay Erickson didn't believe in vampires, until this one skateboarded
into her life and swept her off her feet. Their love was star-crossed,
but held the promise of centuries of passion—if only one of them
would relinquish what they loved best....

Harlequin American Romance #582

LOVE BITES
by
Margaret St. George

Don't miss this exceptional, sexy hero. He'll make your
HEARTBEAT.

Available in May wherever Harlequin Books are sold.
Watch out for more Heartbeat stories, coming your way soon.

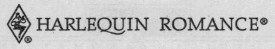

HARLEQUIN ROMANCE®

brings you

More Romances Celebrating Love, Families and Children!

Harlequin Romance #3362

THE BABY BUSINESS

by

Rebecca Winters

If you love babies—this book is for you!

When hotel nanny Rachel Ellis searches for her lost
brother, she meets his boss—the dashing and gorgeous
Vincente de Raino. She is unprepared for her strong
attraction to him, but even more unprepared to be left
holding the baby—his adorable baby niece, Luisa, who
makes her long for a baby of her own!

Available in May wherever Harlequin Books are sold.

With the advent of spring, American Romance is pleased to be presenting three exciting couples, each with their own unique reasons for needing a new beginning...for needing to enter into a marriage of convenience.

Meet the reluctant newlyweds in:

#580 MARRIAGE INCORPORATED
Debbi Rawlins
April 1995

#583 THE RUNAWAY BRIDE
Jacqueline Diamond
May 1995

#587 A SHOTGUN WEDDING
Cathy Gillen Thacker
June 1995

Find out why some couples marry first...and learn to love later. Watch for the upcoming "In Name Only" promotion.

HARLEQUIN®
AMERICAN ◆ ROMANCE®

IS BRINGING YOU A BABY BOOM!

NEW ARRIVALS

We're expecting! This spring, from March through May, three very special Harlequin American Romance authors invite you to read about three equally special heroines—all of whom are on a nine-month adventure! We expect each soon-to-be mom will find the man of her dreams—and a daddy in the bargain!

In March we brought you #576 BABY MAKES NINE by Vivian Leiber, and in April #579 WHO'S THE DADDY by Judy Christenberry. Now meet the expectant mom in:

#584 BABY BY CHANCE
by Elda Minger
May 1995

Look for the New Arrivals logo—and please help us welcome our new arrivals!

HARLEQUIN®

PRESENTS
RELUCTANT BRIDEGROOMS

Two beautiful brides, two unforgettable romances…
two men running for their lives.…

My Lady Love, by Paula Marshall, introduces
Charles, Viscount Halstead, who lost his memory
and found himself employed as a stableboy by the
untouchable Nell Tallboys, Countess Malplaquet.
But Nell didn't consider Charles untouchable—
not at all!

Darling Amazon, by Sylvia Andrew, is the story of
a spurious engagement between Julia Marchant
and Hugo, marquess of Rostherne—an engagement
that gets out of hand and just may lead Hugo to
the altar after all!

Enjoy two madcap Regency weddings this May,
wherever Harlequin books are sold.

REG5

Harlequin invites you to the most
romantic wedding of the season.

Rope the cowboy of your dreams in
Marry Me, Cowboy!

A collection of 4 brand-new stories,
celebrating weddings, written by:

New York Times bestselling author

JANET DAILEY

and favorite authors

Margaret Way
Anne McAllister
Susan Fox

Be sure not to miss Marry Me, Cowboy!
coming this April

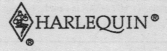 HARLEQUIN®

HARLEQUIN®

Don't miss these Harlequin favorites by some of our most distinguished authors!
And now, you can receive a discount by ordering two or more titles!

HT #25607	PLAIN JANE'S MAN by Kristine Rolofson	$2.99 U.S./$3.50 CAN.	☐
HT #25616	THE BOUNTY HUNTER by Vicki Lewis Thompson	$2.99 U.S./$3.50 CAN.	☐
HP #11674	THE CRUELLEST LIE by Susan Napier	$2.99 U.S./$3.50 CAN.	☐
HP #11699	ISLAND ENCHANTMENT by Robyn Donald	$2.99 U.S./$3.50 CAN.	☐
HR #03268	THE BAD PENNY by Susan Fox	$2.99	☐
HR #03303	BABY MAKES THREE by Emma Goldrick	$2.99	☐
HS #70570	REUNITED by Evelyn A. Crowe	$3.50	☐
HS #70611	ALESSANDRA & THE ARCHANGEL by Judith Arnold	$3.50 U.S./$3.99 CAN.	☐
HI #22291	CRIMSON NIGHTMARE by Patricia Rosemoor	$2.99 U.S./$3.50 CAN.	☐
HAR #16549	THE WEDDING GAMBLE by Muriel Jensen	$3.50 U.S./$3.99 CAN.	☐
HAR #16558	QUINN'S WAY by Rebecca Flanders	$3.50 U.S./$3.99 CAN.	☐
HH #28802	COUNTERFEIT LAIRD by Erin Yorke	$3.99	☐
HH #28824	A WARRIOR'S WAY by Margaret Moore	$3.99 U.S./$4.50 CAN.	☐

(limited quantities available on certain titles)

	AMOUNT	$
DEDUCT:	10% DISCOUNT FOR 2+ BOOKS	$
ADD:	POSTAGE & HANDLING	$
	($1.00 for one book, 50¢ for each additional)	
	APPLICABLE TAXES*	$_____
	TOTAL PAYABLE	$_____
	(check or money order—please do not send cash)	

To order, complete this form and send it, along with a check or money order for the total above, payable to Harlequin Books, to: **In the U.S.:** 3010 Walden Avenue, P.O. Box 9047, Buffalo, NY 14269-9047; **In Canada:** P.O. Box 613, Fort Erie, Ontario, L2A 5X3.

Name: _____

Address: _____ City: _____

State/Prov.: _____ Zip/Postal Code: _____

*New York residents remit applicable sales taxes.
 Canadian residents remit applicable GST and provincial taxes.

HBACK-AJ2